OUT OF CONTROL

Muttering obscenities, Brown released Eric and took a TRW credit report from his leather jacket pocket. "Okay, Garfield, try this out. We'll ruin you. I mean IRS audits, EPA lawsuits every time you break wind. We'll screw with the computers until the credit card companies put you on a blacklist. We'll get the bank to call in your car loan. Your phone will be cut off. We can have Sussman fire you and make sure you don't get unemployment."

"I don't get it. What do you want? Who are you?"

"We told you what we want. You take a little trip to sunny Russia. A few days out of your life. You should be glad to serve your country.

"We tried to do it the nice way; now you'll do it our way."

THE BORZOI CONTROL

THE BORZOI CONTROL

SCOTT ELLIS

TOR ®

A TOM DOHERTY ASSOCIATES BOOK
NEW YORK

This is a work of fiction. All characters and events portrayed in this book are fictional, and any resemblance to real people or events is purely coincidental.

Copyright © 1986 by Scott Ellis

All rights reserved. No part of this book may be used or reproduced in any manner whatsoever without written permission except in the case of brief quotations embodied in critical articles or reviews.

Published by arrangement with St. Martin's Press

A TOR Book
Published by Tom Doherty Associates, Inc.
49 West 24 Street
New York, NY 10010

ISBN: 0-812-50239-6   Can. ISBN: 0-812-50240-X

Library of Congress Catalog Card Number: 86-13808

First Tor edition: October 1988

Printed in the United States of America

0 9 8 7 6 5 4 3 2 1

For Sima

PROLOGUE
1974

"DAMN IT, PHIL, YOU CAN'T DO THIS," ALVIN WINTERS SPUT-
tered.

Phil Dector continued to empty his cluttered desk, his
hands occasionally fumbling as he removed papers, books,
computer hardware and software. He had waited until the
staff had left for the day before collecting his belongings.
He hadn't wanted anyone in the company to know of his
leaving until he was gone. Although corporate breakups in
the burgeoning computer industry were as common as
divorces in Southern California, he knew his departure
would be particularly messy. Alvin Winters was not the
type to graciously let him leave.

Winters' shirt alone cost more than Dector's entire outfit. He was a tall, handsome, forty-five-year-old supersales-
man. Phil was a dumpy, thirty-five-year-old electronics
genius. They had built Vision Electronics up from a work-
table in Dector's garage to a thirty-million-dollar corporation. With Dector designing microchips that were one step
ahead of the competition and Al shmoozing it up with
purchasing agents for the major corporations, Vision had
blossomed.

"I'm begging, okay, I'm begging," Al said.

"You used me. That hurts more than the money. How much did you take?"

"It wasn't much."

"A hundred thousand?"

"Nothing like that."

"Seventy-five?"

"You don't understand," Al said. "My wife spends money hand over fist. We had to get a big house just to hold all the furniture. Then there's the kids' braces, the payments on the Porsche, the credit-card bills that—"

"If you had asked, we could've worked it out. But you treated me like a schmuck," Dector said. "You've done it to me before. Thought I didn't know." He was struggling to keep his voice from cracking. He took off his glasses and buffed them to compose himself.

"I'll make it up to you, I promise. I won't draw a dime for as long as you think fair. I need you, Phil."

"I've already accepted another offer."

"You bastard!" Winters had been feeling the nausea twinges that presaged a migraine. Now the throbbing by his left temple began.

"My attorney will call on Monday," Dector said. He stuffed one last report into his overflowing pockets. The file cabinet and desk drawers gaped open. A pearl-handled Colt .45 automatic lay exposed in the top drawer.

Winters had bought a matched set—and given one to his partner—after a payroll robbery several months earlier. But Dector had looked at the weapon distastefully and stowed it away. It was typical of Al to make a grand gesture in a way that Phil found inappropriate.

Al picked up the gun without thinking. He pressed his other hand against the side of his head, trying to squeeze out the pain. "Don't go," he ordered.

Dector looked up from the box he was taping shut. "Put that away. It's liable to go off."

"It's not fair. You can't do this to me, you fuckin' creep." He clenched his teeth to try to still the migraine.

Dector looked like he was about to cry. "I better go."

Al squeezed the trigger. He didn't know why Phil suddenly had a third eye, a dark, oozy hole in the middle of his forehead. He didn't understand why Dector slumped to the floor, a surprised expression on his face. Then he realized. He was a murderer.

Had anyone heard the shot? He glanced down the hallway, then dashed to the window. There was no sound but the ringing in his ears. The agonizing throbbing got worse. Not now, please not now, he thought. He ran back to the door and locked himself in.

His fingerprints were on the gun. Maybe on other things in the office. What had he touched? He ran around the room frantically wiping. He stopped. His fingerprints *should* be all over the office. Maybe he should just turn himself in, throw himself on the mercy of the court? Could the company attorney help? Winters fell to his knees, nauseous and dizzy from pain. "Oh God, oh God, what do I do, what do I do?" he mumbled.

He dug Glenn Kelly's business card out of his wallet and called the home number written on the back. He said only that he needed to see him urgently, at the office. Glenn said he'd be right over.

Al waited, the gun in his hand, the body cooling on the floor. With his free hand he pressed against his skull, where a cruel giant was banging a hot poker. He was turned so he didn't have to look at Dector's corpse. His panic was subsiding. He could count on Kelly. He felt like a little kid who had done something bad but knew his big brother would take care of it.

Al had met Kelly at a San Diego electronics trade show a year earlier. He never had found out exactly what Kelly

3

did. It had to be something to do with the defense industry—
Kelly always seemed to be around the latest high-tech ex-
hibits, spy-satellite gear, lasers, radar, sonar. Kelly knew
the best hot-spots, the foxiest gals, the wildest after-hours
clubs. He'd pick up the tab smoothly. The men had hit it
off instantly, like old, best friends.

"If ever, and I mean ever, you need help, you can trust
me completely," Glenn had said.

He was a few years older than Winters, but he moved
with a youthful, confident, athletic grace. Kelly was a
get-things-done kind of guy. One of the girls they'd picked
up had said he reminded her of Sean Connery. Kelly had
laughed and hummed a few bars of the James Bond theme.

The knock at the door made Winters jump. "Who is
it?" he asked, lifting the gun. He wasn't sure whether to
point it at the door or his own head.

"It's Glenn."

Winters rushed to the door and unlocked it.

"What happened?" Kelly asked after he stepped into
the room. His penetrating hazel eyes gazed dispassionately
at Dector's body.

"There was a struggle," Al said. "He grabbed the gun.
I wrestled it from him and—"

"It doesn't look like that," Kelly said, bending over to
study Dector's wound. "I'd say he was shot from about
four feet. You better come up with another story."

"What should I do? What should I do?" Al sobbed, the
.45 dangling from his hand.

"Put the gun down."

The distraught Winters did as he was told.

Kelly donned black leather driving gloves. He slid the
gun into his waistband. He typed a few sentences on the
IBM Selectric and showed it to Winters.

"But—this, this is confessing to premeditated murder!"

"That's right," Kelly said. "I'll help you out, make it

4

look like a burglary. But I'm going to keep this. If you get cold feet and think about naming me as an accessory after the fact, remember, it will go badly for you. Premeditated murder carries a much tougher sentence than a crime of passion."

Al looked around the room as if there was something he could find to save him.

"You'll be the sole owner," Kelly said soothingly. "I have access to venture capitalists looking for a company like yours. The company will boom with their funding and you at the helm."

"What do you want?"

"To keep you out of prison. Whatever I ask, you know it's better than that. Right?"

"Yes." Al signed the paper.

"We have to make it look like a burglary and go over the story of how you discovered the body. Listen carefully. Dector was working late. He surprised a burglar. Understand?"

"A burglar."

Kelly began putting Dector's papers back in the file cabinet. "You were also working late. You were in the bathroom when you heard the noise. You saw a figure running down the hall. A black male, in his twenties. Dark clothing. Short-cut hair. Sneakers. That's all you can recall. Don't get fancy and let the cops trick you into saying more."

"I—I can't do it. The cops will be able to tell I'm lying. I can't believe this is happening to me. It's not fair. I'm scared, Glenn, please help me."

"Don't worry. It's normal to be scared when you've just found your partner dead. This is going to work out quite well for you, Al. You're going to be a big success. It's a smart businessman who can turn a liability into an asset."

Kelly knocked a box of papers to the floor. He lifted Dector's corpse, fluttering pages under the body. "Mess up the furniture," he told Al. "Dector died after a heroic struggle."

Al timidly knocked over a chair. Then he got over-enthusiastic, and Kelly had to stop him before he demolished the entire office.

ONE
PRESENT

THE ROOM HAD ONCE BEEN WHERE THE CZAR ENTERTAINED, a cavernous chamber with ornate molding, priceless paintings, and glowing chandeliers. At the center was a rosewood table, with mother-of-pearl inlay, that could comfortably seat two dozen. The massive high-backed chairs around it were rosewood and leather. Fifteen of the seats, which were almost grand enough to be called thrones, were filled.

There was no fixed number of members in the Politburo. It ranged from the low teens to the low twenties, depending on who had the cunning to claw his way from the Central Committee of the Communist Party to the pinnacle of power in the Soviet Union.

Fyodor Levski, the six-foot-three-inch, close-to-three-hundred-pound KGB chairman, liked to loom over his seated colleagues when he spoke. He was sixty-five, with snow-white hair and a face that turned as red as a Ukranian beet at the least emotion.

Levski had begun his Committee for State Security career as a teenager during Stalin's reign of terror. He had switched loyalties at the right time and emerged as a fast-rising climber shortly after Khrushchev's speech denouncing Stalin in 1956. The same year he had helped mastermind the crushing of the rebellion in Hungary.

His first wife had fortuitously died, and he'd married a woman who was a niece of Leonid Brezhnev. As was the case with the old aristocracy, there is a great deal of intermarriage at the upper levels of Soviet society. It makes running the government a family business.

Now, after a lifetime of service, and five years of running the largest intelligence agency in the world, he was telling his fellow Politburo members of his grand plan.

"It will be that easy to destabilize the United States. The ironic part is that all we will be doing is giving the American imperialists exactly what they want."

Levski beamed his toothy smile at the most powerful men of the largest country on earth. He had them cowed. He was confident no one would dare take on the Chairman of the KGB, even though he had admitted breaking the rules by instigating, without a consensus, such an aggressive foreign-policy move.

"We will use the Americans' own capitalistic greed and fear of communism to destroy them," he continued. "I am not exaggerating when I say their cities will be in flames, their economy a wreck, their people begging to accept any offer we make. Russian troops will march down American streets and be welcomed as heroes." He took a sip of Bordzomi mineral water and sat down. The only sounds were the gurgle of the silver samovar standing in a corner of the room and the wheezing of the elderly Politburo members.

Levski smiled at First General Secretary and President of the Politburo Anton Zaroslavski. Zaroslavski's thin shoulders seemed to be wrapped around his ears. He was seventy-five, suffering from emphysema, and had a death-rattle cough. Levski had seen a purloined report from the Krem-

lin Polyclinic. Doctors gave Zaroslavski about three months
to live. Levski had timed his announcement to assure his
own ascension to the number-one slot. He hadn't wanted
to reveal his plan until it was too far along to stop. Better
to go to sea in a leaky boat than to share a secret, he had
been taught. But he had to show his peers he was first
among equals.

Sunlight filtered through the stained-mica windows and
reflected off a jewel-encrusted Fabergé egg resting on a
three-hundred-year-old credenza. Zaroslavski borrowed artwork from the nearby museum in what had once been the
Cathedral of the Annunciation. After the Politburo members savored the priceless work, it was returned for view-
ing by ordinary citizens. A previous Kremlin official had
used priceless czarist china at his daughter's wedding,
causing a minor scandal when dishes were broken by a
drunken guest.

Zaroslavski smiled back at Levski. The dying man gave
the appearance of being unaware of his surroundings. It
was one of the tactics that had brought him to the top.
Ever since he had been a scrawny little boy, Zaroslavski
had thrived by letting the tough kids fight it out, then
moving in when they were exhausted. He hoped he could
follow the same policy with the United States and China.

Zaroslavski had come to power after the premature toppling of Mikhail Gorbachev. The previous First General
Secretary had succeeded in replacing most of the old guard,
but then Andrei Gromyko had led the old-timers in a
rebellion. By the time the struggle was over, both sides
were decimated. Zaroslavski had stepped in, pledging unity
and a giant step forward. Neither promise had been ful-
filled, but at least the suspicious "heart attacks" in the
Kremlin had stopped.

Zaroslavski's bony, pale fingers toyed with the panel of
push buttons next to his chair. There were buttons to
summon security men, if a shouting match became physi-

cal; doctors, if one of the elderly politicians succumbed to ill health; secretaries, if they wanted to pass on their edicts to the rubberstamp Supreme Soviet that met for two weeks a year; and domestic staff, if they needed valets, butlers, or waiters.

Levski glowered, waiting for a response. Usually his supporters immediately rushed to echo his comments, to talk about what a wise move he had made.

"Comrade Levski's plan is a bold and imaginative stroke of genius," the minister of agriculture finally said. But he was a known Levski sycophant, and his words were worthless.

Most of the others avoided Levski's gaze. Despite the Politburo members' impressive titles, what really mattered to each was his place in the Communist Party and whom he owed his loyalty to. Was his mentor in or out of power? Did he in turn have a lot of *blat* on the Central Committee? Or was he bound for a post with the Chukchi Eskimos in the perpetually frozen north? The ministers would have to mull over what was said, what it meant, and who was backing it. There was no room for spontaneous decision.

The samovar gurgled. The egg glittered.

Defense Minister Nikolai Gorchev met Levski's gaze, and Levski held it. Finally, Gorchev blinked and turned to Zaroslavski. "Mr. First Secretary, what is *your* reaction to Chairman Levski's plan?"

The squat Gorchev had a bullet-shaped head and a thick neck; he was a Hero of the Soviet Union medal winner for his actions commanding tank forces against the Nazis during the Great Patriotic War. Some wits said he was modeled after the T-34 tank, others that the tank was modeled after him. He had a surprisingly high voice and hated to speak.

"I would like to hear your opinion, comrade," Zaroslavski said.

"I think it's the most dangerous scheme I have ever

heard," Gorchev said, his voice getting higher. "To have instigated it without consulting the other members of the Politburo reveals dangerous revisionist tendencies, a regression toward the cult of the individual."

"I didn't share the plan before because the more who know, the more chance that tongues will flap," Levski said. "I am consulting with the Politburo today before progressing any further. The operation I have instigated will bring glory to the farsighted leadership of the Motherland. The peace-loving peoples of the Soviet Union can move forward into the twenty-first century without concern over the aggressions of the United States."

"It is brinkmanship at its worst," Gorchev insisted. "It could draw us into a nuclear war."

"Only if the Americans find out, and they won't—unless you intend to tell them." Levski stood up. "We can't depend on the glorious Army," he said, sneering at Gorchev. "It can't even subdue a pack of hooligan Afghans with fifty-year-old rifles."

"You know very well that they are backed by the CIA; otherwise we would have—"

Zaroslavski coughed. "Comrades, please. Sit down, Chairman Levski. Does anyone else care to share his opinion?"

Gorchev didn't expect the other men in the room to help him. The KGB chairman had thick dossiers on them. Of course, Levski was prohibited by law from investigating members of the Central Committee, let alone the Politburo. But their exploits prior to reaching that status would be tucked away in files. They might terrorize their ministries, beat their wives, eliminate challengers in their own department, but they recognized that Levski was more deadly than any of them.

"I think Comrade Levski has an interesting idea," the foreign minister said after a long delay. Gorchev clenched and unclenched his powerful hands. "But I think Comrade Gorchev has a valid point. The chairman of the KGB should have raised this matter before the Politburo years ago when he put it into motion. It could lead to war.''

"Perhaps you are scared," Levski snapped.

"Only a fool wouldn't be scared of war with the United States," Gorchev said.

Levski's face reddened.

"There's no saying there would be a war," interjected the minister of agriculture. "The capitalist system is doomed. We are just helping it to its predestined demise."

"Comrade Levski's plan is dangerously shortsighted," the foreign minister said. "It's better to win the war of ideology slowly than risk total destruction."

"The only way there will be war is if they find out, and the only way they could find out is if you chatter about it," Levski said, pointing an accusatory finger at the defense minister. "Outside this room, only three other people know of the plan."

"That's not possible," Gorchev said.

"Even though your own intelligence service is hopelessly riddled with incompetents and defectors," Levski said with a sneer, "I'm sure someone there can explain to you about compartmentalization. Subordinates may work on pieces of a project and not be aware of the end product."

Levski and Gorchev glared at each other. No one spoke. Some of the men fidgeted or fiddled with papers. The foreign minister scraped a fingernail on the table's mother-of-pearl inlay. He was convinced Levski's plan to topple the U.S. government would not work. But the idea of having an American president they could influence, however slightly, would be invaluable. What if they were able to plant a few people in key positions? How much could an assistant secretary of defense tell them? Or a top man at the State Department? What would it be worth to know exactly what NATO was up to, or the positions of their nuclear submarines? How much faster could they get access to American technology, to pirate designs or come up with countermeasures?

First Secretary Zaroslavski coughed. It was one of his attention-getting coughs, not a death rattle. Everyone looked up.

"The plan will proceed," Zaroslavski said. "But we must be kept informed. At any sign of problems it will be terminated."

"Of course, comrade," Levski said smugly. He slipped his files into a Brazilian alligator-skin attaché case and strode from the room.

He'd won the battle, but not by much. What he'd confirmed was that Gorchev also had his eye on Zaroslavski's seat. It didn't surprise him. Only the commander of the Soviet military forces had as much power as himself, Levski thought, as he passed through the Kremlin's Spasskaya Gate with his two bodyguards.

Though he had an office in the Kremlin Administrative Building, his real headquarters was in the Lubyanka on Dzerzhinsky Square. Much of the KGB's staff had moved to a new compound on the Moscow ring road, but the Chairman stayed close to the Kremlin.

Half of the Lubyanka was a gothic six-story structure built at the turn of the century for an insurance company. The other half was a ten-story addition erected by German POWs and featuring the usual grandiose Stalinesque architecture. The old building had more frills and fancy touches. However, the radiators were cold, the electricity frequently failed, and air-conditioning for humid Moscow summers was nonexistent. The elevators, when they worked, creaked and groaned and took five minutes to climb between floors.

Naturally, Levski's third-floor office was in the newer building. It was a corner office with a view of the square and the statue of Feliks Dzerzhinsky, founder of the Cheka, which had become the GPU, then the OGPU, NKVD, NKGB, MGB, and finally, in 1954, the KGB. Levski had a brass plaque with a quote from Dzerzhinsky: "Trust is good, control is better."

If Gorchev wasn't crushed, the other Politburo eunuchs might get ideas, Levski knew. But taking on a Politburo colleague would demand a delicate ruthlessness. If word of his ambitions leaked, even Levski could get into trouble.

Which was why Levski had brought in Marshal Vladimir Pavlovich Krovili. Krovili could've been head of the KGB if he wasn't such a pervert, Levski thought. Krovili was—besides being the deputy chief in charge of the Second Chief Directorate, which handled counterintelligence and control of the Soviet civilian population—a talented musician and chess grandmaster. But whenever he wasn't using his mind, he was using his prick, generally on a woman under the age of twenty.

Krovili was fifty-eight, in superb physical condition, and said to be sexually active at least twice a day. Georgians had reputations as womanizers, but Krovili boasted a truly prodigious appetite. When he was younger, he had been credited with more bedroom activity than Catherine the Great. During the Great Patriotic War, half the assaults on German women were said to have been by Krovili.

Levski knew of a dozen sex scandals involving Krovili. They had been successfully covered up. But Levski had the details. Krovili would do exactly what was ordered. If Krovili failed, Levski could pass it off as an overambitious attempt by a subordinate.

TWO
1974

MARSHAL VLADIMIR PAVLOVICH KROVILI WAS ENJOYING HIS usual midafternoon break. While other men his age napped or took long lunch hours, Krovili showed his dedication to the cause by interviewing students from Verkhonoye, the House of Love, where the KGB second directorate trained its "swallows" and "ravens." The swallows were women between the ages of eighteen and twenty-two who were prostitute-spies. The ravens were gigolo-spies, who often had to be bisexual. During their four-month training at Verkhonoye, swallows and ravens learned how to arrange seemingly accidental encounters, develop relationships, seduce and set up victims for blackmail, make love unashamedly while cameras were watching and microphones taking in pillow talk.

Marshal Krovili perused the file in front of him with the same intensity he devoted to the copies of *Penthouse* he had smuggled into the country. The girl was eighteen years old, from Estonia, a member of the Komsomol, the Communist young people's organization. She was a hard worker, volunteered often, and was serious in her studies. In her file photo she looked fourteen, and had the clean Scandinavian beauty of so many Estonian girls.

15

Krovili moistened his finger and ran it over his bushy eyebrows. His coarse peasant features had fooled many an adversary. He went to the door. The girl was sitting primly outside, even more beautiful than her photo.

"Come in, *tovarich*," he said warmly.

He sat down behind his desk, every inch the important official. He gestured to one of the big leather chairs. It had cut-down legs and forced her to look up to him.

"Well," he said loudly, and she flinched. "I see you have a great deal of sincerity."

She nodded.

"That is good." He held up her file and thumbed through it so she could see. He made grunts of acknowledgment and wrote a quick note to himself.

"I might be able to advance your career rapidly. Perhaps an overseas assignment. Would you be interested?"

"*Da!* If it served the Motherland," she said dutifully.

The bitch didn't care about the *rodina*. She wanted to be in Paris, shopping for fashions to put on her warm young body, he was sure. "Come here, child."

She stood slowly and came around behind the desk. He indicated that she should kneel on the floor. He stroked her long blond hair. It was as soft as the sable coat his wife had insisted he buy her. He pushed that cow from his mind and thought of the young woman before him.

"Show me what you've learned," he said, unzipping his fly. He intentionally recalled a chess game he had played as the girl went to work. There was no point in making it too easy for her.

He stayed limp despite her ministrations. Finally, he grabbed her hair and tugged. She yelped as he snapped her head up.

"If you fail this test, *tovarich*, you and your whole family are in trouble. *Ponyal?*"

She gulped. "Yes, honored comrade."

"That's good," he said, growing excited by the fear in her eyes.

The Little Czar rose to attention. He shoved her head back down. Her movements were more desperate now. He kept his hand tightly on her hair, pulling at it, forcing the Little Czar deeper and deeper into her mouth. A couple of times she gagged, but she continued.

The girl, coughing and disheveled, scurried from Krovili's office. A contented Krovili came out and said, "I want her back next week for more practice."

His aide nodded. Stefan Blok was Krovili's hatchet man. His duties ranged from fending off subordinates who wanted to bother the deputy chief to procuring women when Krovili wanted to try rougher stuff to occasional special assignments. He was six feet four inches of muscle, with a bristly crew cut and a perpetual scowl. Even hard-nosed KGB operatives were intimidated by him.

The young Blok, a promising athlete with a chance at both the wrestling and weight-lifting teams, had been caught in bed with his male roommate. Homosexuality was a serious crime against the state. He had been given a choice: Work for the KGB or go to Peter and Paul Prison. He found out much later that his roommate had been a KGB raven.

Fifteen years later Blok held the rank of captain. He had worked for the First Chief Directorate, overseas operations, and helped destabilize an African nation by stabbing and mutilating a liberal pro-West politician, making it look like a tribal killing. A specialist at dirty work, *gryaznaya rabota*, he had also eliminated a defector in London, garroting the man with piano wire. But he had nearly killed the Soviet cultural attaché while on assignment in Frankfurt, after an argument over the merits of the Dynamo hockey team. The cultural attaché, the nephew of the editor of *Pravda*, had lost the use of one eye. Blok had almost been dumped from the KGB, until Krovili took him into his unit. Blok repaid him with complete loyalty.

"Comrade Marshal," Blok said, "Chairman Levski asked for you to come to his office as soon as you were done."

"What did you tell him I was doing?" Krovili asked.

"I didn't say anything. He knew. He made a joke about your fiery Georgian blood and how he wished he could bottle it for himself."

A good sign, Krovili thought. He put his jacket on and hurried down the hallway to the chairman's office. The halls had pea-soup-green walls that hadn't been painted in ten years, linoleum floors, and stark fluorescent lighting. Public areas in the building seemed deliberately depressing. Inside the high-ceilinged, spacious offices, however, the KGB brass had plush carpeting, fireplaces, ornate antique furniture—or the most modern imports from Helsinki, if the occupant preferred—and artwork.

Levski waved Krovili into a red-velvet Queen Anne armchair that had once supported Czar Nicholas II's bottom. "Let me hear if you can figure out what happened."

Krovili had expected such a challenge, but he hesitated and pretended he was just coming up with an answer. He glanced at the wall. Levski had life-size oil paintings of Lenin and himself hanging in gilt frames.

"I would guess Gorchev protested. Zaroslavski held back, and the other mastodons lined up to kiss your ass," Krovili said.

"You remain as astute as ever," Levski said, puffing on his cigar. "Can you anticipate what I am going to do?"

"I would guess that, Comrade Chairman, you will mount a bold counterattack. Destroy Gorchev, and no one will oppose you." Krovili paused, and Levski nodded. "Getting to a member of the Politburo is difficult. The top of the tank may be strong, yet if you destroy the treads, it goes nowhere. So perhaps you will attack those under Gorchev, showing him as an incompetent, impotent leader."

"Impotent. I didn't think that word was even in your vocabulary," Levski said with a lewd smile. "Can you handle castrating our illustrious defense minister?"

*　　*　　*

Knowing the weaknesses of these powerful military men will help my career, Krovili mused as he returned to his office. Information, especially secrets, was a valuable commodity.

He thought of an admiral he'd believed was a homosexual and a major general he knew was heavily involved with *fartsovshchiki*, black marketeers. Then there was the man he really wanted to get.

Colonel Anatoli Vasilevich Petrov, a ranking power in the *Glavnoye Razvedyvatelnoye Upravlenie*, the Chief Intelligence Directorate of the General Staff, Soviet military intelligence. Petrov had been his enemy for more than forty years, going back to the time Petrov had pulled Krovili off a plump youngster on the outskirts of Berlin. The marshal would never forget his humiliation.

Krovili had been in charge of one of the units that kept Russian soldiers from retreating. They followed the troops, and shot those who didn't advance. Krovili had found the young German woman, fair and square, hiding under rubble. Three of his soldiers had pinned her down as he ripped her clothes, exposing a great pair of boobs. He squeezed them roughly, and his accomplices had laughed. They knew they would get their turn when Krovili was done.

"Have you been screwing the German soldiers?" he asked her.

"No! No!" She couldn't have been more than fifteen.

"Good, it is fresh *kotik* for us."

She had screamed as he thrust into her, which made him pound harder. Then suddenly he had been pulled off, the Little Czar waggling obscenely in the air. He was surrounded by a squad of regular soldiers.

"You are a disgrace to the uniform," Petrov, then a lieutenant, had said. The girl scuttled away, clutching her torn clothes.

"Girls are not the enemy," Petrov had lectured. "Heroes like you haven't faced combat troops. You don't know what the enemy looks like."

Krovili had only been sergeant, but a sergeant in the NKVD! He swung at Petrov, who blocked his blow and knocked him down. Krovili reached for his pistol. Behind Petrov, Petrov's squad aimed their Tokarevs at Krovili and his men. The regular troopers would have been happy to have an excuse to gun them down. Krovili had zipped up, brushed himself off, and marched away with as much dignity as he could muster.

He had never forgiven Petrov, and had tried to avenge himself several times over the years. He had mounted his campaign covertly, and Petrov did not know who it was in the massive bureaucracy who was out to get him.

But Petrov had stayed clear of every snare. He shunned hetero- and homosexual propositions, avoided the black market, and ran successful operations. Krovili had even arranged for Petrov to be offered a KGB job, to get him into his own domain. Petrov had opted to stay with the GRU. Few who were offered a KGB job dared turn it down. But not Petrov. Somehow he had survived, and prospered, rising to become one of the top men in the rival spy agency. Through untraceable backstabbing Krovili had kept Petrov from achieving the rank of general. That was the only victory the KGB man could point to.

Now Krovili could mix business and pleasure. He told Blok to order up the files of the hundred leading military men. The KGB, which handled internal security for all agencies, had the most extensive files. It would seem like a periodic sweep of the military brass conducted to look for possible defectors. "Tell them it's preventive medicine," Krovili said. "Give them a story about renewed efforts at rooting out ideological subversion."

He didn't care which fish he caught in his net, as long as Colonel Anatoli Vasilevich Petrov was among them.

THREE

ROBERT WELLINGTON SHUFFLED THROUGH THE STACK OF papers on his desk. The reports were marked EYES ONLY. Wellington was convinced that his subordinates would stamp *The New York Times* TOP SECRET if they could. Next to his chrome-and-glass-top desk, the "burn" basket—for the collection and total destruction of classified paperwork—was already filled.

Wellington was a dapper fifty-seven years old. His hair had been gray since his sophomore year at Harvard. He had attended the same schools, played on the same polo fields, and dated the same Vassar women as many of the Agency old boys. Ivy League college, Fletcher School of Diplomacy, house in Georgetown. He knew the right tailors, the right restaurants, and the right way to mix a martini. Or the right service to supply a houseboy to mix it.

He had been a successful investment banker when the president had tapped him, and with a combination of *noblesse oblige* and little-boy fascination with spies, he'd accepted the position as America's premier spymaster.

He had tried tightening supervision when he'd taken

over the Central Intelligence Agency. But the accuracy of intelligence he brought to the White House had declined; confidential information had turned up in newspapers; station productivity had dropped. So he'd made peace with the old-timers, the hard-liners, the cold warriors who were career spooks; and the Agency had gotten back to normal.

In fact, better than normal. They'd bested the National Security Agency and received responsibility and funding for a new satellite-photo-enhancement system. They'd contradicted the Defense Intelligence Agency over the stability of the Marcos regime and been proven right. They'd developed high-level agents in place in the Czech and Polish governments, as well as continued to get vital information from a source deep in the Kremlin. Now his Deputy Director for Operations was promising an intelligence coup that would rank with the Penkovsky papers and the defection of Arkady Shevchenko.

Wellington reread the file. It was marked EYES ONLY, but in this case he agreed with the classification. An operation of this sensitivity would be carried out with access limited to a half dozen people.

The file was headed "Borzoi." Lately, the CIA had been using the names of dog breeds to label operations. They went through groups of categories periodically. There had been the hat era, when "Fedora" was a key agent. Clothing, animals, and liquors were other op names. Columnist Jack Anderson, subject of an Agency probe during the Nixon years, had been labeled "Brandy," his assistant called "Cordial." In the current series they had already run through "Afghan," "Airedale," "Akita," "Basenji," "Basset," "Beagle," and "Bloodhound." But "Borzoi"—the sleek Russian wolfhound—seemed particularly apt.

Colonel Anatoli Vasilevich Petrov wanted to defect. According to the file, he was a career intelligence man, the eighth-most-important official at the GRU. He had remained aloof from GRU in-house politics, and had carved out a niche for himself overseeing their ELINT—electronic intelligence. In addition, Petrov had operated under deep cover at least twice in the United States. He had been picked up and detained in Turkey and Hong Kong, but no espionage charges were ever pressed.

The file alleged that Petrov was behind one of the more clever GRU thefts in recent years, in which they had gotten away with an entire U.S. combat-tank engine. It was not the sort of thing that could be shipped back to the USSR in a diplomatic pouch. All the major ports had been under surveillance by FBI counterintelligence agents, but still there had been an urgent need to smuggle it out. Petrov, using a dummy corporation, had bought a yacht and had the engine mounted into it. By the time the FBI figured out what he had done, the yacht had rendezvoused at sea with a Soviet trawler, and the engine was on its way to Moscow.

In the personal profile Petrov was described as unmarried, with no children or vices. The sixty-three-year-old was an avid fencer—he had made the Soviet Olympic team—had an engineering background, and was fluent in English. He was surrounded by a loyal cadre but known as a loner, a quality not regarded as a virtue by the Soviets.

Petrov could be a bogus defector, a Soviet plant, supplying disinformation, Wellington mused. The fallout from the false defection of Vitaly Yurchenko—the KGB deputy who had given the CIA information for three months before returning home—was still being felt.

Or maybe he had cracked up, not an uncommon problem in the high-stress, high-stakes espionage game. He might even be a well-intentioned but misinformed defector. But why was a loyal, long-time top-ranked Soviet officer deciding to throw his career away, giving up the perks and privileges, and betraying the system he had served so faithfully? On the other hand, if he was the real thing, could the Agency afford to snub him, the way they had initially turned down another GRU colonel, Oleg Penkovsky?

Still, the biggest question stemmed from the conditions of the defection. They were, even by spook standards, bizarre. Wellington glanced at his Rolex. The Agency's Deputy director for operations would be on time. And, Wellington hoped, he would have the answer.

The Agency was divided into four divisions. The largest was Intelligence, which handled the analyzing and writing up of data. Management and Services was responsible for personnel, medical support, training, and security. Science and Technology took care of the "Octopus" computer and electronic intelligence gathering. The most controversial directorate was Operations, known inside the Agency as Clandestine Services.

Clandestine Services Chief James Mitchell Tuttle didn't get along with Wellington. The director figured it was because Tuttle had expected to get the number-one position himself. But the president had wanted an outsider, a fresh perspective.

Tuttle had joined the Agency during the chilliest days of the Cold War, and his attitude toward espionage and the Soviets was as hard-line as J. Edgar Hoover's. The Chief of Clandestine Services was a lean ascetic who jogged five miles a day before driving from his McLean home to the Agency's Virginia headquarters. The few friends who had visited his home reported that it was so meticulous, they felt nervous sitting down and wrinkling the sofa. He was the holder of a record number of "jockstrap medals," the Agency awards so named because they couldn't be worn in public.

The intercom on Wellington's desk buzzed at the precise moment Tuttle was due. Wellington organized his papers, let Tuttle cool his heels for five minutes, and then buzzed him in. Tuttle came in and stood before Wellington's desk at attention, his spine held erect.

"Have you read the material?" he asked.

"Yes. Petrov would be quite a catch. When did the overture come?"

"He made a brush contact with McCarthy in Moscow three days ago," Tuttle said. His pronunciation was crisp and precise. "Petrov was showing off, since McCarthy was under deep cover and not supposed to be known to the hostiles. It was such a slick move, our man didn't even know it until he got home and cleaned out his jacket pocket."

"Why do you think Petrov is doing it?"

Tuttle looked at Wellington condescendingly. "Why do Jews convert to Christianity? Why do husbands divorce their wives? Why does a Redskins fan suddenly—"

"I get your point. But I am concerned about the ground rules the colonel is insisting on. Have you ever encountered anything like this?"

"No, but there's always a first time."

"I just don't understand it. Why does he want this Eric Garfield to escort him out of the Soviet Union? Petrov's been in and out of our country at least twice that we know of. His message said he would handle documentation for his exit. Why this Garfield? Who in blazes is *he?* You said you'd be vetting him. Can you explain it?"

"Garfield is a twenty-eight-year-old white male, a resident of Brooklyn Heights in New York. He's six feet, weighs two hundred pounds, brown hair, hazel eyes, no identifying marks or tattoos.

"His academic record is uninspired, though he has an IQ of a hundred and thirty. He graduated the State University of New York at Stonybrook as a political science major.

"He has been active in politics since he was sixteen. He rose from stuffing envelopes and ringing doorbells to advance work to managing campaigns. All by age twenty-five. He was hired by Winner Political Consultants at eighty-five thousand dollars a year. He lasted a year before having an idealistic break with Winner."

"What kind of idealistic break?"

"He found out that the candidate he was working for was a front for Mafia interests," Tuttle said. "Garfield was surprisingly naive. He left the job and free-lanced, often for longshot or underdog candidates. Three out of the four he has worked for wound up winning."

"Impressive. What're his political beliefs?"

"Eclectic, based on his personal opinion of the politician more than the party line. He's helped two Democrats, a Republican, and an independent. He has no apparent leaning toward communism, if that's what you're getting at. Here's what we have so far." Tuttle dropped a file folder on Wellington's desk, making it a challenging gesture.

"Sounds like an interesting young man, but that doesn't tell me why Petrov picked him as an escort."

"There are several possibilities," Tuttle said. "We have begun a twenty-four-hour surveillance of Garfield to ascertain if he is more than he seems. Currently, he works for an assemblyman in Brooklyn—Brighton Beach, an area with a heavy Russian émigré population. Perhaps that's where Petrov heard of him." Tuttle held up his right hand and counted off fingers with his left. "A second possibility: his father, who ran a restaurant on the east side of Manhattan. Raymond Garfield had contact with the Irgun and later Mossad. Unfortunately, his file was shredded during the Church Committee witch-hunt. I'm hoping to pull backup files out of the archives."

"Is his father still alive?"

"Negative. Both father and mother are deceased. Natural causes, as far as we know. Eric Garfield has no siblings."

"Other possible connections?"

Tuttle lifted a third finger. "His ex-girlfriend had ties to Salvadoran leftists. They met when she was handing out antigovernment literature on the steps of Brooklyn Borough Hall. The relationship lasted eleven months and was quite serious. They lived together. She broke it off. That's all we know about it, for now." Tuttle dropped his hands to his sides. "I'm sure he's done something to earn Soviet attention. The problem is, do we have enough time to find out why without losing Petrov?"

"The problem *is*, do we jeopardize an American citizen who is not under discipline by sending him over to the Soviet Union? I have misgivings about that, as well as the question of why he was chosen. Has Garfield been contacted?"

"It's too early for that," Tuttle said. "We have to know what his vulnerabilities are before we move in."

"What if he refuses to go?"

"I'm sure he can be convinced to do it. Using him is actually in our interest. We give him a week's training. During that period we can continue to look for a Petrov–Garfield connection. If we find it, maybe we can exploit it without Garfield leaving the country. If not, we send him over. If he's caught, the Russians don't get as much information as they would from a less expendable asset."

"I hate to sound like a babe in the woods, but convincing an amateur to go behind the Iron Curtain on a high-risk espionage op rubs me the wrong way." Wellington paused. "Get me more background. Let me sleep on it."

Tuttle nodded and walked from the room.

Wellington leaned back in his chair. He didn't like the idea of endangering the young man. The election, however, was only a few months away. The moderate presi-

dent was being hard pressed by his archconservative foe.
A recent private poll favored the challenger by eight percent. A major intelligence coup, timed just right, might
help the president win.

But why had Petrov insisted on Garfield? Wellington
thought of Winston Churchill's quote: "I cannot forecast
to you the action of Russia. It is a riddle wrapped in a
mystery inside an enigma." The more he dealt with the
Soviet Union, the more he respected Churchill's wisdom.

FOUR

As administrative aide to New York State assembly-man Steve Sussman, Eric Garfield wrote Sussman's speeches, handled his community office, traveled to Albany for weeks at a time, substituted for Sussman at boring community meetings, would run Sussman's campaign, and acted as an interpreter. Garfield, while far from fluent, could make himself understood in Yiddish and Spanish. He was partic-ularly proud of his command of the Russian language, which included several hundred words and phrases the elderly Brighton Beach émigrés delighted in teaching him.

Sitting in the metal folding chair next to Garfield's desk was Benjamin Franklin Sokolov, a refugee from the Soviet Union who had changed his name "in honor of great revolutionary, greater than Lenin." The graying Sokolov, with a small brown bag on his lap, kept wringing a cap as he sat on the metal folding chair in front of Eric's desk.

Sokolov was talking about the *rodina*, the Motherland, and how he missed picking mushrooms in the forests outside Moscow. Eric smiled and nodded along, while scratching off the press list the name of a reporter who had burned Sussman by using an off-the-record comment in a story.

Running the understaffed, underfunded office was a challenge Eric thrived on. He employed his tendency to worry the way a watch used a mainspring. He would "what if" a situation until every eventuality was covered. Four months earlier he had read an interview with Sussman in *The New York Times*. He had liked what the Assemblyman said about crime, the economy, and the future of New York. Eric had volunteered for a low-paying job, and quickly put Sussman into the fast lane.

Eric made a note to himself to call the chairman of the Brooklyn Democratic organization to arrange for Sussman to get a good table at an upcoming hundred-dollar-a-plate dinner. Sokolov continued talking.

"What's the difference between capitalism and communism?" he asked.

"Well, under capitalism the means of production and distribution are privately owned. Under communism—"

Sokolov held up a hand and laughed. "*Nyet*. Under capitalism man exploits man. Under communism it's the other way around."

Eric smiled. "Is there any specific way I can help you?" he asked.

"Is silly, I know, but I still am nerves in government office," Sokolov said. "I talk too much like old woman. Talk, talk, talk."

"There's no need to be nervous," Garfield said. "We're here to help you."

"That's what they say in Russia, too. But you never know how they will help you. Or if you come out of office at all. You know what Lubyanka building is?"

"I've heard stories about it. That's KGB headquarters."

"You know it, buddy. Anyway, you know why Lubyanka is tallest building in Moscow?"

"*Nyet*. Why?"

"Because from basement you can see Siberia."

Eric laughed. "I'll remember that. But you didn't come here just to tell me jokes, did you?"

"No. I came to thank you. Immigration got papers all right. I become citizen very soon."

"That's great," Eric said, shaking Sokolov's hand.

"Thank you. I only wish my brother, Boris, would come here."

"He's still in Russia?"

"In Odessa. He has business on the waterfront, near Potemkin Stairs. He thinks he will change things. He publishes *samizdat.*"

"He must be a brave man. They don't take kindly to underground newsletters."

"He's not brave. He's crazy," Sokolov said. "*Meshuggener* Boris. He drives truck by day and hands out papers at night. Calling for less privileges for *apparatchiki,* less corruption. He is, how do you say, urinating into air."

Eric grinned. "Pissing into the wind."

"Yes." Sokolov stood up and handed Eric the greasy paper bag. "My wife made this. Is only small gift. I hope you are liking it."

"Oh, she shouldn't have." As he opened the bag, the rich smell of the piroshki, meat and potatoes inside crisp dough, filled his nostrils. Eric took a bite and made an appropriate hum of pleasure.

Sokolov said, "I was wondering maybe you could help my friend?"

"What's the matter?"

"He wants his daughter to get into state university, but doesn't know how."

"The school will handle it, but if your friend has any questions, send him over. I'll see what I can do."

Sokolov left beaming. He was growing comfortable with American government.

Shirley Castellano—Sussman's bleach-blond, middle-aged secretary, the only other staff member in the Brighton office—signaled she had an important call holding. "Marty's on line three," she said.

Garfield picked up the phone. "Marty, are you a closet Republican?"

"What do you mean?" the gravelly-voiced man at the other end of the line bellowed.

Garfield spun in his swivel chair and looked at the big sign on the wall. "Ass Stephen Sussman" it said, large letters written on the cheap paper supermarkets use for sale signs. "Some words do not lend themselves to being abbreviated. 'Assemblyman' is one of them."

"What do you want for what you're paying? You told me to make it foot-high letters on a ten-foot banner. Let him shorten his name."

"Everyone calls him Steve. That's two letters right there. We've given you thousands in business, and this is what you do to us?"

Marty grumbled. Garfield got up from his small metal desk and looked out the window. The office was above a bagel bakery on Brighton Beach Avenue, the main thoroughfare for the area. It was a crowded, noisy, dirty street in perpetual gloom—the D train to Coney Island rumbled above the boulevard on tracks that blocked out the sun. Phone pressed against his ear, Eric gazed down on the busy street, looking for suspicious characters. For the past couple of days he'd had the feeling that someone was following him, although he couldn't point to anything or anyone specifically.

Shirley dropped a stack of letters on Garfield's desk. "Tell that *ganef* Marty I'll have my husband break his legs if he doesn't do right by you," she said. Her husband was a mild-mannered bookmaker, but she used the threat of mob violence at least once a day.

Eric smiled and reviewed the papers while arguing with

the signmaker. There were applications for welfare, complaints about potholes, requests for worker's compensation, demands for better police protection. People didn't know who to write to with problems about the city, the state, or the federal government. Garfield would handle those he could and refer the others to the proper agencies.

"Listen, Marty, I'd like to talk to you all day, but I can't. You know the campaign's getting into high gear. We'll be needing more signs than ever. If you can't handle it, I'm sure that Acme Sign can—"

"Those bums can't even spell 'dog.' "

"I know Steve was planning on working the name of the signmaker into a few of his speeches, something about a sign of the times."

"Okay, okay, you twisted my arm. I'll redo it."

"On better stock?"

"On better stock."

"By tomorrow night?"

"You're killing me, you know that?" Marty complained.

"Yeah, by tomorrow night."

"You're a prince among men," Garfield said.

At a little past noon the phone on his desk buzzed twice—Sussman's signal that he wanted to speak to Garfield. Eric rapped on the door to Sussman's office and walked in.

The walls were covered with contact paper that was supposed to look like wood paneling. Dozens of pictures of Sussman shaking hands with more-important politicians, big businessmen, and a few minor celebrities adorned the walls. There were three file cabinets, a TV on a rolling cart, a sofa, and a surplus public school teacher's oak desk. Behind the desk sat Steve Sussman, ten years older than Garfield, clean-cut, with a permanently sincere expression on his face.

"What's going on with you?" Sussman asked without preliminaries.

"What do you mean?"

"You missed the school board meeting last night. I've been on the phone half the morning making excuses to the battle-ax who runs the damn thing."

"Hell. I'm sorry, I forgot."

"That's a first. You're supposed to be efficient. You do the scheduling, the smoothing out, the worrying. I'm the one who's the fuckup around here. I must say, it's almost worth it though, getting to see that even you can make a mistake," Sussman said without rancor.

"I guess I didn't pencil it in on the calendar."

"Let's go out to lunch. You'll tell me what's bugging you. You want a raise or something?"

"That would be nice. Kids who work after school for McDonald's make more." The discussion was part of their usual banter.

"Forget it. Work for McDonald's. Here you get rewarded emotionally. Think of the good you're doing. Something else bugging you?"

Eric hesitated, then said, "I think I'm being followed."

Sussman gave a mysterious whistle.

"I knew you'd be sympathetic," Eric said.

"C'mon. You've got a real problem, tell me. Not some B-movie crap. I know what it is."

"What?"

"You split up with that cute Spanish chick, right? The radical with the outstanding set?" Sussman held his hands in front of his chest and cupped large, imaginary breasts. "You haven't gotten laid in a while. The fluids are building up, causing pressure on your brain."

"Thank you, Dr. Ruth."

"You want to know my professional diagnosis? I'll tell you—you worry too much," Sussman said without giving Eric a chance to respond. "I've got to make two phone calls, then let's go get lunch. I want your input on the election."

Garfield nodded and returned to his desk. He had planned to take the piroshki and eat them by the water. He often spent his lunch hours at the beach. The salt air was clean, the summer crowds hadn't descended on the boardwalk yet, and Eric could almost relax as he watched the waves.

He looked out the window again. Across the street a cop was ticketing the fruit-stand vendor, who had once again blocked off the sidewalk with his wares. Ladies wheeled overloaded shopping carts to the Laundromat. The discount-store owner was putting up a new sign, in Cyrillic lettering. Everything was as it should be. Or at least it appeared that way.

FIVE

"SHIRLEY TELLS ME YOU LOOK OUT THE WINDOW EVERY FIVE minutes," Sussman said as he and Garfield walked down Brighton Beach Avenue. They passed a discount clothing store; the owner saw them and waved.

"Hi, Moishe, how's business?"

"It could be worse, it could be better," Moishe said. "Look at these meters. Only an hour on them. A customer gets a ticket, who does he blame? Me. It's costing me business."

"Jot that down, will you, Eric?" Sussman said, and Eric produced a pad and recorded Moishe's complaints. "I'll see what I can do."

"Jerk," Sussman muttered as soon as they got away from the store. "If the meters were longer, he'd complain people park their cars all day in front of the store. Who would spend an hour shopping in his joint anyway?"

As they walked, shopkeepers, shoppers, and strollers stopped them to complain or chat. Sussman pressed the flesh adroitly, remembering names, making small talk, taking an apparent interest in the most trivial problems. In between, he made cutting comments and talked with Eric about the race for the presidency.

"What do you think about Alvin Winters?" he asked.

"Too conservative for my taste, but I think he's got a good shot. Lots of charm and a tough-guy--Big Daddy image. It's going to be close."

"He's a good speaker. He's got that 'America's the greatest' appeal," Sussman added. "The Fortune 500 provide heavyweight financing for him, and he's got bucks himself."

"Why the interest?" Garfield asked.

A double-parked car was causing a bottleneck and a cacophony of horns. Sussman waited until they passed before responding. "I'm thinking about the future. My future. After I get this congressional seat."

"Are you talking on broad, national terms or selfish, personal ones?" Eric asked with a smile.

"Selfish personal ones. You mean there's some other kind? Seriously. We've got this race in the bag. I figure I stay in Congress a few terms, then the Senate. Stick it out there two terms, then shoot for the big enchilada."

"You've got it all planned. What if the voters don't oblige?"

"With you as my campaign manager, how could those poor dumb bastards resist me?"

"You're thinking of modeling yourself on Winters?"

"Why not?"

"You're not a WASP, not very wealthy, and not from the Midwest. Anyway, you've made a rep as a neo-liberal."

"That's passé. Those other things are minor details. Look at Winters. What's he got going for him, aside from what you mentioned?"

"He's built an electronics-business empire and been governor of Nevada for two terms. He's bright, personable, and plugged into a bunch of PACs. Of course he's slightly to the right of Attila the Hun."

"Details, details. That's the kind of stuff I know you can take care of. So what do you think, Sussman for president?"

"I don't believe you're talking like this. You haven't even gotten a lock on the congressional seat."

"Piece of cake. As long as you don't screw up because of this paranoia. Will you quit looking over your shoulder?"

Garfield had been checking behind them.

"You're going to give yourself an ulcer. If you're going to worry, do it constructively. Think about my career, and how you can further it."

"You know, if I thought you meant what you said half the time, I'd probably quit," Eric said.

"And miss your chance at fancy lunches with powerful and respected members of the community?"

They had walked the length of Brighton Beach Avenue. As they headed into Chaim's Pizzeria, Sussman said, "My treat. Order the deluxe calzone."

"Nyet, nyet, nyet, Mr. Mendelov, I don't want an electric can opener," Eric Garfield insisted. It was midafternoon and he was behind his desk, repeating himself for the fifth time to a pudgy, middle-aged man with shifty, deep-set eyes.

"Sokolov told me about the piroshki," Mendelov said. "I know food is not enough to get my daughter into state school. If not can opener, how about radio? AM and FM."

"Mr. Mendelov, I will be happy to help your daughter apply to the state university. I don't need or want a radio. It's my job to help you. Ben Sokolov didn't *have* to give me a gift."

"Apply, shmapply. I want her to get in. This radio is Japanese. In original carton. With warranty."

A man appeared in the doorway. He had a gray three-piece suit on his large frame, stylishly cut hair, and a self-confident walk with a light tread. He spoke briefly to

39

Shirley and was led into Sussman's office. Eric wondered what his business was. He hadn't been listed on the appointments calendar.

Mendelov continued to badger Eric. Eric finally had to interrupt. "Mr. Mendelov, you say your daughter had a ninety-one average. I'm sure she'll be accepted, if she has good scores on the SATs and the Regents exams. Does she know you came down here like this?"

"Of course not." Mendelov snorted. "She's too innocent. Okay, you've got my back to wall. A brand-new television set. Color. You pick the brand name."

"We don't do things like that here. It's a merit system."

"It's merit system in Soviet Union, too. Only Party members have more merit," Mendelov said. "You mean to say, if Governor of New York's son wanted to get into state school, he would have to apply like everyone else?"

Eric looked off, unsure whether to smile or shout with frustration. "Well, maybe not *absolutely* like everyone else, but—"

"Ah-ha," Mendelov said triumphantly. "Use your *blat*. If you are as good as Sokolov says, you can find way. I will get you Sony Trinitron." Mendelov stood.

"I tell you what—why don't you just send your daughter over here, with her school records?" Garfield said.

"Okay. But don't tell her we have deal on side. Right?"

"You can bet I won't mention it."

Mendelov strode out triumphantly. Shirley came over.

"I'm going to kill Sokolov," Eric said when he saw her giggling. "How can they even think like that? All we need is some hotshot reporter to hear how we get paid in appliances."

"I could use a new freezer," Shirley said. "Maybe get Marty to print up a big sign. 'Tipping Is Prohibited.' "

"You're a real comfort to me, Shirley," Eric said. "Who's the guy in with Steve?"

"Dennis Brown. State Department."

Before he could ask any more, Eric was buzzed into Sussman's office. After introductions, Sussman took over the conversation. Brown sat motionless on the sofa.

"Boy, are you lucky, Eric," Sussman said. "You're going to get a one-week, all-expense-paid trip to Moscow, courtesy of your Uncle Sam."

"What?"

"As my aide, the government has arranged for the trip for you. First class all the way. I only wish I could go."

"I've never heard of anything like that," Eric said.

"We don't publicize the program," Brown said. "It's a mixture of government and private enterprise working together. Certain companies wish to demonstrate their services to us. In this case, it's World of Wonder Travel in New York. It won't cost you, or the taxpayers, a cent."

"The campaign is just gearing up," Eric said, studying Sussman. Why was he being so cooperative on this strange offer? "I can't do it."

"Don't worry. They'll be arranging for a paid political consultant to take your place," Sussman said. "You go and enjoy."

"I'll pass," Eric said, getting up. "If you'll excuse me, I ought to get back to work."

"You'd be better able to help the constituents if you knew, as they say, where they were coming from," Brown said.

"They're more concerned with adapting to the U.S. than how things are in Moscow, Mr. Brown. It was nice meeting you."

Eric returned to his desk. He called directory assistance and asked for World of Wonder Travel. It was listed with an office in lower Manhattan.

"Hi, do you have trips to the Soviet Union?" Eric asked when he called.

"It's our specialty. Would you like a brochure?" the cheery receptionist responded.

"No, thank you." Eric hung up, feeling rather foolish.

Shirley was standing over him. "What's the State Department want?"

"To give me a free trip to Russia."

"First piroshki, then a TV, now travel. What's your secret for success?"

Eric forced a laugh. He was upset. He liked traveling on other people's money, but Brown's offer troubled him. He looked up as the State Department man left, giving Eric a polite wave. A few minutes later Sussman buzzed Eric in.

"Why'd you kiss him off like that?" Sussman demanded.

"The offer stinks. I think it's some sort of scam."

"He showed me his ID. He used the names of people I know in Congress."

"It doesn't make sense."

"You didn't let him finish the spiel. The good work we've been doing for all these Russian immigrants has paid off. Word's gotten back to the Soviet Union. There's some hotshot dissident the Russkies are letting leave the country, and he wants you to escort him out."

"You believe that?"

"Don't look a gift horse in the mouth. We're talking a trip worth thousands."

"It's crazy. I don't believe you want me to do it. Haven't you heard any of our constituents' stories? Russia isn't like Club Med—you don't just fly in and out."

"I told you, the Russkies agreed to let this guy out. Hey, I wouldn't get you killed. You know how hard it is to get good help these days." Sussman flashed his grin.

"I'm not going."

"You're crazy. This is the chance of a lifetime. Think of all you'll learn about Russia. Firsthand."

"Did Brown tell you to use that argument?"

"No," Sussman said, in a way that Eric knew meant yes.

"What did they offer you? A development contract for the district?"

"Don't get obnoxious," Sussman snapped. Eric could tell he had struck a nerve. "You're limiting yourself," Sussman continued. "This crap about being followed, turning down this great opportunity. What do you think, the KGB is after you?"

"No. Maybe the FBI."

"I'm sure they've got better things to do than follow you. Like unbend paper clips."

Eric stood. "I have work to do."

Sussman gave an exasperated snort. "Listen, Eric, you're like a kid brother to me. I want what's best for you."

"Steve, have you heard any of the stories about Russia? People disappear there all the time."

"The State Department will be behind you."

"That'll warm the cockles of my heart while I'm looking through the barbed wire at the gulag. I've got papers for you to sign, if there's nothing more to discuss."

Sussman just shook his head in disgust.

SIX

TUTTLE FINISHED A FIFTEEN-MINUTE RECITATION THAT IN-cluded everything from Eric Garfield's blood type to the reason he had broken up with his leftist Salvadoran girlfriend. While the chief of operations spoke, Wellington listened and eyed the surveillance and driver's-license photos of Garfield.

"But what it boils down to is, we still really don't know why Petrov wants him," Wellington said.

"The analysts in psy ops are in the process of preparing a report," Tuttle responded, not answering the question. "It should be available late today. From what I ascertained, however, it isn't of much substantive value."

"Maybe we should try another soft contact?" Wellington suggested.

"He rejected the first one out of hand," Tuttle said. "I think it would be a waste of time. We should move on to the next recruitment phase."

"What about approaching him straight out?"

"The problem with that," Tuttle said condescendingly, "is we have to tell him too much. We can't hazard that without knowing why Petrov wants him."

"But if the Russians are behind it, how can they know less than we do?"

"Sometimes they run an operation just to see how our system works. They don't know how much we know about what they know."

"It sounds like a Catch-22 to me."

"We know Garfield is not inclined to go to the Soviet Union. At least that is the posture he's assuming. We have to take control of him, of the situation."

"What if we do force him into it and the Russians catch him?"

"In any field operation there is a certain amount of risk. Agents who are not under discipline get caught all the time. If you're worried about bad publicity, we'll have Damage Control set it up so he looks like a psycho. The forged scrapbook in his apartment, the letters declaring himself the savior of the world, et cetera."

"We still don't know why this Petrov wants him over there," Wellington said.

"No. But I am reasonably confident Garfield has not had access to any classified information. If we were to lose him, I don't believe national security would in any way be compromised," Tuttle said. "He was never in the military. This is his chance to serve his country. I've already determined the best man to assign as his handler. We'll give this Garfield a few weeks' training in operating as an illegal if you want."

"He should have some preparation. But isn't that risky, too? Won't that jeopardize our means and methods?"

Tuttle gave an exasperated sigh, clearly resenting what he saw as his boss's ill-founded meddling. "He won't be sent to the Farm. He'll receive individual training. His exposure to Agency personnel will be limited."

"Which case officer did you plan on using?"

Tuttle had hoped Wellington wouldn't ask. "You probably don't know him."

"Try me."

"Bert Slater," Tuttle said, quickly moving on. "Petrov did give us a time limit. We have to get the operation going."

"Slater. Slater. The name is familiar. What's his background?"

"He was one of the best scalp hunters we had when he was in the field. He recruited assets for us in East Germany, Poland, and the Soviet Union itself. A Harvard man, like yourself. He speaks three Slavic languages. Passed Special Forces training and Paratroopers' School and—"

"I know how I know it," Wellington said. "Didn't my predecessor have to work out a confidential trade to get him back? Wasn't he caught by the Russians or something? Developed emotional problems? I didn't know he was still with the Agency."

"We take care of our own. He's been in the training division, teaching new agents recruitment techniques."

"Do you really think it advisable to have someone like that in on this sensitive an operation?"

"Definitely. He's top-notch, a master at recruiting and handling. I've kept tabs on him, and he's been performing admirably. The incident in the Soviet Union was three years ago. He's completely recovered."

Wellington stroked his chin. "Okay, Slater is authorized to recruit and prepare Garfield. But before we send Garfield anywhere, I want a level-three investigation on him and Petrov. I insist on knowing the connection before we send Garfield overseas."

As he strode down the blue-carpeted hallway to his office, Tuttle allowed himself a tight little smile. He had to make sure Wellington saw sanitized reports. It was important that unprofessional meddlers didn't foul up the way the Company was run. Amazing that he remembered Slater.

The Tuttles and Slaters went back several generations. He had helped get Bert Slater into the Fletcher School of Diplomacy. Slater had been a bright, patriotic young man during the political upheaval of the late sixties. Tuttle had run him as a field man throughout the Soviet bloc. He'd won numerous jockstrap medals.

Then he'd been betrayed by a potential defector while running an operation in Leningrad. He'd been interrogated for two months, injected with drugs that caused psychoses and agonizing convulsions. He'd cracked and divulged an entire network. Anyone would have cracked eventually, Tuttle knew—so did Slater. But it didn't ease the pain. Twisted balls, the Russians called it. A man who had been tortured once easily could be broken again.

Slater had been traded for three Soviet illegals caught in the U.S. He'd been assigned to low-level desk jobs at Langley after a suitable period of treatment and observation by CIA psychiatrists. The only symptom of Slater's bad experience was his consuming hatred of the Soviets. He'd been promoted to instructor.

Slater would never get the clearance to be a field man again. But he could work as a case officer, under supervision. Tuttle's supervision. He could play on Bert's desire to get back into action, let Slater know who was behind his rehabilitation.

The Agency compound sprawls over two hundred and twenty heavily wooded acres south of the Potomac River in Virginia. In the seven-story main building there are more than a million square feet of space. It took Tuttle a full ten minutes, walking at a good clip, to get to the igloo-shaped auditorium.

Fifty men and women, largely whites but with a half dozen blacks, Latinos, and Orientals mixed in, were listening to Slater speak. None were taking notes. Paper, they had been taught, could be incriminating. At the front of the room Slater was erasing his own words from the blackboard. He was a sinewy forty-two-year-old in a dark suit, with shortcut blond hair and don't-mess-with-me eyes.

"What you've just described sounds like something a cult would do to a new member," a fresh-faced young man said. "Remove the subject from familiar surroundings, sleep deprivation, absolute control of all factors in their life, supply a strong figure for the subject to identify with."

"Don't forget providing an ideological system," Slater said. "Yes. The techniques are similar. You'll find the same sort of programming in the military. There are a limited number of ways the human mind can be controlled. Okay, let's review field recruitment. Sue, what are the four motivations?"

"MICE. Money, ideology, compromise, ego."

"John, give an example of compromise."

"You pay someone for an innocuous job, then covertly photograph them accepting the money. You use the picture to blackmail them."

"Be careful to avoid words like 'blackmail' in reports. You never know if a Freedom of Information Act abuser will get his hands on it and leak it to *The Washington Post*. 'Biographic leverage' is a better way to phrase it. Any questions?" No one raised a hand. "Fine. Next week we'll talk about keeping an asset once you have him. Class dismissed."

The students silently filed out of the auditorium.

"You make an excellent teacher, Bert," Tuttle said when he was alone in the cavernous room with Slater.

"Thank you, sir."

"Do you like it?"

"It can be rewarding."

"Would you be interested in coming in on a covert op? As a desk man, but you'd also handle a domestic recruitment."

"I would give my right arm for the chance," Slater said.

"That won't be necessary." Tuttle sat down in the front row and motioned for Slater to join him. Then Tuttle outlined Operation Borzoi.

"That's a great kick in the balls to the Reds. But why this Garfield, if I may ask?"

"We've been asking the same question. I've got a detailed dossier going back to his kindergarten teacher noting that he threw up when he had to sing in front of the class. But no explanation why Petrov wants him. We hope you'll make that determination while you're training him. Teach him Russian, how to pass casual inspection. Build his confidence. Find out everything you can from him. Don't give him anything that would hurt us if the Soviets learned it. You know the routine."

"Yes, sir."

"Soft contact was already made, and he turned us down. Use your discretion. Keep me posted."

Eric Garfield made it home by a little past midnight. He'd been stuck at a community planning board meeting that had degenerated into a shouting match over whether a residential area should be rezoned to allow a video arcade to operate. His whole body felt like an overtightened guitar string. As he opened the three locks on his apartment door, he was looking forward to a hot bath and a glass of cognac.

He reached for the light, and someone slammed him against the wall. He was thrown to the floor and pinned to the ground. The beam of a powerful flashlight blinded him.

"What the—"

A hand clamped over his mouth. "You scream and you'll regret it. Understand?" the man who used the name Dennis Brown growled. He waited for Eric to nod before removing the hand from his mouth. "All right, asshole, where have you been?" Brown demanded.

"At—at a planning board meeting. Who are you? What do you want?"

"I ask the questions."

"Where are you from? What's going on?"

"Shut up, scumbag," Brown said.

Slater took the flashlight off Garfield's face and turned on the overhead light.

"I recognize you," Eric said to Brown."You're from the State Department."

"What do you want, a fucking medal?" Brown snarled. He grabbed Eric's lapel and tugged him to his feet, then threw him onto the couch and loomed over him. "We tried to do it the nice way, but you wouldn't listen, would you?"

"I don't understand."

"There's a job for you to take, and you turned it down," Brown said. "Your country doesn't ask much, and still you don't do it. You're probably a draft-dodging Commie wimp, ain't you?"

"Who are you?"

"Have you reconsidered?" Slater asked.

"Breaking into my apartment and scaring the hell out of me doesn't seem to be the way to get my cooperation," Garfield said. "If you leave right now, I won't press charges."

Brown grabbed his lapels again. Eric tried to push his hand away. Brown slapped him. "You think we're playing games? I ought to bounce you off the walls."

"Brown, stop it," Slater said. "Remember what happened the last time you did that?"

Muttering obscenities, Brown released Eric and took a TRW credit report from his leather jacket pocket. "Okay, Garfield, try this out. We'll ruin you. I mean IRS audits, EPA lawsuits every time you fart. We'll fuck with the computers until the credit-card companies put you on a blacklist. We'll get the bank to call in your car loan. Your phone will be cut off. We can have Sussman fire you and make sure you don't get unemployment.''

"I don't get it. What do you want? Who are you?''

"We told you what we want," Brown said. "You take a little trip to sunny Russia. A few days out of your life. You should be glad to serve your country."

Garfield stood up. "I don't know what this is all about, but you can bet by tomorrow every reporter I know, and I know plenty, will hear about this. And I have friends on quite a few congressional staffs. Get out!''

"Remember that Salvadoran couple with the young daughter who hid at your place for a few weeks?''

Eric nodded.

"That's illegal. Conspiracy to circumvent the immigration laws of your country.''

"Big deal.''

"It will be, especially after the jury hears how you molested the little girl.''

"What! What are you saying? I didn't do anything like that," Eric sputtered.

Brown shoved him down. "You know it, and I know it. But what about when the jury hears her and her parents testify about the gringo pervert? Or how about when your jailhouse bunkmates find out they have a short eyes in their midst?''

"They'd never say that.''

"They would if they knew they were going back to their beloved country if they didn't. We've got the affidavits on file.'' Brown chuckled. "Some people will do anything for a green card.''

"You blackmailed them. You really suck, you know that?'' Eric said.

Brown stepped forward menacingly. He took out a passport and dropped it on Garfield's lap. "Open it up, tough guy."

It was his ex-girlfriend's.

"She's being held at the INS detention facility on Flushing Avenue," Brown said. "Unless we get the answer we want, she goes back to El Salvador on the next flight."

"But that's a death sentence," Garfield said, feeling the control he had briefly gained slipping away. "They'll kill her."

"Oh, too bad," Brown sneered.

Slater had been standing off to the side while his accomplice raged. He stepped in and put a hand on Brown's shoulder. "Take it easy. Let me talk to the kid alone, okay?"

Brown looked at Eric like a lion eyeing a piece of raw meat, then reluctantly agreed. He walked into the kitchen and helped himself to a soda, careful to wipe off his fingerprints after touching the refrigerator.

Slater sat on the sofa next to Eric. "You've got to excuse Brown. There was no need for the rough stuff." Slater's tone was gentle. He produced a badge case with FBI identification and flashed it.

"I can't believe this. I'm being smacked around by the U.S. government."

Slater patted his shoulder. "Brown's a hard case. Don't judge everyone by him."

"Does that mean the threat of deporting her is a bluff?"

Slater stared at him wordlessly.

"You really will do it, won't you?"

Slater nodded.

"Shit! What do you want me to do?"

"Visit the Soviet Union, meet a dissident, and escort him back. He specifically asked for you. You'll get details later. You have to put yourself in our hands. We have your interest, and the country's interest, at heart. You can work with me. I'll make sure you don't have any dealings with

Brown." Slater was not a very large man, but he had a confidence that inspired confidence. He gazed at Eric warmly, as if to say, "I'll help you. Trust me."

Brown swaggered into the room. "Enough of this crap. I say we drag him to headquarters and sweat him."

"Give him a chance to think."

"What do you mean, telling me no? You don't have seniority."

"Back off."

"Oh yeah?"

It happened faster than Eric could follow. One second Brown was pushing Slater. The next he was lying on the floor. Slater had a foot on Brown's throat.

"Don't ever do that again," Slater said in the same level tone of voice. He eased his foot off Brown's throat, who sat up, coughing. "Go wait outside."

Rubbing his throat, Brown slouched out.

"We're not going to disappear," Slater said when he was alone with Eric. "I'll do what I can to help you, kid, but you've got to do exactly what I say. You start improvising, ad-libbing, or getting cute, and we'll both get our dicks in a wringer."

"I'll go to Russia."

"Good. Pack your bags and come with me. We'll train you."

"No one said anything about that."

"Remember what I said about not questioning me?"

"But—but my job?"

"It will be taken care of," Slater said. "This is top secret. Between you, God, and your country. You'll be signing a security agreement."

"Under duress."

"It's your word against mine. Now, pack."

"I don't believe this is happening. Why do you have to train me? I go there, I meet this guy, we come home."

Slater sighed. "This is your last chance to question me,

kid. Normally, if we're just going to debrief a civilian after a trip to the Soviet Union, we make a point of not contacting him beforehand. Amateurs have a tendency to boast or skulk around over there calling attention to themselves. We prefer to rely on basic powers of observation.

"Unfortunately, we have to come to you beforehand. It's important to give you certain minimal skills, a quickie course, mainly to keep you out of trouble."

"What will I learn?"

"The first thing is obedience. Pack your bag. You've got fifteen minutes. Let's go, let's go, let's go."

Slater watched Garfield as he selected apparel from his drawers. Much of his clothing came from the hamper, where it was waiting to be washed. Slater made sure he didn't try to slip a weapon into his suitcase. All indications were that Garfield was a peaceable type, but Slater had stayed alive because he was careful.

At 2:30 A.M. Eric Garfield began his journey.

SEVEN

"WHY'D YOU LET YOUR SUBSCRIPTION TO *ESQUIRE* LAPSE?"
Brown demanded of Eric.

"Why's that relevant?"

"You haven't had a tetanus shot in ten years. What
happens if you step on a rusty nail, huh?"

"What are you asking me this for?"

"How come you sold your stocks? Are you a Communist? Did you cheat on your chem finals at Stony Brook?"

Brown fired questions at Eric and noted his responses.
A silent Slater kept glancing at the rearview mirror, all the
while making unnecessary turns, stopping abruptly, and
scooting through lights just as they turned red.

After they dropped Brown off in front of FBI headquarters at Federal Plaza, Slater told Eric, "Your girlfriend will
be taken care of. Brown will handle straightening it out."

"I want to file a complaint against him."

"It'll all be in my report," Slater said. "You're no
longer a civilian. You don't ask questions unless you're
invited to. You don't file complaints. You don't talk to
outsiders about what you do. Your life depends on it." His
words hung in the car like stale cigarette smoke as they
drove through the Holland Tunnel.

"Where are we going?"

Slater gave Garfield a look that chilled him. "Did you hear what I said?"

There was silence in the car for a long time. They drove through Newark. Slater made U-turns and sudden rights and lefts on the bleak city streets. He handed Eric a pair of wraparound sunglasses. "Put these on."

Garfield did as he was told. The glasses had tape on the inside. He tried peeking, but couldn't see anything.

Slater continued to drive, heading south, doubling back once or twice. He knew that for the blindfolded Eric, time would seem to have slowed. Every minute would be like ten. Slater shoved a fifties rock-and-roll tape into the Blaupunkt. It would keep Garfield's mind busy as well as block out exterior noises that might provide location clues.

They got on and off the New Jersey Turnpike, then U.S. 9, making their way south. They headed west again on Route 70. The safe house was about ten miles south of Fort Dix. Far enough to escape the routine Soviet surveillance of military bases, but close enough for the Agency to use Army facilities.

The sun was beginning to rise as Slater guided Eric up the steps. The isolated split-level was sheltered by a large pine grove. There was no indication from the outside that it was anything other than a typical suburban home.

Slater opened the door cautiously, hand on the 9mm Browning Hi-Power he carried in a belly holster. The house smelled of air freshener and looked tidy.

Slater left Garfield standing in the middle of the living room, still wearing the glasses. He went to the hall closet and removed a plywood panel from the back wall. The indicator lights on the hidden console winked at him reassuringly.

The two-bedroom house had been bought for eighty thousand dollars. Nearly twice as much had been spent on improvements, including concealed heat and motion detectors, polycarbonate glass, a pistol range in the basement, jamming gear, and sensitive radio equipment in the attic. It was used for training agents who were to be sent behind the Iron Curtain. While a certain amount of basic training was done at the Farm, located at Camp Peary near Williamsburg, Virginia, ops going into high-risk situations were trained individually. If captured, they couldn't betray hundreds of classmates.

Slater reset the detectors that had been disconnected to allow their entry, replaced the panel, and went back to Garfield. Eric was swaying slightly from exhaustion and the difficulty of keeping his balance without the benefit of sight. "You can take them off," Slater said.

There were light-brown love seats and a sofa, with matching armchairs around a chrome-and-glass coffee table; a well-stocked bar; an entertainment center with VCR, TV, and full stereo setup; and assorted modern end tables and lamps.

"You can go anywhere in the house," Slater said. "But do not leave the premises for *any* reason without my permission."

"I'm under house arrest?"

"I wouldn't characterize it like that. You're my responsibility. I don't want you jeopardizing yourself or the security of the mission."

"I still don't understand. Why me?"

"Maybe it'll come to you. For now, let me show you your home for the next two weeks."

"Two weeks! I thought we were talking a day or two. How long are you sending me to Russia for, anyway?"

"It doesn't matter if it's only for five minutes. You'll be playing Moscow rules, in a hostile environment. Think of yourself as an athlete. You may be in training for months to get that one javelin throw just right. Or work out at a gym full-time for years to be able to hold up for ten rounds in the ring."

"That's me, Rocky Garfield."

"When I'm done with you, you will be. Wait until finals."

Slater led Eric to his room, which had a laminated-wood dresser, a night table, a small desk, a chair, and a platform bed. The furniture was the kind sold at layaway stores.

"You get to sleep," Slater said. "I'll bring your bag in from the car."

"I don't know if I can. When do my classes start?"

"They've started. First, you've got to learn to follow orders. Don't worry about time of day. We'll be adjusting your biological clock to Moscow time."

Slater left. Garfield undressed and slipped under the covers in his undershorts. Slater returned, set the suitcase down, and pulled the shades shut.

"Can you tell me what's going on?"

"In time. A wise man once said, 'If you can't flee it or fight it, flow with it.' "

"What would happen if I did 'flee it'?"

"I'd hunt you down."

"And?"

Slater smiled. Remembering his smile made it hard for Eric to sleep.

Eric awoke, and it took several moments for him to realize where he was. Four o'clock. He decided that meant four P.M., judging by the light filtering through the curtains. He looked out the window. There was a well-trimmed lawn and a thick line of trees about fifty yards away. If he could make it to the trees . . .

He lifted the window. It only went up about six inches— enough to let air in, but not him out. He pushed the glass in the frame. It was thicker than regular glass, and though hard, it had a plasticky feel.

"I'll expect you downstairs in ten minutes," Slater said from the doorway.

Eric looked from Slater to the window that he'd opened. "You *knew* I was up. Is this thing wired?"

"Very good. Get dressed. You're going to learn to eat Russian. Dress casual. This course includes phys. ed."

Garfield found that his dirty clothes had been washed and put in the dresser. He put on a pair of jeans, a T-shirt, and sneakers, and then went downstairs to the kitchen.

Slater was there with a middle-age man with thinning red hair, a pot belly, and an intense air about him.

"Eric, this is Sam."

"Pleased to meet you," Sam said, not looking up from the meat he was slicing. "You're in luck. Russian food is one of my favorites. Everything from *bitki* to *zakuski*."

"You do this a lot?" Eric asked.

"Some people speak different languages. I cook different cuisines," Sam said. "Let's say, and of course this is theoretical, we were sending someone to Kuwait. You take on the odor of the food you eat. Like, I went out with a Japanese girl once, said I smelled too much of red meat. She taught me how to make a California roll you wouldn't believe. For the sesame—"

"You'll talk later," Slater said, taking Eric's elbow and guiding him from the kitchen.

"What's *your* name?"

"Call me Bert."

Slater led Eric to the mini-gym in the basement. There was a rowing machine, a stationary bicycle, and mats on the parquet floor. Speed and heavy bags were suspended from the exposed wooden beams. Off to a side was a one-lane pistol range, twenty feet long. "I can teach you to shoot, if we have time," Slater said. "You won't need those skills for this operation."

"That's reassuring. I don't like guns."

"They're a tool, just like anything else."

"But the only job they do is kill people."

"Or protect them. You and I will spend two hours a day

61

working out down here." Slater patted Garfield's belly. "I'm going to knock some weight off you, get you in the best shape you've ever been."

"That move you used on Brown was pretty slick. Which martial art did you study?"

"It's a mixture of jujitsu and aikido, with karate, Special Forces hand-to-hand combat, and ghetto street-fighting techniques thrown in. If nothing else, you'll feel better riding on the subway late at night."

"That's tempting, but before you start training me or telling me anything, why don't we just call the whole thing off? It's some sort of mistake. There's no reason in the world for this Russian to want me."

"No turning back."

"Don't you think my boss will be suspicious about me disappearing?"

"We told Sussman your uncle in Chicago took a turn for the worse. You had to rush to his bedside."

"My uncle in Chicago died two years ago."

"We know that. Sussman doesn't. We arranged for a temporary assistant to fill in for you," Slater continued. "The temp has a lot of experience doing political work."

"What did he do before? Overthrow Latin American governments?"

Slater gave him a sharp look. "What's that supposed to mean?"

"You say you're FBI. This assignment sounds more like CIA. Since you haven't been up-front with me on anything, I don't believe that badge you flashed was real."

"Lesson two," Slater said, holding two fingers a few inches from Garfield's nose. "Don't show off. What does your remark accomplish? Nothing. But you've made yourself a liability. If you discover someone else's secret, usually there's no strategic value in letting them know. Got it?"

"Yes."

Eric followed Slater into the den. The walls were covered with book-filled shelves. Titles ranged from economic treatises to classics by Tolstoy and Chekhov to sociological textbooks on the Soviet Union. There were also books with titles like *Deal the First Deadly Blow* and *Confessions of an Undercover Op*.

The other, larger bedroom had furnishings similar to Eric's but included a second bed. "Sam or I will be here all the time, if you need us."

"How about if I need to get away?"

Slater didn't answer.

"Soup's on," Sam called from the kitchen.

There were cabbage rolls and borscht, and *lagman po Uyegursky*, a thick, savory lamb-and-noodle soup. By the time they got to the main course, roast suckling pig with an apple in its mouth, served on a bed of kasha, Eric was already stuffed.

"You've got to leave room," Sam said. "Russians do everything on a grand scale."

"Uhhhh. I don't think I can eat any more."

"Prepare half portions," Slater said to Sam, making it clear who was in charge. "He won't do anyone any good if he's living on Alka-Seltzer."

Sam pouted but nodded.

To Eric, Slater said, "Practice eating European style, with knife and fork."

They ate and made small talk about sports. Garfield thought he detected a hint of a Boston accent in Sam's voice. He was about to comment when he remembered Slater's lecture on not showing off.

"Starting tomorrow, we'll speak only Russian at the dinner table. It'll be good for you to use it in other than a classroom environment. The operation you're going on is an easy one, but a careless mistake and you wind up in a Soviet labor camp or one of their so-called mental hospitals."

"You're really building my enthusiasm," Eric said sarcastically.

"A little fear is good," Slater said. "Adrenaline does wonders for properly trained reflexes."

"Don't worry. I've heard enough stories about the KGB and blackjacks and rubber hoses from the immigrants I work with," Eric said. "I'm scared, believe me."

Slater shook his head and wiped tomato sauce from his mouth with a paper napkin. "In general, the KGB doesn't use blunt-force trauma anymore. They favor haloperidol and other psychoactive drugs."

"What does it do?"

"It makes you stiff and restless at the same time, as well as giving you excruciating cramps," Slater said.

"It's sophisticated stuff compared to what they do in some of the Third World countries," Sam added. "There they like shoving cattle prods into the anus, or pouring acid into eyes and ears, or . . ."

Garfield gulped and set down his fork.

"I guess it isn't the best dinnertime conversation," Sam said.

"It's all true," Slater said to Garfield. "Thank your lucky stars you're living in America."

"Where we export the equipment that they use to torture people in South America or Africa."

"If we send a cattle prod to Argentina, who's to say what they use it for?" Slater demanded.

"If we're sending it to gauchos, that's one thing. If we're sending it to a secret-police captain or head of a death squad, that's another."

"What do you want, an end-use certificate for cattle prods?" Slater snapped.

While Sam fetched the dessert, candied milk, Slater and Garfield continued their argument.

"You don't appreciate how great this country is," Slater said. "Wait until you see the rest of the world. You're very lucky, kid, and so are the countries we've protected over the years.''

"Like Haiti, or Guatemala, or Chile, or Vietnam, or—''

"What do you know about Vietnam? Do you know that—'' Slater stopped in mid-sentence. He was about to reveal part of his past. He mentally chastised himself for slipping. "You'll wise up when you get older.''

"I bet you think Alvin Winters is the answer for America.''

"Damn straight,'' Slater said. "The only thing the Soviets respect is dealing from strength. Winters will do that. Remember the Cuban missile crisis, how we backed them down? They're like any other bully. Face to face, they're just a bunch of cowards.''

"What if they don't back down? What if the Russians decide they're as macho as Winters?''

"Enough talk. We'll begin expanding your Russian vocabulary in a half hour. Go to the library and list every Russian word you can recall.''

Eric went to the library, but he couldn't focus his thoughts. How could he escape? And to where? They knew everything about him. How long would it take the government to find him? Who would protect him? Who would believe him? Why was this happening?

Slater came in and saw Eric hadn't written anything. "We're going to establish discipline. Get downstairs. We don't have time to waste.''

"What if I refuse?'' Eric asked, folding his arms across his chest.

Slater cupped his hand and put the fingertips under Eric's jaw near its hinge. Then he lifted hard.

The pain was dizzying. Eric scrambled out of his seat and clutched the pressure point. "I—I can't believe you did that.'' The pain subsided as quickly as it had come.

"I like you, kid. I've put up with more shit from you than I'm supposed to. I have to show results. If I have to beat them into you, I will. Get your butt downstairs, double time.''

EIGHT

"ALL RIGHT, I WANT TO ATTACK," SLATER SAID, BECKONING Eric into the middle of the mat.

"Do you like to hurt people?"

"Only if I have to. Come on. I can't cripple you—you couldn't do the job. Charge me, you pinko wimp."

"You're not going to provoke me that crudely."

"Your old girlfriend was right. You do have no *cojones*."

"She wouldn't say that."

"I'll play you the tape. Of course, I shut it off before I hopped in the sack with her. How would your little Latin lovely feel if she knew she had fucked an agent of this imperialist, war-mongering government?"

"Bullshit."

"You know it as well as I do. Those radical meetings at your apartment, when you were working late at the office, I think she fucked half the guys there. She got all hot over some radical cause, then glory to the revolution with a comrade's dick up her ass."

"If you're trying to get me to take a swing at you, you're wasting your time."

Slater smiled. "Okay, I'll make you a deal. If you hit

me one solid punch, the mission is canceled. You go home like none of this ever happened.''

"Really?"

"Take your shot."

Before the words were out of Slater's mouth, Eric swung. Slater easily sidestepped the blow.

"C'mon, be serious," he taunted.

Eric threw another punch, and another. Slater blocked them both. Garfield tried to grab Slater in a bear hug. The agent slapped his hands aside.

Garfield was breathing hard, angry snorts of air expelled through his nose. He pretended to turn away from Slater, then spun and reached for his throat. The agent seized Eric's arms and then spun his own body. Eric crashed to the floor. Slater's hand was on his face, fingers an inch from Garfield's eyeballs.

"Lesson three. Read the body language. That fake turning away wasn't bad, but you telegraphed your attack with your shoulders. Always watch the opposition's shoulders, the hands, the feet. Forget about the head and eyes. A smart op will fake you out."

Eric lay on the floor, panting.

"I'm going to teach you a very simple system of self-defense. It's based on a block, a throw, a blow. The system won't be much good against a trained professional, but for your average goon, it should be enough. If you ever think you're up against a professional, attack first, and give it all you got. You won't get a second chance.

"Better than half of the untrained attackers begin with a left jab, or feinted jab, and then go into a right that's supposed to be a knockout punch." Slater feinted with the left, and then threw a roundhouse right. "You do that, and we'll go through the defense slowly."

As Garfield threw the left, Slater blocked his hand from the inside. He spun under the right and landed an elbow, gently, in Garfield's solar plexus. The same arm went up and braced itself under Garfield's armpit. Bending at the hips, Slater tossed the heavier man in a classic judo throw, *morote seoi-nage*.

Again Eric lay on the floor, gasping for air. "I guess I should teach you how to fall," Slater said.

They went over basic breakfalls—slapping the mat with an extended arm, keeping legs apart without the ankles smashing, making sure the tongue was never between the teeth.

Then they returned to the blows and throws. Slater emphasized balance and speed. After a half hour of repetition, he switched to another move—blocking a dagger thrust, snapping the palm under the chin, and finishing the assailant off with an *osoto gari*. The throw, in which an opponent's legs were kicked out from the rear, suited Eric's long legs much better than the *morote seoi-nage*.

"I have a few books upstairs for you to look at," Slater said when Eric was soaked with sweat and breathing hard. "Remember to always step in on an adversary. It throws them off and prevents them from getting leverage. Also, use your hips wherever possible. Even a girl has a lot of power in her hip," Slater said with a mildly lecherous grin. He patted Eric's shoulder. "You did well. Would you like a drink?"

Eric hesitated, then nodded.

Slater got a bottle of lemon-flavored vodka and poured them glasses. *"Nazdorovye."*

"Bottoms up."

"Think Russian," Slater said.

"Nazdorovye," Eric said.

Slater belted his drink back. Eric sipped his.

"You've got to learn to drink like a Russian," Slater said, refilling his glass. "To the glorious worker's paradise known as the Soviet Union," he said sarcastically in Russian. He gulped his down. Eric did the same.

"Your Russian sounds *kharasho*. Have you been over there?"

Slater nodded. "Did you ever have any interest in seeing the Soviet Union?"

"I guess maybe a passing interest. I think I'd rather spend a week in the Virgin Islands," Eric quipped.

"Especially in the winter. What do the people at the district office tell you?"

"How wonderful the country is, and how the government sucks. They're homesick."

"It's a collective culture," Slater explained. "The harsh climate, the oppressive conditions, have forced the individual to subordinate his needs to the group's. If someone leaves Mother Russia, it's that much harder on everyone left behind. They've been brainwashed to have team feelings. But they're on the wrong team, a pack of corrupt, incompetent bastards. What were the stories you heard?"

They kept drinking vodka, and Garfield recounted the stories Sokolov and others had told him. He was careful to avoid giving names or details that might allow Slater to identify the storytellers.

Eventually, Garfield began to slur his words. Slater, who also sounded drunk, kept probing, asking questions, searching for anything that might connect Eric to Petrov.

The combination of hard physical exercise, liquor, and disrupted sleep patterns took their toll. Eric's face dropped to the table. Slater helped him to his bedroom and put him to bed.

The only visitor Eric would have over the next two weeks was his scholastic instructor, a Georgetown professor who was a frequent CIA consultant. He was a red-haired, gray-bearded man with a slight paunch and a foul-smelling pipe. Sam fussed over the odor. He brought along Russian classical and folk music, icons and paintings, and films. Eric learned how the Mighty Fistful, the five great Russian musicians of the nineteenth century, developed Russian folk music and themes into symphonic works. In the background, the professor played works by the five: Borodin, Mussorgsky, Rimsky-Korsakov, Balakirev, and Cui. Sometimes he'd pause in his lecture to hum along.

While going through a portfolio of prints of Russian artwork and icons, the professor explained, "The deep-seated Russian urge for iconism prevails to this day. Since its religious manifestation has been squelched by the Communists, it has surfaced with paintings, murals, photos, and busts of Lenin. They are everpresent."

During the cinema lessons, they concentrated on Sergei Eisenstein, the director active in the twenties and thirties who had invented the montage. Eric also learned of the Soviet rating system, which ranged from "one," films fit for everyone, to "four," films that no one could watch without supposedly endangering his ideology.

The teacher grew excited when he began talking about Russian history. Even though one-on-one with Eric, his voice boomed. He used the blackboard, drawing family trees and time lines. "We will examine the history, the geopolitics, in essence the socioeconomic parameters of life in the Union of Soviet Socialist Republics," he said. "We shall begin with the history, for to know a people you must first know their memories.

"I don't expect you to memorize all the facts and figures I offer. But it is vital that you grasp certain concepts. The minutia can be especially damning. Imagine if you met someone who said he was an American and didn't know there were fifty states. Yet how many real Americans could name the capital of South Dakota? There are certain basic facts that every citizen of any nation will know. Russians are particularly proud of their heritage. But they are also very secretive. Let us begin."

Eric, who had expected a pedantic lecture, was caught up by the academic's enthusiastic gestures. The professor waved his arms and paced around the room as if he could barely contain the ideas.

"The two hundred and seventy million people living in the U.S.S.R. are not a homogeneous mass. There are a hundred and four nationalities speaking a hundred and twenty languages living in fifty-three nationality republics or regions. They include Ukranians, Lithuanians, Armenians, Uzbeks, and Georgians."

He told Eric about the different ethnic types and their various contributions to Soviet culture. He raced through a history recital beginning with Rurik, a Viking king from 862 A.D. and ending with the final days of the monarchy. The blackboard was filled with the czar's family tree. The professor painted a picture of an oppressed, hungry populace; a cold, unforgiving landscape; frequent invasion by neighbors; and a brutal, decadent ruling class.

"It is axiomatic that revolution often follows when expectations are raised. Czar Nicholas II was vulnerable when he was forced, after the revolution of 1905, to create the Duma. That parliament was a sham, but it fostered hope of liberalization. Then World War One came. There were shortages, defeats, and a hopelessly inept bureaucracy. Nicholas responded to complaints with vicious repression."

He summarized the organization of the first soviet and the provisional Kerensky government.

"Flashback to 1848. A German economist working in Great Britain had come up with the theory that would revolutionize the world. Who was he?"

"Uh, Karl Marx," Eric blurted in response to the sudden question.

"Right! Fifty years after it was published, the Russian Social Democratic Party was formed. Among the followers was a young man whose brother had been executed by the czar, who had spent three years exiled in Siberia, and who, aside from Marx, is the most influential Communist ever."

"Lenin."

"Exactly. To a people who had been treated worse than

72

cattle, he promised dignity, equality. Socialism would be hard going. Communism would be utopia. He was an impassioned orator. Imagine the crowds as this frenetic fellow belted out Marx's 'Workers of the world, unite!' or 'From each according to his ability, to each according to his need.' '' The professor mimicked a demagogue delivering an address to a feverish crowd. His hair was mussed, his eyes bulged. He glanced at his watch. ''Well, that's enough for today. Tomorrow we discuss the revolution itself. Ten days that shook the world. Bolsheviki, Mensheviki. Lenin, Trotsky, Zinoviev. Then the dark force of the Russian soul personified, Josif Vissarionovich Dzhugashvili.''

''Stalin?''

''Very good.'' He ran his hand across his hair, smoothed out his jacket, and walked out.

Slater's tradecraft lessons began with the fundamentals of disguise. He showed Eric how to improvise with items like shoe polish, cigarette ash, or hydrogen peroxide. He taught Eric to use a towel under the jacket, across the shoulders, to build up bulk, or a pebble in the shoe to change his posture and the way he walked.

''From a distance, the way you walk is more of a giveaway than individual features. You walk like an American. Sort of an arrogant-cowboy swagger. Russians move with a belligerent waddle. Work on that. Let's move on to specific features.''

He gave Eric a half dozen household items and had him try to change his appearance as much as possible.

''The hairline is the feature the eye first seizes on when identifying a face. A quick change of your hairstyle—say, brushing it back when you're used to wearing it in bangs—can make the difference. The shape of the face can't be changed, but you can put tissues, cotton, or whatever in your mouth and puff out your jaws. Sunglasses, a hat—

these are simple but effective props. They draw the observer's eye away from natural features.''

In subsequent classes, the lectures became more espionage oriented.

"First, some terms. There's pocket litter. That's the junk we have in our pockets that helps establish our character. Possibilities include coins, key rings, pocketknives, rabbit's feet, worry beads.

"The wallet is another story. The rudimentary false identification is flash alias documentation, which will only pass a casual inspection. For more sophisticated use, backstopping is needed. As an example, if there is a phone number given out, someone should be on the other end, ready to back up the story. Like when you called World of Wonder Travel and got a receptionist.''

Slater launched into a discussion of dead drops, places where agents could leave messages for later pickup by their handlers. "They are crucial. Urban dead drops have the advantage of easy access. Rural dead drops offer greater seclusion, however—'' Slater noticed Eric's quizzical expression. "Am I going too fast?''

"No. Why are you telling me all this? I thought I'm going in to meet a dissident. This is heavy-duty spy shit!''

"It's just routine.''

"Routine? This is routine! When do I get the pen that squirts poison and the flammable code book?''

"They won't be necessary.''

"Then why this training? What the hell are you sending me into?'' Eric shouted.

"It's routine,'' Slater lied. He didn't explain that he was deliberately slipping in minor inaccuracies, nothing critical, in the hope that Eric would correct him. The technique had been effectively used by the British during World War II. A captured German spy had refused to give up any information, even after rough interrogation. The Brits had then put him in a classroom where an English colonel was giving a lesson on tradecraft. The colonel kept deliberately bungling things. The German corrected him once, then again, and before the proper Prussian knew it, he was telling the class things he had never intended to.

Garfield didn't have the Prussian spirit of precision, but he did have a cocky soul, Slater had decided. Garfield would have felt it necessary to correct him. Much of Bert's tradecraft spiel had been bait. Garfield hadn't taken it. The big question remained: Why had Petrov chosen Eric Garfield?

"Russian is a difficult language to master," Slater said during one of their linguistic sessions. "There are thirty-three letters in the Cyrillic alphabet. You have to teach your tongue to move in new ways. On the positive side, there are numerous words that are the same as in English, like *telefon* or *teatr*. That's theater. But Slavic translation can kill you. Remember Jimmy Carter's translator, who told a Polish crowd Carter 'lusted' after them? For years scholars have been referring to Ivan the Terrible. Actually, the proper translation is Ivan the Awe-Inspiring.

"Keep your conversations to a minimum, especially with officials. Don't volunteer anything. Act stupid, like you have to think about every word before you speak."

He rattled off two long sentences in Russian. "Those are Russian proverbs. What do they mean?"

"I didn't understand. Something about an ox horn and a mouth."

Slater repeated the sentences, a little slower.

"An ox gets caught by the horn, a man by his tongue," Eric said.

"Good. And the second?"

"Could you repeat it please?"

"We'll have to work on your comprehension. What I said was, once a word is out of your mouth, you can't swallow it again."

* * *

Sam taught Eric about popular culture and the day-to-day routines that made up Soviet life. Eric found Sam the least threatening. He didn't realize it was part of the setup. If Eric was going to confide in anyone, it would be Sam, Slater hoped.

"I'm glad I don't have to make the food that the vast majority of Russians eat," Sam told Eric one time, as Garfield watched him preparing a meal. "Boiled cabbage, potatoes, beets, bread. Maybe some greasy sausage now and then." Sam wrinkled his nose. "Shopping over there is a nightmare, an absolute nightmare. Russian women always carry an *avos'ka,* a little 'maybe bag.' They never know when scarce jelly or fresh meat will appear on the shelves. They scoop up as much as they can. Which adds to the shortages."

"What about the muckety-mucks?"

"There's a special network for them, called 'the Distribution.' The best food, clothing, assorted creature comforts, get slipped out of the system before the masses can get it."

"The food I've been eating here isn't so bad."

Sam looked hurt.

"No, don't get me wrong. It's delicious. How come you're feeding me good food, though? Does that mean the person I'm meeting has access to this network?"

"Oh, look, the water's boiling over," Sam said, turning his attention to a pot.

Garfield had no time to himself, no time to brood. Whenever he wasn't being tutored, he was being supervised by Sam or Slater, developing his body. He'd spend a half hour on the rowing machine, while a Russian-language tape or Russian music played. He had hand-to-hand combat sessions with Slater, which left him feeling bruised and exhausted. He stretched, did aerobics, and powerlifted.

"I'm teaching you only three throws," Slater explained.

"Better to know a limited amount reflexively than a hundred throws awkwardly. Striking will be limited to the fist, the knife edge of the hand, the palm, and the elbow. The elbow is the hardest striking surface of the body. It can be particularly effective if you move in on an adversary."

At night Slater would take him into the nearby woods and teach him survival skills and orienteering. "You can go for three weeks without food, three days without water, but only three hours under adverse weather conditions," Slater said, as he demonstrated how to build concealed lean-to, foxhole, and trench shelters. Eric learned to orienteer by the stars and, during the daytime, to use his watch to find due south. He was shown how to read an existing trail or blaze a new one, and how to sight on a landmark to find his way home.

Eric tried to figure out how to escape, but he had trouble enough finding his way on the path right behind his teacher. Even if he got away from Slater, he wouldn't have known where to run.

A week passed and the facts kept pouring in. The Georgetown professor taught him the structure of the Soviet government, the constitution that was virtually ignored, the various strengths of the Central Committee, the Politburo, the *nomenklatura*, the ministers, and the power of the Communist Party of the Soviet Union—the CPSU—which included about six percent of the population.

He learned about "golden rubles," the pay to the elite, actually worth eight times more than regular rubles, and usable at the stores that sold deluxe foreign goods to those in power; about restricted cities, where foreigners couldn't go, and Moscow, where every resident had to have a pass and other Soviet citizens couldn't stay for more than three days; and about labor camps and psychiatric hospitals for dissidents.

*   *   *

"I don't know how much more of this I can take," Eric said late one night. "I've never been so beat. I think sneaking across the Soviet border would be easier."

"That's the idea," Slater said as they downed vodkas. "I have a reward for you. Tomorrow we leave this area."

"Let me guess: This has been a mistake. I'm free to go." Eric had gotten better at holding his liquor, but Slater could still drink him under the table.

Slater shook his head. "I'm going to teach you counter-surveillance. To do that right, I also have to teach you surveillance techniques. Make you into a real pavement artist."

For the first few hours they tailed randomly selected people on New York streets. At one intersection Eric was nearly struck by a car, so intent had he been on watching one subject. Another time he was spotted by a woman he was following. As she hurried to a policeman, Slater hustled him away.

Slater showed him how to spot a tracker by slowing down and speeding up, using reflections in store windows, jaywalking, observing a scene from high ground. He demonstrated how to shake a tail by entering a building with multiple exits, taking a cab and then jumping out around the corner, and using the acting coach's tricks to quickly change one's appearance.

They went to the Soviet mission on East Sixty-seventh Street. Slater stared at the building malevolently, as if his hate could tear it down. He had Eric observe the mission for a minute, turn away, and then describe it in detail.

"Twelve stories. The bottom is polished black granite, the upper eleven white glazed brick. A narrow garden in front with a few shrubs. Gray spiked fence. Entranceway two steps down. Astroturf leading up to it. Cement canopy on two metal poles. Three flagpoles on the second floor."

"Good. What about exterior security?"

"Surveillance cameras trained on the entranceway and street. New York police booth to the east of the entrance."

"Take a look at it. You see the fifth floor, the one with the unwashed windows?" Slater said. "That's for their spooks. Even their own people aren't supposed to know that. KGB agents go to the sixth floor and walk down a flight. GRU operatives go to the fourth floor and walk up. KGB have the front of the building, GRU a much smaller section at the rear."

Eric nodded. Slater had hoped Garfield would correct him. The intelligence services actually were based on the seventh floor.

In a building doorway concealed from the cameras, they waited until Slater spotted a familiar face. "That's Borchov coming out. KGB resident chief. Follow him."

The canny Borchov rushed through midtown Manhattan on foot, by cab, and subway. He lost them after a half hour of tailing.

"That's lesson nine," Slater said, holding up all but one finger. "With only a couple of people on his tail, any op can shake loose."

"What's lesson ten?"

"I'll tell you after your final."

NINE

NEVADA GOVERNOR ALVIN WINTERS ENJOYED THE VIEW IN his hotel-room mirror. He was by any estimate a handsome man, central casting for high political office. His optimistic message about America was always well received. Audiences sensed that when Winters spoke of how the nation was destined to be number one, it wasn't just a politician putting on a show. Winters was a true believer in "the greatest country on earth, now or ever, which has been very good to millions of people, and particularly generous to me."

Phil Dector's unfortunate accident had been the turning point in his life, he thought as he adjusted his tie. Winters, with Glenn Kelly's guidance, had reorganized the company and renamed it Alvin Winters Electronics, and soon the AWE logo was appearing on hundreds of hi-tech products. The company had moved to a sprawling fifty-acre compound in Nevada to avoid oppressive corporate taxes. Kelly had provided secret information and access to financing. All he had asked for in return was gossip, trade tips, insight into state-of-the-art technology. Some of the material was classified defense work, but that hadn't bothered Winters. Those government bureaucrats overclassified everything anyway.

After a couple of years Winters had gotten embroiled in the debate to keep Nevada from passing a corporate tax. Fellow businessmen had suggested he run for office. He won by a sizable margin. The cheers of the crowd were even more of a kick than large deposits in the bank.

Right before the election, Glenn Kelly had disappeared. He'd been replaced by Vince Persico. They didn't look the same—Persico was younger, and a bit of a fop—but they had the same ruthless aura.

Winters had figured that Kelly and Persico were Mafioso. They both drew resources from a powerful, secret organization, and had that cold killer soul under a civilized veneer. Winters had made peace with that fact. Neither man had tried to get him to do anything against his nature. So they lent money a few points above the prime rate. Whom did it hurt if they paid off a cop or inspector? Or maybe they took bets where it wasn't legal. Who cared? Winters' opinions meshed perfectly with those of his secret supporters. They were ambitious, successful businessmen, just like him. It was in their interest, as much as his, to keep the relationship hidden.

They had made no effort to alter his politics. He was a hard-liner on crime, offering to pull the switch on the electric chair. Welfare was freeloading. The Reds had to be stopped wherever they reared their ugly heads. A strong military was the only way to ensure peace.

It didn't hurt that Winters had benefited from several million-dollar defense contracts, he thought, smiling at himself. If he was elected president, he'd have to put it into a blind trust. Hell, he'd give it up in a minute. President Alvin Winters. It had a nice sound to it.

"I'm glad you could make the time to see me," Agency Deputy Director for Clandestine Services James Mitchell

Tuttle said, tearing off a piece of fresh-baked sourdough bread.

"I've been looking forward to meeting you," Winters said, taking a sip of his chablis.

The two men were at Sonny Brown's, a marginally chic eatery in the Washington suburb of Roslyn. The food was excellent, the restaurant dark, and there were no CIA staffers, members of Congress, or reporters about.

"We've been watching the race with great interest," Tuttle said. "We appreciate your strong anti-Communist stance. The present administration is too knee-jerk."

"That's good to know. The present administration doesn't appreciate you. The CIA does a fine job for this country. Only the bad news gets into the newspapers."

"How true. I admire your platform. Abolishing the Freedom of Information Act would be a godsend. Scores of employees would be freed for chores vital to our national security. The information that has leaked out because of that act is frightful."

"I sometimes think that act was dreamed up by the KGB," Winters said. "I'd like to see your budget increased. By at least twenty percent."

"We could do a lot of good with that kind of funding. There's always a need for new personnel."

"Definitely. But I think it's important to keep old hands around. I hope whoever wins recognizes your contribution to our nation's security. Have you considered becoming the Director of Central Intelligence?"

"I'm flattered."

"You deserve it," Winters said. He took a mouthful of julienne string beans with toasted almonds. "The food here is excellent."

"Thank you. I think our association can be mutually beneficial. I would be pleased to recommend very astute political consultants."

"I'd value your suggestions."

After a few minutes of chitchat and compliment swapping, Tuttle lowered his voice to a whisper and said, "We have an intelligence coup coming up. The defection of a prominent Soviet intelligence officer. It could be arranged to prolong the debriefing, keep him on ice until after the election."

"Whatever's in the country's interest I would support wholeheartedly."

"This coup will hit the Central Committee like a torpedo amidships. It could be bigger than Shevchenko or Penkovsky."

Winters grinned. "I won't be audacious enough to ask who you're talking about, but I must say I'm extremely curious."

"A top man in their intelligence community. That's all I can tell you at the moment. There are rather unusual conditions surrounding his defection. Once we get it sorted out, perhaps I can fill you in."

"I love a good spy story."

"So do I. As long as the right side wins," Tuttle said, taking a sliver of capon. "The food here really *is* good, isn't it?"

Back at Langley, Tuttle snapped at his secretary when she reminded him he had a meeting in an hour with Wellington. The director of the Agency would want to be updated on the Garfield–Petrov operation. Tuttle was trying to keep him as far from it as possible. Its success, and then delay until Winters took office, could guarantee Tuttle the post he coveted.

Tuttle shut the door to his office and punched his access code into the Octopus computer. Slater, working with a scrambler and modem-equipped microcomputer, had been filing daily reports. Tuttle called up the Borzoi file.

Slater's program was more than Tuttle thought necessary, but that was to be expected. Remembering his own traumatic experiences as a Communist prisoner, Slater would naturally be overcautious.

Tuttle skimmed the latest entries. Slater was meticulous, detailing Garfield's reactions under stress, what he said during boozy conversations, his academic performance. Still there was no clue as to why Petrov had chosen the young man.

TEN

"WHAT IS YOUR NAME?" SLATER GROWLED.

"Konstantin Petrov."

"Where were you born?"

"In Moscow," the young man answered in Russian.

"Liar," Sam shouted. "Where in Moscow?"

"Just off Leningradsky Prospekt."

"What was your father's name? What was your mother's name? Who was your group leader in the Komsomol? Who is the vice chairman of the Communist Party? Where do you work? What is your boss's name?"

Eric stumbled over a few words.

"Fake laryngitis," Slater said.

"I have no boss. We are all equals under our glorious system," Eric answered in a Marlon Brando-as-Don Corleone voice. Giddy from exhaustion, he broke out laughing.

"What's so funny?" Slater bellowed.

"I'm sorry," Garfield said. "But do you realize what a scene this is?"

"One slip behind the Iron Curtain and you won't laugh ever again. Don't get cocky, or sloppy. There's a good chance you won't need any of this. But if you do, it has to be perfect, whether you're talking to a *babushka* in the street or a KGB interrogator.''

"Let's continue,'' Garfield said in Russian.

"We'll start over again. What are your three cover stories?''

"Eric Garber, a U.S. citizen looking to get Eisenstein films for a festival. David Lee, a Canadian with an import-export business. And Konstantin Petrov, Soviet citizen.''

"When do you use each of them?''

"Garber on entry, Petrov while I'm over there, and Lee on exit. Why do I need a fake passport to leave? I thought I just waltz out of the country with this refusenik.''

"It never hurts to have a fallback plan. Tell me Garber's background.''

Eric groaned and began his recital.

It was the evening of Garfield's last day. He hadn't had a full night's sleep, it seemed, since he had first been brought here. He had gotten used to a permanent state of tiredness. He pounded the speed bag, his steady rhythm making a pleasing thumping noise. Stravinsky's *Firebird* played in the background.

Eric could relate Vladimir Ilyitch Lenin's life story or discourse on Gogol's *The Overcoat* and explain how it presaged the Russian Revolution. He could understand and speak enough Russian to carry on a simple conversation. He was able to improvise a disguise, alter his mannerisms, and spot a tail within minutes. He paused in his pounding and admired his biceps.

"Do you like what you see?'' Slater asked.

Garfield, as usual, had not heard him approach. Embarrassed, he relaxed his muscles. "It's time, isn't it? I still don't believe it. I'm not ready for this.''

"I'm the professional. You have to trust my assessment. Let's go out and celebrate. You're in the Konstantin mode from the moment we leave the house. It's time for you to get used to it.''

Slater still insisted that Eric wear the opaque sun-glasses after they left the house. They drove a good distance before he let Eric take them off. Half an hour later, they pulled up by a roadside bar. It was a wood-shingled, single-story building with a busted neon sign that sputtered "Dew Drop Inn." There were two huge, chopped motor-cycles parked out front.

"This is where we go to celebrate?" Eric asked.

"I have to see someone."

Inside, country and western music blasted from a juke box. On the wall behind the bar a Nazi flag was hung amid a jumble of biker paraphernalia. Two thuggish men and a couple of trampy women were swilling beer. The red lighting in the room was muted by the pall of tobacco and marijuana smoke.

"This place has a real ambiance," Eric whispered.

Slater smiled.

Eric looked over the motley crew and tried to figure out who was Slater's contact. The slovenly woman with the watermelon-size breasts and no bra? Or her boyfriend, who was missing more teeth than he had? Or maybe it was the bartender, whose mammoth arms had tattoos of snakes, spiders, and naked women?

"Two beers," Slater said to the bartender as they stepped up to the bare pine counter.

"Five bucks," the bartender said, slamming dirty steins on the bar. The regulars chortled.

Slater paid the tab without comment. He wiped the top of his glass and gulped the liquid down. Eric nursed his.

"I've got to go to the john. Be right back," Slater said. As Slater passed a bruiser in a ratty leather vest, he leaned over and said something quietly in his ear. Garfield was amazed at the openness of the contact.

The bruiser in the vest strutted over. "Who the hell are you to call me a faggot?"

"What?"

The bruiser threw a right without warning. Instinctively, Eric dropped under the punch, slammed the back of his fist into the man's nose, and planted him with a *taoitoshi*. For an inestimable amount of time, he felt like he was in the eye of a hurricane. Later, all he could clearly recall was standing in the middle of the bar, surrounded by smashed tables, chairs, and dazed or unconscious bodies.

As they climbed into the car, Slater said, "You did good."

"I—what—what happened?"

"You just passed your final with honors."

"Someone could've gotten killed!"

"Those animals deserve to die." Slater neglected to say that he actually had incapacitated two out of the five people in the bar.

"We should call an ambulance for them."

"Would they have called one for you?"

"But we—you—provoked it."

"Who threw the first punch?"

"I don't believe this," Garfield said. He had a few minor cuts and his right shoulder was sore from where he had blocked a punch. "What if they had seriously injured me?"

"You can knock yourself, but don't knock my training," Slater said. "Time to relax. The only condition is, you have to stay in the Konstantin Petrov identity. No matter what. Agreed?"

Shaking his head in disbelief, Eric said, "Okay."

They rode to a gentrified Hoboken neighborhood and entered a bar in a former warehouse. Half of it was set up as a conventional tavern, with a long redwood bar, two dozen oak stools, red booths, and dim lighting. The other half was a dance floor, where loud music thumped, lights flashed, and patrons swirled.

"What do you think of them?" Slater said, indicating two women sitting together at the far end of the bar.

One was a blonde, slightly overweight, with a sweet, pudgy face. The angular-featured brunette looked like an aerobics buff. Both were in their mid-thirties, fashionably dressed, and perfectly made-up.

"They look pleasant enough. But I've never been very good at pick-up lines. And right now I—"

"Speak only Russian," Slater ordered. "My name will be Fred. I'm an import-export businessman."

Eric toyed with his drink and watched as Slater drifted over to the women. Slater said something and they laughed. The brunette laughed harder. The trio talked for a few more minutes. As they came over, Slater put his arm around them. Neither shied away. Eric could tell from the women's movements that they were tipsy.

"Konstantin, this is Roseann," Slater said, indicating the brunette. "And this is Gina."

The women said hello. Gina asked, "Are you really a Russian defector?"

Eric was about to answer, when he realized he wasn't supposed to understand. He put a quizzical expression on his face.

"He's cute," Gina said, as she sat down next to him.

Slater and the two women talked while Eric nodded along amiably. Slater would periodically "translate" something for Eric. At one point Slater left to use the men's room. Gina and Roseann spoke as if Eric wasn't there.

"That Fred's got roaming hands," Roseann said. "He's feeling me up under the table."

"I don't see you complaining," Gina said with a giggle.

"He's got what it takes. What do you think of the Russian?"

"Seems nice. Are you sure it's okay to talk like this?" Gina asked, looking suspiciously at Eric.

Roseann turned to Eric. "Hey, you horny Commie, wouldn't you like to ball me and Gina right here on the table?"

91

"Roseann!"

Eric looked innocently at Roseann and mimicked her nod.

"He doesn't understand a thing," Roseann said.

They wound up at an apartment in Fort Lee with a breathtaking view of Upper Manhattan. Eric wasn't sure if it was Gina or Roseann's place. He was a little drunk, and all he cared about was Gina's soft body. There was no question what they were there for, and Slater and Roseann quickly disappeared.

In the bedroom, Gina's girlish silliness disappeared. Her movements became bold as she reached into his pants and wrapped her cool hands around him. Her grip was strong, almost painful, then gently stimulating. He nibbled her neck and murmured Russian nonsense words.

The next morning, back at the safehouse, Eric wondered about Gina. Had he slipped and said anything to her in English? He didn't think he had, but his actions had been clouded by alcohol and passion. Had the whole night been a test? Bert had picked the women up so easily.

Slater was all business, and refused to talk about their double date. He brought out the equipment Eric would need for his Russian trip. It included a reversible jacket and a suitcase with a small concealed compartment. Inside the compartment was makeup, a mustache, a fake Canadian passport with Eric's picture and the name David Lee, and a Russian internal passport with Eric's photo above the name Konstantin Petrov. An American passport and visa, with the name Eric Garber, showed the undisguised Eric.

"Does the name Anatoli Vasilevich Petrov mean anything to you?" Slater asked casually.

"No."

"Are you sure?"

Eric thought for a moment. "Positive."

"He's the one who insisted on you making the trip."

"He must've been crocked on vodka when he did. Ten to one I get over there, he sees me and goes, 'Oops, I made a mistake.' What does he do?"

"He's a minor clerk in the government," Slater said.

"I don't believe that. Why would you spend so much time and energy on a minor clerk? He's very important, isn't he?"

"As far as I know, he's a nobody," Slater said. "Let's go through it again, kid. What's the parole?"

"The 'parole'?"

Slater had tried one last time to trip Eric up. "It's a recognition code, a password. What is it?"

"I don't believe you, Bert. I think this Petrov is a big deal. I think you're putting me in over my head."

"*You* thought you were over your head in the Dew Drop Inn. This won't be difficult. And you'll have the satisfaction of knowing you've served your country."

"If all goes well. That's a big if. I can't handle this. Is there anyone you can check with, see if maybe I'll get a last-minute pardon?"

"To show Uncle Sam appreciates you, I've arranged for you to get paid," Slater said, ignoring Eric's remarks.

"Does that include life insurance? Maybe you'd like to be my beneficiary?"

"For the time spent training, and your three days over there, your generous uncle will give you ten thousand dollars. That's cash. Okay, what's the parole?"

ELEVEN

MAX GOLDSTEIN LIVED IN A ONE-BEDROOM APARTMENT IN Flushing, Queens. The fifty-four-year-old bachelor would've been quite handsome, with hard Slavic features, if it hadn't been for the raccoonlike rings under his eyes.

Goldstein was a cabbie, a loner at the job and in his neighborhood. At work he turned down offers to go to the track or play poker with the boys. From his neighbors he rejected matchmaking attempts with widows and divorcees. He was pleasant to everyone, but had no family or friends.

His gossipy fellow drivers believed he had a tragic past: one of the Jews who had gotten out of the Soviet Union. There were rumors that he had left, or lost, his whole family.

Max Goldstein was, in reality, a KGB captain, dispatched to the United States with the papers of a Jewish tailor who had died of a heart attack in a labor camp. Goldstein had been using the identity for so long—eleven years—it took him a moment before he could remember his real name.

He worked around the United Nations, and diplomats or

U.N. staffers who confided in the cabbie did not realize the resources he could draw on. Like the African ambassador who wanted two white girls and a whip, or the European trade minister who cruised Times Square and mentioned his interest in meeting a willing young man, or the South American who was troubled by gambling debts. Goldstein relayed the word to the KGB, and these and other pigeons had been snared and were now working for the *Komitet Gosudarstvennoy Bezopasnosti*.

But recruitment was not Goldstein's job, merely a fringe benefit that increased his value. Goldstein worked for Directorate S, Department Eight, and his job was to kill. He had eliminated seven foes of the Soviet Union, all defectors or émigrés.

It had been nearly two years since his last bit of *mokrie dela*, "wet work." He'd been excited when he had been activated through the dead drop under the trunk he left in the basement.

The name Eric had been written in code on a piece of paper, as well as a date and time in Central Park. There was a photo of Eric and another envelope. The instructions were very strange. Goldstein frowned as he reread them.

He took the paper with the message and tore it into a hundred pieces. He went to his bedroom and removed a K-bar knife from the night table. With whetstone and leather he sharpened the already deadly blade.

Eric paced the hotel bedroom. Did he dare try to escape? It always came back to the same question. Where? They would track him down. Had Bert been bluffing when he threatened him and his ex-girlfriend? Could they do anything worse to him than what the Russians would if he was caught? What if it really was an important mission and he blew it? How could his own government shanghai him like this?

He tried to psych himself. He was about to start on a

bold journey. He could imagine how Columbus had felt before sailing west, or Neil Armstrong's anticipation as he stepped on the moon. Great, he thought, I'm having delusions of grandeur.

How would Petrov contact him? Why was the U.S. giving him all that money? Why had they spent so much time on him? Who was this Petrov, anyway? And most important of all, why me? Garfield thought. Like a patient with a terminal disease, he tried to convince himself it would turn out to be a mistake. He wouldn't even sue. He just wanted to go back to his old life.

Eric Garfield, cold warrior, protecting truth, justice, and the American way. Or was he just a patsy in some game of intrigue?

These people loved secrets and playing games, Eric had decided. He wondered how much of espionage was useless tradecraft, like Loyal Order of Moose members exchanging secret handshakes. Silly people.

The euphemisms had caused nearly as much hostility between Eric and Bert as their political differences. "Surreptitious entry" meant burglary. "Biographic leverage" meant blackmail. "Terminate with extreme prejudice," "demote maximally," "sanction," "neutralize," "liquidate"—they all meant murder.

"They're still crimes," Eric had argued.

"Crime means criminal intent. Our motive is national security."

"Sure. If you're caught, you were only following orders," Eric said with a mock German accent.

"You don't give a shit about our country, do you?"

"Wrong. Just the opposite. I care a lot more about it than you do. I care about the Constitution, civil liberties, obeying the laws not only of—"

"Cut the schoolboy crap," Bert had snapped.

The phone rang, cutting into Eric's recollection and making him jump. It rang again. He snatched it from the cradle, hoping it would be a wrong number, or Bert cancelling the mission.

"Hello, Mr. Garber?"

It was a man's deep voice, with a strong Slavic accent.

"Yes?" Eric asked, struggling to keep his voice level.

"Have you seen any good movies recently?"

"Not since—not since—not since *Alexander Nevsky.*"

"I might be able to recommend some. I suggest meeting in Central Park. Bethesda Fountain. Six o'clock. Did you get that?"

"Six o'clock. Bethesda Fountain. How will I know you?"

"I'll know you," the man said, and broke the connection.

TWELVE

BETHESDA FOUNTAIN IS LOCATED JUST NORTH OF THE SHEEP Meadow, on line with Seventy-second Street. The circular fountain is two dozen feet high, with the statue of the Angel of the Waters on top. Layered like a wedding cake, the statue has cherubs on the second tier and small columns on ground level, surrounded by a large circular pool. The Angel's copper skin has turned green with age.

As Eric approached the stairs down to the fountain, the lake north of it came into view. Shadows of the pin oaks in the Rambles fell across the edges of the lake. They were a relatively recent addition, only forty years old, and initially the center of controversy for interfering with the planners' wishes for an unobstructed view.

It was getting dark quickly. In the apartment houses in the distance, high-rise residents were turning on their lights.

Senses humming, Eric walked down the stairs. It was a cool spring evening, with a damp, fertile smell in the air. The heads protruding from the bas-reliefs on the sooty stairway walls were chipped. A few seedy people lounged around the fountain. The park had long been a meeting place for lovers. During the sixties it had become a site of "happenings." Now, especially in the evening hours, dope dealers used it as a marketplace.

"Loose joints?" a man hissed, looming up suddenly on Eric's right as he reached the foot of the stairs. Eric instantly raised his hands in a defensive position. The dealer, a skinny man in his early twenties, grinned, baring a tooth with a gold star embedded in it.

"You need to calm down—best weed in town," the dealer said.

"I'll pass," Garfield said, and moved on. He watched the grass dealer head out of the park. Eric walked toward the fountain. He felt eyes upon him. What beasts were hiding in the trees?

Goldstein watched Eric approach the fountain. He counted eight people in the area, six men and two women. One of the men was lying on the ground, drunk or stoned. The kind of scum he'd never pick up in his cab. They were probably in the park to deal dope. If they were there to prey on him, they'd be in for a rude surprise. He felt the K-bar clipped under his jacket, in a special holster that allowed a quick draw. He would carve them up, his contribution to the Cleaner New York campaign.

He leaned against an oak tree, in black pants and jacket, barely visible. His assignment was simple enough. He patted the knife for good luck and walked to where Eric fidgeted.

Garfield saw the man approaching. No doubt about the Slavic features. He had a slow, deliberate pace. Circles under his eyes gave him an ominous look. Both hands hung at his sides as he came closer. He wore dark clothes.

The man was a few feet away now. He had a humorless smile on his face. His mouth opened to speak as his hand reached under the coat.

There was a whistling sound, and he fell suddenly. His

hand reached deeper into his jacket. A second whistle, and his body jerked.

Eric spun, looking to see what was going on. The loungers on the other side of the fountain hadn't heard the whistle, but they'd seen the man fall.

"Police. Everybody freeze!" someone shouted.

All but two men took off, dropping plastic bags filled with green leafy substances or white crystalline powders. They disappeared in a little more than a second. The remaining two loiterers raced over.

The man with Slavic features lay on the ground, cursing in Russian and English. A stunned Eric saw moist patches glistening on his knee and shoulder.

Bert came running down the stairs, a rifle with a night sniperscope over his shoulder. He tossed the gun to one of the loiterers, a burly man with a Navy watch cap.

"Why'd you abort?" asked the other loiterer, an Hispanic with a scrawny mustache.

"This is Max Goldstein," Bert said. "KGB wet work pro. Fix him up."

Mustache took out a compact first-aid kit and tied pressure bandages around Max's wounds.

"But we had orders to let the meet go—"

"Screw that." Bert took a syringe from a case in his coat pocket. He rolled up Max's sleeve and plunged the needle into his arm.

"All right, Max, this is a painkiller. It's more than you deserve."

"I don't know what you're talking about," Goldstein said through gritted teeth.

Slater dug under the coat where Goldstein had been reaching when he dropped him. The agent expected to find a gun or Goldstein's characteristic knife. Instead, there was an envelope. Slater slipped it into his jacket pocket. He felt around. The knife was on the other side.

The lounger who had taken the gun from Slater had reduced it to several pieces, each no longer than a foot.

"You'll take responsibility for this?" he asked Slater.

Slater nodded. Eric watched numbly as the backup agents helped Goldstein to his feet. Goldstein's head drooped, his mouth hung open. There were two puddles of blood where he had been lying on the terra-cotta tile and cement floor. The puddles joined into one big pool.

Slater grabbed Eric's arm and tugged him away.

They scurried from bush to bush, heading south along the park's perimeter, pausing occasionally to listen for sounds. It was like the cross-country exercises Bert had taken him on, but this time Eric's pulse was pounding so loud, he thought everyone in midtown could hear it.

"What's going on?" he asked.

"Quiet."

There was a knock at their door almost immediately after they got in. Eric had no reaction, sitting on the hotel bed, staring straight forward.

"Who's there?" Bert demanded, his hand on the butt of his 9mm Browning.

"I've got Mr. Borzoi's suitcase."

Slater opened the door, his hand still on the gun. The bellboy handed him the suitcase and hurried away without waiting for a tip.

Slater locked the door. He laid the case on the bed and opened it. Inside, cushioned by foam, were a portable phone and scrambler, a jamming device, and a Magpie Board. The Board was a mini-survival kit with amphetamines, barbiturates, plastic explosive, a lock-pick set, and other compact gear an agent might need.

He activated the jamming device. It generated a modulating signal that would turn a conventional mike into a feedback generator. Anyone eavesdropping would get a painful electronic screech.

He went into the bathroom and dissolved an odorless, tasteless pill in a glass of water. He returned to Eric and offered the glass. "Have a drink of water."

Eric gulped it down.

"Did you talk to anyone, anyone at all, when you were alone in the hotel?" Slater asked. Eric had been under constant surveillance, but it was always possible there had been a slipup.

Eric shook his head.

"I don't know what happened out there, but we're going to find out." Bert tore open the envelope he'd taken from Goldstein. Inside was a Bolshoi Ballet ticket for a performance in Moscow and a two-sentence password.

At CIA headquarters Tuttle received word of the trouble on Borzoi. He decided he had to inform the Director immediately.

Wellington was sitting behind his desk, fingers steepled, with the Petrov and Garfield files before him.

"This really intrigues me," the CIA director said as Tuttle entered. "It reminds me of the jigsaw puzzles I used to enjoy when I still had time to myself."

"There's been another piece added. A known KGB killer showed up at the rendezvous point and had to be incapacitated. The reports from the field are sketchy, but I'm sure you want to be kept posted. Borzoi may have to be aborted."

"What do we know so far?" Wellington asked.

"The killer is claiming he's a cabdriver who was just delivering an envelope. He says a fare gave him twenty dollars to do it. He's unlikely as a mere courier. He has been linked to three murders and a kidnaping at KGB behest, and he was armed. We've put him on ice. Maybe the Soviets will make a trade for one of our illegals."

"How many hours until Garfield's plane is due to take off?"

"Two."

Wellington toyed with the files. "Did you know Petrov went to Frunze Military Academy? He used to fence with their current defense minister. He knows most of the top brass in the military and four of the members of the Politburo. The insight he could offer us would be phenomenal."

"Yes," Tuttle said impatiently. "He's an important bastard, all right."

"He's got psychological value, too. A Hero of the Soviet Union medal winner," Wellington said. "His exploits with the freedom fighters in the Odessa catacombs are the stuff legends are made of." Wellington took Eric's file and Petrov's file and slapped them against each other. "If I had a handle on why Petrov wants him, I could make a much better decision."

"I can't go through with this, Bert," Eric said, his eyes drooping. The tranquilizer had taken effect. "I'm scared and tired. I feel really out of it. Starting like this, it's a bad sign. Please call it off."

"Stage fright," Slater said. This was his big chance to run an operation, to prove himself once again to the Company. But his instructions were to sit in the room and wait. How long? The first reaction of the bureaucrats was always to pull back, sit tight, wait out the storm. If Eric missed the flight from Kennedy, the whole mission could be terminated.

"I've never seen someone get shot," Eric murmured. "Right in front of me. Because of me."

The secure phone in the case on the bed rang and Slater lifted it. He recognized Tuttle's voice.

"You jumped the gun with Goldstein," he said harshly. "It looks like he was just a messenger boy on this op."

"He's a killer. Why risk him when they could've used a dead drop, or a brush contact, or an embassy flunkie?"

"I don't know. You're the one who took the envelope. Did you plan on sharing it with us? Or were you going to hold on to it as a souvenir?"

"There's a ticket to the Bolshoi and a parole."

"You know you should have sent it to us forthwith. We could've had it at the lab by now. In your rush to protect Borzoi, you exceeded your authority. Just hold Garfield there. We'll get back to you."

Slater set the phone down in the case.

"What's the matter?" Garfield asked.

"Nothing. They told me to get you to the airport."

"I can't do it."

"You can and will. We'll be protecting you. We'll always be watching. Just like in the bar. Just like in the park. You're as safe as in your mother's arms."

"Even in the Soviet Union?"

"Even there. It's time to go."

The sedative in Eric's system had flattened his emotions. He was too exhausted to protest. Slater took his suitcase, and they stepped into the hall.

The bellboy who'd delivered the suitcase was hanging around near the elevator. "What's going on?" he asked.

"Go wait by the stairs," Slater ordered Eric.

Slater indicated for the bellboy to follow him into the room they'd vacated. "I spoke to Langley. They want me to move Borzoi to another hotel," Slater said. "They're afraid the whole op may be compromised."

"I haven't heard anything like that."

"I told you, I just heard. I've got to hustle him out of here forthwith."

"I better check."

"Of course."

The bellboy turned his head slightly. Suspicious, he twisted defensively as Slater raised his right hand. The bellboy blocked the knife edge that was aimed at his temple and launched a kick. Slater blocked it with his thigh, stepped in, and planted a raised-knuckle fist in the bellboy's solar plexus. Slater hit him on the side of the neck, shocking his carotid artery and vagus nerve. The bellboy collapsed. Slater ripped the cords off two lamps, bound the man's hands and feet, and gagged him.

"What happened?" Eric asked when Slater returned. It was an effort to speak without slurring his words.

"Bureaucratic foulup," Slater said. "I straightened it out. Follow me. We're going out through the basement. If anyone stops us, let me handle it."

Slater took his arm and guided him down the stairs.

"What's going on?" Eric asked.

"We're just being careful."

Eric Andrew Garfield was born in Manhattan in 1959, the son of Anna and Raymond Garfield. Raymond had been held at the concentration camp at Dachau. Anna was a U.S. citizen. They met in the garment center where they were employed.

Raymond had contact with Israeli government founders based on his World War II experiences. Details are not available, but he apparently rejected a postwar solicitation they made.

The Garfields opened a coffee shop on the East Side of Manhattan in 1955. Tax records indicate it was a typical struggling business. By 1966 the business was showing a small profit. In 1970 Anna developed breast cancer. She died in 1972. Two years later, Raymond was struck by a hit-and-run driver and died of resulting injuries. He had not remarried.

Garfield was a normal, heterosexual teenager. He had no drug arrests or associations with . . .

Wellington shut the folder. He was nearing the point where he could recite it from memory. He spread out an Immigration photo of Eric's father, a passport photo of Anna, a high school yearbook picture of Eric. He added a surveillance head shot of Petrov, a similar shot of Garfield's ex-girlfriend, a photo of Assemblyman Sussman at a banquet.

He played with the photos like a Las Vegas dealer with a fresh deck. He laid Eric and Petrov out, then all the other photos under Eric. What was the connection?

He picked up the picture of Eric and the one of Petrov and stared into the frozen faces. He squinted, blurring the details until only shapes remained. The images began to look the same. There was something similar in the line of the jaw and around the eyes—vaguely Oriental, but with a slightly Slavic cast, a look that showed up in neither Anna nor Raymond.

Wellington tore through the folders. Eric was blood type O. His mother was type O. Raymond Garfield was type AB. Anatoli Petrov was type O. He hurriedly called the Agency's medical section and had a call patched through to their chief hematologist. He presented the situation, without using any names.

"If the individual identified as the father is one of the three percent of the white population with type AB, that means he has both A and B antigens," the hematologist said. "One or the other *must* be passed on to the progeny. The child can be A, or B, or AB, but not Type O. Type O genes are recessive. If you get me blood samples, I can check other factors."

"Are you sure about the AB parent?"

"Absolutely. An AB parent cannot produce an O child."

Wellington thanked the expert and hung up.

He checked dates. Petrov would've been in New York when Eric was conceived.

"The prodigal son coming home," Wellington said to himself.

"I can't go any farther," Slater said as they stood at the

end of a long airport corridor. "If the KGB sees you with me, you're blown."

"I can't do it."

"There's no backing out. People have risked their lives for you. Matters of national security. You must get Petrov. The country is counting on you," Slater said. "We'll be watching."

His words sounded more threatening than protective.

THIRTEEN

DETSKY MIR, CHILDREN'S WORLD, IS THE SOVIET VERSION of F.A.O. Schwartz—though nowhere near as colorful or well stocked. The mammoth, high-ceilinged Moscow department store bustles with parents, grandparents, and eager youngsters. The slow-moving lines at counters and cash registers are always long. The harried sales staff ranges from unpleasant to surly.

Colonel Anatoli Petrov leaned over a counter, admiring a wooden toy sword. He was searching for a birthday present for his five-year-old nephew. The lean, gray-haired colonel's cold hazel eyes and aristocratic bearing commanded obedience. He held top Russian honors: a Hero of the Soviet Union medal, a Red Star, and a Red Banner. Most honorees wore their decorations every place but the shower. The small gold star and red ribbon in the left lapel meant respect and numerous privileges, from lifetime free use of public transportation to reserved seats at the Bolshoi to special shopping privileges. Petrov, however, had lived much of his life as a covert operative, and calling attention to himself, even in his homeland, was anathema. He was entitled to jump the line, or shop in the Special Section—

reserved for Party officials, leading academics, and honored military men. Instead he chose to wait with the masses.

He got in the line for the sword. He tried to focus his attention on his copy of *Izvestia*, but all he could think about was the impending arrival of Eric Garfield. No meeting had ever meant as much to him.

The normally alert GRU man didn't feel the eyes of the KGB agents watching him.

The idea to bring his son over had started with a gallstone. Petrov hadn't known it was a gallstone when he had felt the first stabbing pain. Proper diagnosis had taken a week, and during that time Petrov had had flashes of his own mortality. He didn't want to die without meeting his son.

He could've arranged to slip back into the United States. But how would the young man receive him? Could he expect Eric to greet him with anything but suspicion? If not hatred? He wanted his son to see Russia. He hoped the magnetism of the *rodina* would catch and hold Eric the way it held him.

A half hour passed, and he was nearing the counter. A pudgy, middle-aged man shoved into line. The man, well dressed in Western-style clothing, banged into a pretty blonde. She fell against Petrov.

"I—I'm sorry," she said, still leaning against him. She smelled sweet with perfume. Her blouse was low cut, her hair pulled back from her heart-shaped face.

"Apologize and get in the back of the line," Petrov barked at the pushy man as he helped the woman upright.

"Who do you think you're talking to, shithead?" The intruder had a sadistic face, with small eyes buried in folds of flesh. "You want to step outside and get your ass kicked?"

The colonel slapped the young man across the face, with

a crack that was heard halfway across the store. In earlier times it would've been the challenge to a duel.

The foul-mouthed man whipped out a red wallet case. "You're under arrest for striking an officer of the Committee for State Security."

The shoppers kept their distance, but stayed near enough to hear what was happening. The woman who had banged into Petrov rushed away.

"What is your name?" the KGB agent demanded.

"Colonel Anatoli Vasilevich Petrov. GRU."

The crowd listened attentively. Although not as well known as the KGB, the GRU was highly regarded. It spied on enemies of the Soviet Union, not on the Russian people.

A third man, a near giant, ambled over. "Blok. KGB. What's going on here?" If Petrov was a rapier, Blok was a broadsword.

"He struck me," the foul-mouthed agent said. "He says he's with the *sosedi*."

"He *is* with the neighbors. You're Colonel Petrov, correct?" Blok asked.

Petrov nodded.

"I'm sure there's been a misunderstanding," Blok said. "Please accept my apologies."

Petrov nodded again and strode from the building. He was furious, more at himself than at the squat KGB man. He usually kept control of his emotions. And now was the worst time to lose his temper.

The GRU, the Chief Intelligence Directorate of the Soviet General Staff, was headquartered by Khodinka Field, an airport closed to commercial traffic. The site makes it convenient to fly the latest Western technology in for dissection by the technical staff.

The surrounding grounds include three aviation and one rocket-construction plant, as well as the Institute of Cosmic Biology. The facilities do classified work and are protected with security cameras, barbed wire, armed men, and vicious dogs. The two-story GRU building has a nine-story windowless tower. The only other building in the area of similar height is an apartment house that is a residence for mid- to upper-level GRU officials.

Even the park benches in the neighborhood are part of the security plan. GRU operatives of more than twenty years spend their retirement on the benches, gossiping with cronies and watching for any suspicious activity.

The agency has four major divisions—operations, information, training, and auxiliary. Although much smaller than the KGB, with about five thousand operatives, they have had spectacular successes. They predicted Hitler's invasion of Russia. The ring credited with stealing American atom-bomb secrets was run by a GRU case officer. GRU-run operations had saved the Soviet Union hundreds of millions of rubles in research by stealing American, French, and German fighter-airplane technology.

In the elevator on his way to his fourth-floor office, a captain in counterintelligence tried to make conversation with Petrov about a soccer match the GRU team had had against the Ukrainian Locomotives. The colonel nodded noncommittally. He got off and walked to his office, exchanging curt greetings with those he couldn't pretend not to see. His secretary had no messages.

He entered his office and shut the door. He sighed.

The leather armchairs glowed like a general's boots and the carpet was thick. On one wall were a framed photo of Lenin, Petrov's Olympic medals, and blowups of satellite photos of the Motherland. The room was dominated by a massive safe, which had been serving the country longer than he had. Classified documents went into the safe at night, and a wax seal was pressed over the door. Even he, an honored colonel, could get in trouble for leaving papers unsecured. It didn't help that it was the rival KGB who handled internal-affairs investigations. They loved to catch a GRU man being sloppy.

Somehow the KGB had kept him from being promoted to general. He could never find out who was behind it. He had made enough petty enemies at Lubyanka. He had beaten their best fencer in competition. He had run operations in areas where the KGB thought no one was recruitable. And he had earned more medals than their best people. It was frustrating that he had seen others getting the promotions due him.

Petrov dug into a pile of paperwork. He was chief of Electronic Intelligence, and his division was responsible for satellite data collection as well as interception of signal traffic. There were reports of a satellite that had just been launched straying from geosynchronous orbit and sending back pictures of the Canadian Rockies instead of the American Midwest. This great-grandson of Sputnik would have to be destroyed. It was losing altitude, and there was a good chance it would crash.

Every day more than a hundred Soviet satellites circled the globe, half of them for military purposes. The assembly plants at Leninsk, Plesetsk, and Kapustin Yar turned out satellites and launch systems. The annual payload rate was 660,000 pounds, ten times that of the United States. Yet because of malfunctions, his country and the king of capitalist nations were running neck and neck.

He slapped the papers down on his desk. Why couldn't his people master technology? Thirty years after Hiroshima the Japanese had challenged the United States where it hurt the most, right in their capitalist hearts. The Germans could rebuild and market precision instruments. The Americans produced consumer goods like there was no tomorrow. In Russia the wheat didn't grow, the furniture fell apart, and satellites went astray.

He hit the buzzer on the intercom. "See if you can find Yuri for me," he told his secretary.

He reviewed the notes for a report due the next month on the orbital antisatellite system, ASAT. He was pushing instead for more civilian satellites, like the GORIZONT, to aid communications. The Soviet Union covered eleven time zones, with a land area of 8.66 million square miles. The *rodina* was two and a half times the size of the United States and had 37,000 miles of borders. Improved telephone service, television, and radio would do more to unite the people than another killer satellite.

There was a strong knock at the door, and Yuri Karabian stepped in. He was freshly shaved. Yuri had to take a razor to his jowly face at least twice a day or he looked so much like a caveman that people would stop and stare.

Aside from his coarse appearance, Yuri could've been the consummate politician. He had an easy, back-patting charm, remembering jokes and associates' birthdays. He knew everyone and could get things done, overcoming the clunky incompetence of the system. Although his rank was captain, as Petrov's *tolkach* he held a lot more clout. In the Army they're called "dog robbers," in private industry, expediters. In the Soviet Union, they're "*tolkachi*," and they are as vital as grease to a machine.

Yuri and his five brothers, three sisters, and members of their extended families had thoroughly infiltrated the Soviet government and carved out niches for themselves. Whether it meant swapping a vanload of hair curlers for a hundred pairs of Czech shoes, or arranging a pass for a shopping trip to France in return for a color television, video cassette recorder, and five American movies, Karabian and his brothers and sisters were powers in *nalevo*, the black market and influence peddling.

"You wanted me?" Yuri asked, standing at attention.

"I'd like to hear that new cassette," Petrov said.

Yuri walked over to the bookcase, took a tape recorder he had given the colonel from the shelf, and set it next to a potted plant. He turned it on, and Russian folk music filled the room.

The colonel had discovered the bug in the plant shortly after it had turned up unannounced. It was nothing to get alarmed about—the KGB was always snooping.

"Tell me what gossip you've heard," Petrov said.

"General Polozhentsnev is in trouble again," Yuri said. "At a party last week at the Premier's house, he got drunk and starting telling jokes."

"Were they that offensive?"

"Communism is just over the horizon," Yuri said deadpan. "But the horizon is an imaginary line that recedes as you approach it. Then he asked what alcoholism was, and answered it was a state between socialism and communism."

"Comrade Premier is not known for his sense of humor."

"Then, not realizing that the commissar of the Chukchi National Okrug was present, he began telling Chukchi jokes. Like the one about the Chukchi abortion clinic, with the ten-month waiting list. What are the three most difficult years for a Chukchi? Second grade. There were more."

"They must have been very well received," Petrov said with a sardonic smile.

"Like an army of Tartars. I understand someone had to keep the commissar from attacking Polozhentsnev."

Petrov let his smile broaden. It was a sign of his fondness for Yuri that he showed any emotion. Yuri had told him once, after several glasses of vodka, that he was called "Tundra Face." Yuri had instantly regretted the revelation, but Petrov had rather liked the nickname.

"Marshal Krovili knocked up a fourteen-year-old," Yuri said. "The KGB took care of it by giving her an abortion and allowing her parents a vacation in Finland."

"It's a tradition to have perverts at Lubyanka," Petrov said. "Going back to Beria and his lust for deflowering young teens. It's funny how the KGB depends on the honey trap so much, when they are the worst lechers."

Karabian nodded. "They have parties where they listen to tapes. Most of the *nachalstvo* spend at least one weekend a month testing the skills of the swallows at the House of Love."

"I should talk to the defense minister. I saw him a few weeks ago at the gymnasium. Maybe Gorchev would bring the matter up at the Politburo. Maybe get *Pravda* to take a look at the sorry state of the KGB."

"I hope you don't. I don't wish to visit you in Tiksi. Or to be posted there myself. I only have three pairs of thermal underwear my sister got me in Finland."

Petrov inhaled as if about to say something, then released the air in a long, slow sigh. "I'd never be that stupid. Just the musings of an old fool."

"You're not old or foolish. Is it the American that's bothering you?" Yuri asked softly.

The operation had been motivated by his paternal need to see his offspring. But then it had grabbed him on a professional level. This was his first time running an operation strictly for his own benefit, and not the *rodina*'s.

And by putting his only child in jeopardy, he was risking his own immortality. Somehow knowing he had a son had always given him courage. He was like a gambler betting everything on a high hand. He felt confident he would win, but there was the chance the dealer would have an ace up his sleeve.

"He arrives in a few hours," Petrov said after a long silence. "I haven't let myself hope for so long. It only leads to disappointment. After the Revolution, there was hope. After the concessions Stalin got at Yalta, there was hope. After Stalin was revealed as a barbarian by Khrushchev, there was hope. After Khrushchev was ousted as a buffoon, there was hope. Always, there is hope. Maybe not bread, maybe not shoes, maybe not freedom, but always hope."

"Nothing will go wrong," Yuri said. "I can make sure

the internal surveillance files are misplaced. Your son will be safer here than on the streets of New York."

"Risking my life is my business. But to endanger you . . ." His words trailed off.

Yuri stood up. "I would be insulted if you didn't let me take part. There'll be matters that you can't get away to handle. If need be, I would say that you ordered me to do it, that I didn't know it wasn't being done in the interests of Mother Russia."

Petrov allowed himself another smile. "I have put you in for a promotion."

"There's no need."

"Yes there is. Not for you, for the country. If we don't get fresh blood to the head of this organization soon, it'll topple over like Brezhnev," Petrov said. "You did an excellent job arranging matters in New York. I'm surprised the Americans didn't kill Goldstein."

"I didn't question why you wanted it done like that. I am curious."

"I wanted Eric to see American intelligence operatives in action," Petrov said. "So far it's gone well. They have no doubt twisted his arm to get him to go, and he's witnessed CIA bloodshed firsthand. He'll be able to accept me and the realities of the intelligence community by seeing how his countrymen behave."

"Do you want him to work for us?"

"No. Just to understand."

"I hope he appreciates the careful planning you've put into this," Karabian said. He walked over to the cabinet and retrieved a bottle of premium Armenian brandy. He poured a snifter for Petrov. The colonel gestured, and he filled a glass for himself.

"Eric owes me nothing," Petrov said, taking the snifter. He rolled the brandy, watching it coat the glass, then flow down into a warm amber pool. "It's strange how nervous I am, like a young man going to meet his bride.

Did you ever think you would see Tundra Face this agitated?''

Yuri gave a noncommittal shrug.

"I dreamed of his mother again last night. So many years since I've seen her, and still she comes to me. What a woman, Yuri," Petrov said. He sipped and mused silently for a moment. "Memories. But you seem troubled. Is everything okay?"

Yuri cleared his throat. "My cousin, the one who works as a clerk at the *sosedi*. She was updating files at Lubyanka and noticed a number were missing."

"Yes?"

"Someone has pulled the files of the top military people. Yours was among them. There's rumors of a purge in the offing."

The foul-mouthed KGBer from *Detsky Mir* and Stefan Blok stood before Vladimir Krovili in the Marshal's office.

"Old Tundra Face lost his temper," Krovili muttered. "Interesting. That confirms what we have heard about his recent irritability. He has *something* on his mind."

"He struck me hard enough to knock my fillings loose," said the pudgy man, whose name was Viktor Vesky.

Krovili had no doubt that Petrov, though twice Vesky's age, could thrash him. Vesky was a classic *stukach*, a snitch who had risen through the Young Pioneers, the Komsomol, Moscow University, and into the KGB solely because of his skill at tattling on his friends and associates.

"But the swallow failed. As soon as he raised his voice, she ran away."

"I'll see to her," Krovili said. "I wonder what has put the bug in Petrov's behind. There has to be a way to use it to our benefit."

"I'm sure it won't take that long for Comrade Marshal to get Petrov," Vesky said. "Should we try again? Put a round-the-clock watch on him?"

"This is not some low-level hooligan," the Marshal said. "He lives on Kutuzovsky Prospekt. Two deputy ministers live in the same building, as well as the editor of *Izvestia*. And Petrov is a cunning fox. If he detected any watchers, he could cover his tracks."

"Of course, Comrade Marshal," Vesky said. "I should have known you'd have everything figured out. Could we make up some believable *amoralka?*"

"Vesky, we have to have Petrov so that there can be no way out," Krovili said. "His supporters, and he has many, will try to protect him. If they can discredit our investigation, it will blow up in our faces."

"I have much to learn," Vesky said. "I am lucky to have such a good teacher."

Krovili turned to Blok and patted the stack of files on his desk. "We have what we need on the others I targeted?"

"Two are involved heavily in speculation in the black market. An admiral and another general are using government money to keep mistresses. One of the deputy defense minister's top aides is a faggot," Blok said without any sign of emotion. "He is with a different lover every night."

Krovili leaned back in his chair. "The greater the man, the more demanding his prick."

FOURTEEN

THE ROAR OF THE AEROFLOT IL62M INCREASED AND THE PLANE descended into Sheremetyevo Airport, thirty kilometers from the heart of Moscow.

Eric had slept for several hours. When he woke, he realized Bert had slipped him a mickey. He felt like a shanghaied sailor, doped and kidnaped to do a job.

He passed through disbelief to resentment to resignation.

He'd tried reading the heavy-handed propaganda pamphlets provided in lieu of the slick travel magazines on U.S. flights: "The U.S.S.R. has become the first country in which all the peoples, ethnic groups, and races got their freedom and independence," the propagandist had written. He went on to explain how other nations "had united with the Russian people of their own free will" and discussed Russia's "peaceloving foreign policy." There were obviously staged pictures of happy workers grinning for the camera. The pamphlets only added to his unease.

After a smooth touchdown Eric followed the flow of passengers to Passport Control. Two khaki-uniformed men were sitting inside the bulletproof-glass-enclosed booth. Eric slid his passport into the slot.

The passport inspector had a pubescent, unreadable face with Asiatic features. His review of Eric's papers was painfully slow. A bead of sweat bubbled on Eric's brow.

"Name?"

"Eric Garber."

The inspector repeatedly compared Eric's face with the passport photo. He asked Eric questions, in stiff English, and checked his answers with those on the forms.

"You are not travelling Intourist?" the guard challenged.

"No. I'm here to see an official at Goskino," Eric explained.

"Why?"

"I'm trying to arrange an American screening of the works of Sergei Eisenstein." He handed over a business card, with the name Eric Garber and a bogus address where the fictional East-West Cinematic Cooperative was housed. The guard looked at it, fingered it, and gave it back.

"I hope to exhibit films that have never been seen in America," Eric said. "He's very important to the history of cinema."

"Yes," the guard said, unimpressed.

Finally, Garfield was directed through a metal detector— the first time he had been searched coming off a plane. Two soldiers with Stechkin machine pistols watched him.

The machine beeped. They moved in. He had to remove the change from his pocket, then his belt buckle, before the machine would let him pass without wailing. The guard gestured for him to move on.

Eric retrieved his bag from the groaning steel carousel and brought it to the customs counter, which had X-ray machines built in. The blue-uniformed guard, also Asiatic-looking, had a military cap sitting cockeyed on his short-cut black hair. He peered into the X-ray tube for what seemed like hours, then looked up at Eric.

Behind him more scowling young men, automatic weapons slung over their shoulders, prowled back and forth. A few feet down the counter, a guard ordered a woman to open her suitcase. He reached in quickly and held up a jar of pills.

"Narcotics?"

"No, no. Allergy medicine."

The backup guards stepped forward. They hadn't unslung their weapons, but they were ready.

"Come with me," an older uniformed man indicated. The woman and her bags were taken to a row of rooms behind the counter. The door was shut. A guard stood outside.

Eric tried not to think of what would happen if they found out his name wasn't Garber, or discovered his fake documents or disguise kit.

"Don't worry about appearing nervous," Bert had told him. "If you're too at ease, then they'll wonder. When you're undercover, remember you don't have a neon sign hanging on you. Beginners assume the opposition knows. They don't."

"Open your bags," the customs agent ordered.

"It's normal, they do this to everyone," Eric reassured himself as he unsnapped the latches. He stretched casually and tried to relax his shoulders.

The customs man went through the suitcase thoroughly, checking it against the declaration form. He tapped around the interior, but didn't find the hidden compartment.

"I'd like to give you a few rolls of toilet paper," Bert had said during one of their vodka end-of-day sessions. "The Russians use sandpaper. But only savvy travelers know to carry that. You're going to have to suffer." Eric hoped that was the worst that would happen to him behind the Iron Curtain.

"Ah!" the guard said, and Eric's heart began to pound.

The guard lifted a copy of *Playboy*.

''Is something wrong with that?'' Eric asked innocently. Bert had included it, like a piece of meat for Cerberus.

''Decadent American filth. Prohibited to bring into Union of Soviet Socialist Republics.''

''I'm sorry, I didn't know. Will you dispose of it for me?''

The guard nodded officiously and slipped the magazine inside his personal cubbyhole under the counter.

There'll be a fun time in the customs office tonight, Eric thought, as the guard gestured for him to close his bags. Then Eric was back in the flow of passengers, moving into the Soviet Union.

Inside the terminal were signs in Cyrillic and some in English, saying things like WELCOME TO MOSCOW—THE HERO CITY and THE SOVIET WORKERS INVITE YOU TO A HAPPY JOURNEY THROUGH THE CCCP. There were duty-free shops, snack stands, currency-exchange offices, bars, and banks of telephones. The businesses were neither crowded nor inviting.

The woman with the allergy medicine rejoined the rest of the visitors. She looked around nervously, as if the guards might still take her away.

Garfield stopped at the currency-exchange store and traded two hundred of the thousand dollars expense money for rubles. He was so anxious, he nearly filled out ''Eric Garfield'' on the forms. He caught himself as he reached the ''a'' and was able to smoothly finish the form under the scrutiny of the hovering clerk. He understood now why Bert had chosen a name similar to his own.

He shared a cab with an American and two Italians. During the forty-five-minute ride the Italian chattered, and he and the American spoke briefly.

At the edge of the city the cabdriver pulled over and got out in front of a statue of two gargantuan soldiers. ''The Germans were stopped here,'' the cabbie said in broken English. He gestured grandly, as if he personally was responsible for the rebuff, though he would've been no more than five at the end of World War II. The American took a picture, which pleased the driver.

The city was a disquieting jumble of architectural styles. There were impressive buildings dating back to the 1800s, battered by the fierce weather but still standing proud; structures from the Stalin era, trying to look grand but looking more gaudy; boxlike modern buildings, almost intentionally ugly; and construction everywhere. The colors were muted—muddy reds, dirty yellows, washed-out oranges. There were occasional clusters of hardy evergreens lining the broad boulevards and frequent squares.

Some of the urban scenes—traffic jams and clouds of fumes, crowded sidewalks with scowling pedestrians, tall buildings and a gray sky—reminded Eric of New York.

A closer look, and he instantly knew how far he was from home. Signs were in Cyrillic. The cars were clunky-looking: small Moskviches and Zaporozheches, Fiat-like Zhigulis, official Volgas and ZIL limousines. And it seemed that every fourth person was wearing a military or police uniform.

Garfield didn't know whether it was the Russian or U.S. government that had decided where he was going to stay, but he was assigned to the top-rated National Hotel on Marx Prospekt. There was a narrow door with a portico shaped like a piano lid, a small lobby with a couple of sickly plants in pots, and a few hard chairs that looked uncomfortable.

After Eric received his hotel pass at the front desk, the elevator operator—an old man in an even older brown uniform—took him up to the sixth floor.

Next to the elevator a stocky *dezhurnaya* sat in a wooden chair that matched the ones in the lobby. She wore a gray-and-white polka-dot dress and a sneer. Her job was more that of a police informant than a concierge. While the *dezhurnaya* carefully checked Eric's hotel pass, he appraised the corridor for exits, distances, dead ends. She led him to his room.

Eric entered and locked the door behind him. Safe at last! Or sort of. He felt like giving a triumphant whoop. He threw himself down on the bed, which creaked and groaned in protest.

The room was a shabby three by four meters square. No phone or television. The curtains were stained and frayed, the sheets yellowed, the mattress lumpy. The chair, small desk, and bureau were decrepit. They could've been the originals used by Lenin when he lived there.

When he was done looking over the room, Eric undressed and took an unsatisfying shower under the tepid stream that dribbled from the rusted showerhead.

He opened the window. Red Square was visible, as well as a pinch of the Kremlin and the gaudy turnip domes of St. Basil's, their rainbow colors outstanding in the Moscow pall. To prevent anyone else from having such an edifice, Ivan the Terrible had ordered the architect blinded.

Eric dressed in the clothing Bert had provided. A coat from Poland, pants from Romania, shoes from Czechoslovakia. He'd pass as a Russian, albeit a wealthy one who could afford foreign quality goods.

Before going out he opened a drawer exactly the width of his thumb; he sprinkled talc in the bottom of his suitcase, closed it, and pasted a hair with a drop of saliva to the outside.

Moscow is laid out in a series of concentric circles, with Red Square at the center of the bull's-eye. Eric was just out of the center. The avenues were packed with pedestrians fighting their way to work in the morning rush hour. There were fewer cars than in an American metropolis, but more trucks. Streets were either narrow and overcrowded with traffic or grandiose twelve-lane boulevards that appeared larger than life. Elderly women with kerchief-wrapped hair and long straw brooms swept sidewalks. Eric had been warned that littering was a crime that could lead to arrest. An unwashed car would receive a ticket.

He took a cab, easy to spot with its checkered sides and green "available" lights in the window, and asked to be taken to Goskino. ·

"You lucky, I speak English good," the driver said, turning around and flashing stainless-steel teeth. "I give you good ride. You have blue jeans?"

"What?"

"Blue jeans. I make you good deal on them. Maybe T-shirt? Rock-and-roll singers. I give you goodest price in all of Moscow. Guaranteed." As he gave his pitch, he guided the car through Moscow traffic.

"Sorry, I just have my own clothes."

"My name is Dimitri. Find me at National, or maybe the Rossiya. I give good prices. Guaranteed. Would you like tour? Only five rubles. Or two American dollars. You want change currency, I give good prices. Guaranteed."

"Another time," Eric said.

On the way there Dimitri offered to sell Eric precious icons, old coins, and a sable hat. He asked what sort of possessions Eric might have that he would part with.

"We partners," Dimitri said. "We split profits fifty-fifty. Guaranteed."

"You know, you'd make quite a capitalist," Garfield said with a grin.

"Too much competition," Dimitri said, flashing his metal teeth again. "The black market here is busy as capitalist stock market."

A black Volga limousine with MOC license plates zoomed by in the restricted traffic lane next to them.

"Who was that?"

"The *Chaika* lane is for big cheese. MOC license plate means member of Central Committee," Dimitri said. "Special cars, special traffic lanes, special homes. We equal, only some more than other."

They reached the Goskino building—a four-story, Italian-ate structure dating back to the turn of the century. Dimitri made a last-ditch attempt to make a deal, but accepted his failure graciously and pumped Eric's hand.

The Goskino officials were not as pleasant. They bounced Eric from office to office, from bureaucrat to bureaucrat. He had to fill out a half dozen lengthy forms and sit for an hour in a waiting room under the squinty eye of a surly secretary.

Finally he got to see a fidgety mid-level functionary.

As a radiator hissed and a translator converted Eric's words to Russian, the bureaucrat stroked his chin, pursed his lips, nibbled a pencil, and massaged his neck. Then he repeated the procedure in a slightly different order.

Bert had told him not to reveal his Russian, explaining, "If they interrogate you, you get extra time while they're translating."

Garfield praised Eisenstein, saying, "His bold imagery, stylized compositions, and powerful editing rhythms in masterpieces like *The Battleship Potemkin* mark him as not just a great Soviet director, but an artist of world stature."

In listening to the translation, Eric discovered his words being twisted.

"He says Eisenstein was a very good director for a Russian," the translator said.

"I would like to share his lesser-known works with the American people," Garfield said.

"He wants to exploit the works of Eisenstein for his own capitalistic gain" was the translator's interpretation. The opinionated translator smiled blandly. Garfield smiled back, feigning ignorance.

The functionary was not encouraging—hardly surprising considering the way Garfield's words were distorted. Finally, Eric got the answer he wanted. He had to come back in a few days to see the Deputy Minister. Eric's cover story for staying in Moscow was now confirmed.

He found the nearest Metro stop, signaled by a large illuminated "M," and rode the escalator seven stories down to the platform. There were vaulted arches, gleaming tiles, paintings on the walls, and spotless floors. For the first time in the city, he gawked. As a New Yorker he had always assumed subways meant garbage, graffiti, and urine puddles.

The two-tone blue-and-green train roared into the station and the passengers shoved on. He eavesdropped on neighbors' conversations. Men talked about women and sports. Women talked about men and running a household. Many passengers stared glumly off into space, dozed, or read the newspapers. The mood didn't seem very different from the Lexington Avenue express on a Monday afternoon.

Eric got off near the Kremlin. He noticed two men in belted black trenchcoats and hats about twenty meters back.

He strolled cobblestoned Red Square. Towering over him were the red-brick, battlemented walls of the Kremlin, a fortification a mile and a half in circumference encircling museums, old cathedrals, and the offices of the Supreme Soviet and Palace of Congresses. It had been the seat of Russian government since a prince built a wooden fort on the site in the twelfth century. When Columbus was just a boy, Red Square was already a bustling marketplace.

He gazed at St. Basil's, whose turnip domes symbolized Moscow the way the skyscraper skyline meant New York. In front of the cathedral was the *Lobnoye Mesto,* an elevated stone platform dating back to 1534. Imperial decrees were once posted there. Later it was used as a scaffold for executions.

As he approached the sixty-five-foot-high, twenty-foot-thick Kremlin walls, he passed the black-and-red stone mausoleum where Lenin's body lay. Two white-gloved soldiers, as serious as the guards at Buckingham Palace, stood at attention outside the squat, modern building. The tomb was known as Security Post Number One, and when the guards moved, they goose-stepped with precision, proud of the great honor of being assigned there. Each held a bayoneted rifle by the butt, an awkward display requiring more balance than soldierly abilities. The inevitable long line of Russians was queued up to see the revered corpse.

Eric turned frequently, pretending to admire the buildings. The men in black coats were still behind him, about the same distance. He slowed. They slowed. He sped up, they sped up. It made him nervous, but not panicky. He'd been warned that tourists, especially Americans, not part of a tour group were subject to routine surveillance.

He reached the massive Czar's Cannon. Tourists were clustered about the forty-ton artillery piece, which was cast in bronze in 1586. Eric paused to take a picture for a Japanese family. While they were arranging themselves, he checked his tail. Still there, a little closer. He could see their faces. Both had neatly trimmed mustaches and indifferent expressions. If they were always assigned to foreigners, they must be sick of Soviet culture spots, Eric mused.

He took the picture and moved on. He wanted to make sure they were bored, convince them he was just another tourist. He went from museum to museum, admiring old ivory thrones; delicate clocks made by gold- and silversmiths; chain mail and helmets; maces and sabers; vestments of silk, velvet, and brocade, encrusted with jewels.

The descendants of peasants and serfs eyeballed the splendid trappings that their grandparents could only have dreamed of seeing close up. Even though it was an off hour, the Kremlin halls were as crowded as the Museum of Natural History on a Saturday afternoon. Adults cooed as loudly as the children as they studied the antique finery. The KGB tails were conspicuous by the way they made the most casual pretense of looking at the showcases.

Bert had told him to just be a normal tourist. Until the

rendezvous time, his only responsibility was not calling undue attention to himself.

"It's a piece-of-cake assignment," Bert had claimed. "Once you hook up with Petrov, just follow his lead." Eric kept wondering how Petrov would get them to the Leningrad CIA contact. Did he have forged papers? Could he travel freely? How could he escape surveillance? Why did he need Eric?

Garfield spent the rest of the day sightseeing, scurrying from museum to museum like a frenzied tourist. He took in presentations of Russian history (Battle of Borodino Panorama Museum), literature (Mayakovsky Library and Museum), art (Ostankino Serf Art Museum), and science (Moscow State University Museum).

He kept as busy as he could. If he slowed down, his doubts would catch up with him.

FIFTEEN

THERE WAS A NEW STERN CONCIERGE BY THE ELEVATOR IN Eric's hotel who gave him his room key and a penetrating glance. He shut the door to his room and put on the radio. The Voice of Moscow was playing a concerto by Rachmaninoff.

Eric checked to see if anyone had been snooping. The telltales had been disturbed. The hair was gone from his suitcase, and the partially opened drawer was shut. But the powder on the hidden compartment was undisturbed.

While at the Kremlin, several times he'd felt swept away by the grandeur of Russian history. Back in his depressing hotel room, however, he dwelled on the oppression.

In a few hours he had an appointment at the Bolshoi. He tried to rest, but couldn't. He tuned the radio until he got martial music, and exercised to force the tension from his muscles. He took another tepid shower and dressed in a dark suit.

He double-checked that the door was locked and turned up the radio. The announcer was boasting that the Kazan collectives were exceeding their five-year goals. The announcer's strong, masculine voice masked the sound of Eric's popping open the hidden compartment. Bert had warned that hotel rooms were bugged.

He removed his forged documents and disguise kit and put them in special pockets in his trenchcoat. The kit, a little smaller than a paperback book, contained a packet of dehydrated dye and a fake blond mustache and matching wig. The "hair" looked remarkably natural, considering it was made of compressible plastic.

He slipped on his trenchcoat and looked at himself in the mirror. It seemed to him that the contraband bulged like grotesque tumors. He patted the coat and shifted. Maybe it wasn't so bad.

He sat at the desk and wrote on a postcard:

> *Dear Joe,*
> *I met a cute Russian chick, and she's invited me back to her place. I'm doing my best to establish good international relations. She's a student at Moscow U, a real fox. I've got a shot at spending a night with her. I'll let you know how my foreign affair works out.*
>
> *Best,*
> *Eric the Stud*

He left the card on the desk. He hoped that would make the KGB hold off on putting out an alert for him, at least for a day, when he didn't return to the hotel room. If he was lucky, they might even wait until he missed his appointment at Goskino before going nuts.

It was time for "dry-cleaning"—getting rid of his watchers. He strolled to GUM, the State Universal Department Store, housed in a beautiful, glass-roofed building from the nineteenth century. There were wrought-iron railings, gushing fountains, and ornate archways leading to the separate shops. Catwalks on the second and third floors stretched across the open center court. GUM's exterior gave it the mood of a New Orleans bazaar, a touch of exotic elegance.

The walls inside, however, were a sickly green; the floors were worn. In the shops Eric found limited-quantity, shoddy-quality Soviet goods. The aisles were barely navigable, crowded with stocky, aggressive shoppers. They had the desperate air of last-minute bargain hunters at a pre-Christmas sale. They searched for better-quality foreign goods. To call a product "domestic" in the Soviet Union was an insult.

He bought a cap and tucked it into his pocket. His watchers stood twenty meters away. Eric sauntered, covertly studying the interior. Bert and he had reviewed a blueprint of the place, but Garfield had been warned to check it out for himself. Stores were often *zakrito na ushchot*, which literally meant closed for inventory but could mean the workers were out drinking, or the store was out of stock, or a bigwig was shopping and wanted privacy. A shop closed, a passageway barred, a minor change in route, and Garfield's plan could be ruined.

But the shops were open; the long courtyard appeared exactly as Bert had shown him on the blueprint. Eric joined a line at the busiest store, Section 330, which sold housewares and hardware. Several dozen people were waiting to talk to the saleslady.

"How's your shopping?" Eric asked the man in front of him in Russian.

"Better than usual. Once I'm done here, I go home."

"You're not going to get shoes?"

"Shoes?"

"At Section Two Fifty. I heard they got a shipment in from Czechoslovakia," Eric said in a stage whisper. "They want to keep it quiet, but they're putting them out in five minutes."

Eric said it loud enough for the man, and three people in front of him, to hear. They all bolted toward Section 250. Eric joined them.

Passersby shouted the rallying cry *"Chto oni dayuti?"* which translates to "What are they giving out?" Along the way they picked up forty more people. Other shoppers saw the movement and guessed that someone had inside information on a hot shipment, and their group snowballed. By the time they reached the store, more than a hundred people were eagerly expecting a hard-to-get item.

There were already many shoppers at Section 250, and when they saw the action by the shoe counter, they swarmed it and yelled at the sales clerks.

Eric maneuvered until his back was against the wall, then reversed his beige trenchcoat, baring the blue side. He put on glasses and his new cap. He edged out a side door as the two KGB watchers at the main entrance searched for him.

Eric moved briskly to Gorky Park. Following Bert's instructions, he stifled the urge to look over his shoulder, and didn't check to see if he was being tailed until he reached the park.

A Ferris wheel and carnival attractions with Socialist themes were crowded with patrons. The blue-gray rowboats on the lake blended with the color of the water as the sun began to set. Ducks and geese quacked and honked as they retired to their nighttime shelters. Men sat hunched over chessboards at long tables, oblivious to the dying sun. The lawns, shrubbery, and trees offered a dozen different shades of green. Bunches of flowers lay at the foot of the statue to Maksim Gorky.

Everywhere in the park couples were flirting. The perpetual housing shortage forced young lovers to search for romantic spots outdoors. Despite the scolding of the *babushkas*, the elderly women who could be as stern as KGB agents in enforcing morals, love blossomed on benches, under trees, and on blankets.

He sat on a bench next to a grizzled man feeding bread crumbs to pigeons. The man gave Garfield a slice of stale black bread. Eric thanked him, tore off chunks, and tossed them to the birds. There were no signs of a KGB surveillance team.

"I was in Leningrad during the Great Patriotic War," the grizzled man said as if apologizing. "I caught pigeons and fed my family. Today there is enough that I can feed the pigeons. We live in wonderous times."

Eric nodded along. The man still seemed to be embarrassed at wasting bread on the birds. He smiled awkwardly at Eric and walked away. When the birds saw there was no more bread forthcoming, they left too.

The shadows lengthened, the sky turned purple, and the stars became visible. Memories of the night at Bethesda Fountain flashed through Garfield's mind. At one point he thought he was being watched by a sinister man with a furtive manner. Gorky Park was a center of illegal transactions. Everything from T-shirts and jazz records to Turkish marijuana and icons could be bought.

Eric went into the public bathroom and pasted on the false mustache. Back outside he wandered around, took a rowboat out on the lake, and strolled the park. Finally, he decided he was safe and headed over to Sverdlov Square— the home of the Bolshoi Ballet.

GRU Colonel Anatoli Petrov dropped the garbage bag into the metal trash can next to his house. Having a genuine galvanized can was a sign of his importance. For four hours he had been cleaning like an Army recruit anticipating his first inspection.

His dacha was fifty kilometers outside Moscow, a weekend retreat in Toyma given by the state as a reward. The modest two-story wood-frame home was well kept but undistinguished. The big advantage was its privacy. Located on a two-acre lot, its high hedges and dense clumps of trees made it seem even more isolated.

The various dacha communities were occupational enclaves. Zhukovka was for government officials and their families. Svetlana Stalin returned there after her brief stint in the West. Nikolina Gora was for favored journalists; Zavidovo for academics, Peredelkino for writers, and Toyma for military men. The house nearest Petrov's, one hundred yards away, belonged to an Army general—Grigori Grigorevich Vasilev.

"Yo, Petrov, are you expecting a woman?" the general bellowed from his side of the wooden fence that separated their property. Vasilev had a froggy' voice, and his guttural Russian made every word sound like a command.

Petrov closed the can. "No. Just doing a few chores."

"I've been watching you. A GRU colonel cleaning up like a maid. Don't you have any aides?"

"I felt like doing it myself."

The edge in Petrov's tone caught Vasilev by surprise. Usually Vasilev would brook no such disrespect from a colonel. But Petrov was a special case.

"I wondered if you had time for . . ." The general made a dueling motion with his hand. "I owe you from last time."

"I'm expecting company. I want everthing perfect."

"Is she worth this trouble?" General Vasilev's head seemed too large for his body, and his features too large for his face. His lecherous wink was an overwhelming gesture.

"It's a he. My nephew. I haven't seen him for years."

"You're better off. Three of my children are out of the house, luckily. Two of them work on the pipeline in Siberia. Even better. But the one I have at home makes up for the others. She's more trouble than NATO."

Petrov had seen the general's daughter, Katya. She was a pretty girl in her early twenties who wore flashy Western clothes and makeup.

"What do you say?" Vasilev asked. "Will you give me a chance to regain my honor? Your nephew won't care if he can't bounce a coin off the sheets."

Petrov hesitated and looked at his watch. Eric was not due for a few hours. A match with Vasilev was just the tonic he needed.

"Okay. Five touches?"

"Weapon of your choice."

"Saber," Petrov said, knowing that it was Vasilev's favorite. He wanted a challenge to overcome.

Foil demanded the most delicacy, with hits restricted to the upper torso and strict rules of attack and riposte. The epee was the same length as the foil—a half inch shy of three feet—but with a heavier blade that stung on impact. Any part of the body was a fair target.

The shorter, heavier saber was similar to the old slashing cavalry sword. The point and the cutting edges could be used to score. It led to fiercer bouts; flashing, slashing blades; and attacks that looked like a madman's rage.

In Vasilev's pine-paneled basement, Petrov selected a saber from the rack and put on one of Vasilev's spare canvas fencing jackets. As he cinched the straps across his body, Petrov felt at ease. The familiar ritual. He was moving into a realm where few were his equal. The crusty Hungarian who had first taught him had called it "chess at ninety miles an hour." There was no time for brooding.

Vasilev donned his mask, and his coarse features were gone. His face became an impassive wire mesh.

Petrov pulled the leather gauntlet onto his hand and the mask over his face.

The general swished the air with his weapon. "Prepare to be beaten."

Petrov gave a slight bow.

The general had a fencing platform in the middle of his basement—smooth wooden boards a foot off the floor. They lifted their swords to their faces, blades straight up, and then slashed them down.

"En garde," Vasilev said. His left hand was on his hip; his right held the sword in tierce, handle at waist level, tip of the blade pointed at Petrov's eyes.

The general attacked fiercely, forcing Petrov to retreat. Vasilev tried a cheek cut and then a head cut. The tip of his blade flashed, inches from Petrov's face.

Petrov lunged on a riposte; Vasilev parried and then struck the GRU colonel's ribs with a solid flank cut. The blow would raise a bruise. Vasilev was prone to giving too much steel, landing hard blows that intimidated an opponent but left the general overcommitted to a move.

"Ha, I told you I would give you a thrashing," Vasilev said.

Petrov knew what the problem was. He had not been able to push Eric Garfield from his thoughts. Petrov tapped twice with his right foot, signaling he wanted a break. He peeled off his mask and Vasilev did the same.

"Do you wish to hoist the white flag?" Vasilev asked.

"Not quite yet. I had forgotten how skilled you are," Petrov said.

"Hmmmph. You'll try to get me off guard with flattery and then close in for the kill. I need competition. I'm getting to be a fat desk sitter," Vasilev said, shaking the sizable roll of flesh at his middle. "Does your nephew fence?"

"Ah, no."

"What a pity. Does he have proper attitudes?"

"It's been a while, but I've heard only good things. Why?"

"We can introduce him to Katya. They can talk about whatever young people talk about while we cross swords. I want to make sure he isn't a hooligan. She has enough of that kind of friends."

Petrov put the mask back on. Vasilev had given him an idea. "I'm ready," Petrov said. *"En garde."*

A half hour later they set down their blades. Vasilev was grumbling. Petrov had beaten him four to one.

SIXTEEN

ATOP THE SPOTLIT PEDIMENT A STONE CHARIOTEER STRUGGLED to control four rearing horses. A hundred or so people lingered on the steps below, socializing, being seen. They were dressed casually, sport jackets on the men and plain dresses on the women. The Russians had no reservations about mixing plaids with houndstooths, tweeds with stripes. They had strong faces, heavy jowled. They were the ones with *klass* and connections, who could get the coveted seats.

Eric approached the door slowly, scanning the crowd, dreading the flash of recognition that meant he had been spotted. What if the ticket was marked? What if a trap was about to spring shut? When the ticket taker did nothing but rip his ticket in half, Eric gave him a breathy *"Spassibo."*

In the grand lobby, with sweeping staircase and detailed reliefs on the wall, there were loud greetings, hugs, men kissing men unashamedly. The marble wainscotting and parquet floors gleamed.

Garfield was handed a program by a blue-uniformed usher and directed to his red-velvet seat, twenty rows back from the stage. The theater was about half filled. There were crimson curtains over white walls, six tiers of gold-trimmed boxes separated from each other by graceful, glittering chandeliers. The lush carpet was scarlet. Everywhere was red, *krasnaya*, the Russians' favorite color.

The hum of voices from the audience was muted by the size of the theater and the well-designed acoustics. Every now and then the sound of an instrument being tuned escaped from the mammoth orchestra pit. Just to the left of the stage was the special box for the First Secretary and ranking party officials. If they didn't attend the performance, the box was kept empty, though the show was always sold out.

Eric nervously patted his mustache. It simultaneously felt too tight-itchy and too loose, as if it might fall off. Could the KGB pavement artists have picked up his scent? Perhaps Petrov had been caught and was telling the KGB about him?

The seats around him began filling up. Would his contact arrive and whisper the password? What would happen then?

Eric stood to allow a pair of heavy-set ladies to pass. They sat on his left and chatted. Could they be messengers for Petrov? Or KGB plants? The seat to his right, between him and the aisle, was still empty.

The lady next to him tapped his shoulder. "It's commendable you like the opera," she said. He hoped she hadn't noticed the way he flinched when she startled him.

"*Da.*"

"Your generation listens to that roll-and-rock junk from America. Noise."

"I like classical music," Eric answered in Russian. He smiled nervously. Was this the prelude to the password?

"What is your favorite?" the lady asked. She leaned in close. She had eaten an onion recently.

Eric thought for a moment and chose a work that was rarely presented outside the Soviet Union. "*Sadko.*"

"By Rimsky-Korsakov," the woman said, clearly pleased. She indicated the empty seat next to Eric. "Waiting for your girlfriend?"

"No. A friend. A man," Eric said. He realized he had made a mistake. What if Petrov didn't come in person? What if a woman was his contact? He had broken one of Bert's rules: "Volunteer nothing."

"I don't recognize your accent," the woman said. "You aren't from Moscow?"

In New York he would've been able to fend her off. By American standards she was being too pushy. By Russian standards she was showing a normal interest in a comrade.

"I've been away. In Vladivostok," Eric said, choosing the farthest community he could think of.

"My daughter, she's your age. I know she would like to go to the opera. Do you get tickets often?"

"Unfortunately, I'm married, or I would take her."

The woman grunted and turned back to her friend. Her matchmaking attempt had failed.

But where was his contact? Virtually all the seats were taken, except for the one next to him. It was seven minutes to show time. Twice he had false starts as suspicious-looking individuals walked down the aisle, seemingly headed right toward him.

Then abruptly a man sat in the seat. He had coarse, Arabic features, was well-dressed, and had an easy, insincere smile on his lips.

"I like the ballet more than the beach," the man said after settling his plump frame into the plush seat.

Eric's body throbbed with every beat of his heart. He spoke the response to the recognition code. "Especially at this time of year."

The man leaned over and whispered in British-accented English. "My name is Yuri. The colonel sent me."

"What do you mean, the colonel? Is he in the Army?"

"The GRU."

Eric understood why the CIA was so interested.

"You're very pale," Yuri said. "Go to the bathroom and throw cold water on your face."

"I'm okay."

"Go," Yuri ordered. "I want to see if anyone follows you."

Garfield walked to the washroom, threw water on his face, and returned. Yuri was more relaxed. "It appears to be fine," Yuri said, and the lights dimmed.

Ivan Susanin, a patriotic opera by Glinka, began on a restrained note, but by the end of the fifth and final act, the stage was packed with the giant cast and props, and the hall echoed with the chorus of "Glory to you, Russia!" Elaborately costumed men and women sang from the stage as if their life depended on it. In a way, it did. They were at the pinnacle of Soviet *kultura* and a fall from grace could mean losing apartment, dacha, car, and privileges.

The opera told the story of the Polish invasion of Russia in 1612, and how a heroic Russian led Poles into the woods, where he and the Polish troops froze to death.

The women next to Eric were crying, as were dozens of other men and women in the audience. Even Yuri appeared moved. Eric was too scared to appreciate the drama.

After several tumultuous ovations, the curtain came down for a final time. The crowd started to edge from the theater.

"Follow me and don't say anything," Yuri said.

While everyone shoved to the rear, Yuri led Eric toward the front. As they neared the stage, an usher blocked their path. "The exit is the other way, comrades," he said.

Yuri flashed identification. "KGB. Where is the nearest exit?"

The usher, a young man in a blue-and-gold uniform, snapped to attention. "Right this way, comrade."

He pushed open a door, and they entered a backstage

corridor, cluttered with the ropes, props, and trunks found behind the facades of all theaters.

"The Sword and the Shield is my favorite program on television. It's a chance to learn of the glorious work of the organs of State Security. It's the best show," the usher gushed as he led them briskly down the hall. "I want to join the KGB, but my school grades were poor."

"Study hard, learn languages," Yuri said tersely. "And keep your meeting us a secret."

The usher made as if buttoning his lips. Then they were at a door and he held it open. The cold night air rushed in.

"You have served the *rodina*," Yuri said, patting the usher on the shoulder with one hand and propelling Eric out the door with the other. "Remember, tell no one."

Yuri hurried Eric down the street.

"In here," he said, pointing to a parked black Zhiguli. The late-model car was the size and shape of a Fiat.

Eric got in and, following Yuri's directions, crouched low. He felt squeamish, breathing stale air, his body uncomfortably twisted. Yuri slammed on the gas, and the car surged into traffic. Eric raised his head.

"Sit up. Take off that silly mustache," Karabian said. "The colonel will want to see how you look."

Eric removed it and rubbed the adhesive from his upper lip. "Why does he care how I look? Why did he insist on *me?*"

Yuri didn't answer.

"Tell me about the colonel. What does he do? What is your relationship with him?"

Yuri didn't answer.

"Can you tell me where we're going at least?"

"Out of Moscow."

"Where?"

Yuri didn't answer again.

Frustrated, Eric slumped into his seat and stared out the window. As far as he could judge, they were zigging and zagging, the same kind of maneuvers Bert had taken him on.

An hour later, Yuri said, "About a half hour more and you will meet the colonel."

Soon there were more trees than houses. Many of the homes were set back from the road. Those that Eric could see looked like the kind found in any metropolitan suburb: one or two story, many ranch style, a garage at the side, a car in the driveway.

They turned off the avenue onto a smaller street near a *Beryozka*, the well-stocked store that sold foreign goods. A four-meter-high barbed-wire fence ran parallel to the road. They passed a guardhouse, and behind it Eric saw a small military base whose quarrel of antennae reached high above the flat landscape. They turned again, down a country lane. They were surrounded by a birch forest. After a few hundred meters, they pulled onto a gravel road. The stones crunched under their wheels.

For one grisly moment Eric thought Yuri was taking him to be executed—shot dead and left in the woods. It didn't make sense, but then again, neither did being in Russia in the first place.

Two houses came into view and the road forked. Yuri took the right fork. They drove up the driveway to a two-story house with rough wooden siding. It had a sharply peaked roof and freshly painted trim and shutters. The yard was well landscaped with flowers just beginning to blossom.

Yuri got out of the car and removed a suitcase from the trunk. "This is for you," he said.

"What?"

"Clothing."

"You know my size?"

Yuri looked at him as if he was an idiot and handed over the suitcase. Eric stood in front of the house. There was no name or number. A yellow light next to the oak-paneled door lit the open porch.

Eric followed the blue-slate slabs that led to the front door as Yuri got back into the car.

"You're not coming in?" Eric called to Yuri.

"You will want time alone together, I'm sure," he answered, somewhat hostilely.

"What . . ." Eric's words were drowned out as Karabian pulled away.

Eric heard crickets chirp and the sound of the departing Zhiguli. At the nearby house, which he could barely make out through the trees, he thought he saw a curtain move, a figure at the window, watching.

A nation of snoops and snitches, he thought. He stepped up to the door and knocked. A tall, lean man opened it. The light was behind him. Eric couldn't make out his features.

"Colonel Petrov?"

"Come in, come in," the colonel said. His face remained in shadow.

The house was nicely furnished. Not lavish, but the furniture appeared to be good-quality antiques, gleaming with polish.

"I've prepared a bedroom upstairs for you," Petrov said. His voice had a quiver to it.

"All I want to know is when you'll be ready to leave."

They'd moved farther into the house. They were in the dining room, which was lit by a chandelier suspended over the teak table.

Eric could see the man's face now. It radiated wide-eyed love. First he thought the colonel was gay, but then realized there was no lust in his expression.

Eric met the Russian's eyes. There was something familiar about them. He had a sense of *déjà vu*. Where had he seen those eyes?

149

"You haven't realized yet, have you?" the colonel said, struggling to control his voice.

"Have we met?"

Petrov laughed, a strange, nearly hysterical sound. Eric was worried—alone with a madman in a deserted woods in the Soviet Union.

"You don't know?" he asked again.

"Know what?"

"You have your mother's nose. The shape of your face too. But your eyes . . ."

Eric gasped and felt dizzy. He knew where he had seen the colonel's peculiar hazel-flecked-with-yellow eyes before. In the mirror.

"My son!" Petrov said, and he threw his arms around the young man.

SEVENTEEN

THE COLONEL SMILED AND GESTURED TO A SEAT IN THE LIVING room. He poured them glasses of Armenian brandy.

Eric was shocked by the unexpected bombshell, and angry over the way Petrov, and the CIA, had knocked the legs out from under him. Even the fear that had been with him since he had boarded the Aeroflot flight was overwhelmed.

"I don't believe it," Eric said.

"I can understand your feelings," Petrov said. "I ask you to try and understand mine. Please, sit."

Eric sat in a comfortable wing chair, Petrov on the neighboring sofa. The colonel took a sip of the brandy and spoke:

"I was stationed in New York at the Soviet mission. My title is of no importance. Your parents owned a coffee shop on the east side of Manhattan. Not a very large place, but Anna was an excellent cook, Raymond a good host and businessman. Many people went there, including agents from the FBI office, which was then on Sixty-ninth Street, and executives from several of the largest capitalist corporations. I was assigned to become a familiar face at the restaurant and see what I could find out.

"I struck up a friendship with the couple. It was not hard. Raymond had lived in Warsaw. I had access to the file on him. I knew his likes, his dislikes. He was a man of refined taste in music, art. I ingratiated myself. I didn't realize they had their eyes on me as much as I had mine on them."

Eric had never had any inkling that Raymond was not his natural father. Could he have been wrong about such a fundamental part of his life?

"Don't make conclusions until I'm done," Petrov said, reading the turmoil in his son's face. "You must hear me out."

Grudgingly, Eric nodded.

"They knew who I was, though not that I was GRU. I was relatively honest with them. It makes for an easier cover story. They were intrigued by my schooling and my participating in the Olympics. They drew out details of my role in the war against Germany. Somehow, it came to pass that I began to spend more and more time with your mother. Raymond was always busy at the restaurant, and he seemed grateful if I would take her to a movie or horseback riding, give her a break from the routine.

"She drew out even more of my past, my family history. At one point I thought they were FBI, trying to turn me," he said, chuckling. "Your mother had captured my heart. She was an incredible woman. She was tender, gentle, and yet underneath as strong as any man. Stronger. Here I was, a trained intelligence officer, and she had me wrapped around her finger. I suppose you know about her only as a son knows his mother. You can't see her for the incredible woman she was. I wasn't the only one to see it.

"I remember once we were walking hand in hand in a lower-Manhattan neighborhood where we weren't known. There was a dog that had been hit by a car. He was in great pain, snarling at anyone who came near. A policeman was going to shoot it. Your mother stopped him. She spoke softly to the dog. It was a big mutt, with yellow teeth like a shark's. But she kept going closer and closer. His snarls turned to growls, and then purrs.

"She had me carry that dog to a veterinarian, then convinced the vet to treat the dog for nothing. She kept the dog for a week, but he was too big for their small apartment. She insisted on getting him a home. The people who came for the dog had to pass a questioning worse than the KGB gives a dissident. She could be tough."

Eric vaguely remembered hearing something like it, though of course Petrov had not been mentioned. What could have made a life-loving American fall for a Russian spy?

"I could tell you many stories about her," Petrov continued. "However, you're not here to listen to me ramble. Suffice it to say she was an exceptional person."

Eric nodded.

Petrov took a few sips of brandy. "One afternoon she suggested we go to a hotel and make love."

"You're saying it was her fault, not yours?" Eric asked accusingly.

"It was no one's fault," the colonel said. His eyes had softened, as if he was seeing back into the years. "It happened again, and then again. For six months. Then she confessed to me."

The colonel paused, milking the moment like an actor.

"They wanted a child, but Raymond was sterile. They had decided to select someone with good genes, and she would bear a child by that person. She was thirty-nine when she conceived. She had not counted on falling in love. Though she still loved your father.

"She was pregnant and should have ended our relationship. She could not. In the months that followed, I saw her grow heavy with you. I worried that she would have a miscarriage or even take her own life. She loved passionately, and loving two men was tearing her apart."

"What about my father? What was happening to him during all of this?"

"You mean Raymond?" Petrov said. "He was very understanding. A remarkable man. I stopped going to the restaurant, but would see her whenever she could get away. When you were born, I visited the hospital as much as he did. I saw how Raymond treated you, truly like his own son.

"Your mother and I tried many times to break it off. We kept coming back to each other. A year and a half after we met, I could take it no longer. I requested an emergency transfer to Moscow Centre. There were questions, but I was able to get around them. I left without saying good-bye."

The colonel's voice had a strained quality again.

"I kept track of you over the years—one of the advantages of being with an intelligence agency," Petrov said. "I wished I could have come over and been with you so many times. Never more than when I heard Anna died." The memory deflated Petrov. He swirled the brandy around his glass and sighed deeply.

"I don't know what to say," Eric said finally. "It's possible, I guess, but I never had any indication. Why didn't they tell me?"

"What would it have accomplished?"

"It's my right to know."

"You Americans, you like to get things out in the open. To air every private matter. You don't help a wound by rubbing salt in it."

"It's my history. Why couldn't you have written me, after both of them had passed away, and told me the truth?"

"Would you have believed it? Wouldn't you have dismissed it as some sort of sick joke? I want you to understand what your father does for a living. That is why I arranged for you to come to me like this, for the CIA to get you here. I wanted you to see them in action, to see that we are all the same."

"We?"

"*Nash*. The intelligence community."

"You set up that messenger getting shot in Central Park?"

"I could anticipate how the CIA would behave."

"What if they had killed him?"

"He was a KGB contract agent who had murdered many people, some unauthorized. He was no longer an asset. It was an effective way to get rid of him and teach you a lesson in the great game," Petrov said.

"Game? It's a great game?"

"I was merely quoting Rudyard Kipling. Your corporations have a colonial mentality as oppressive as the British Empire did in Kipling's day."

"But nobody does as good a job of oppression as the KGB."

"I see you've been brainwashed. Your agents are no more moral than ours."

"Not brainwashed, educated."

"Do you know how your corporations play with lives in small countries, oppressing the workers, stealing their resources, polluting the air and water, working them to death? Have you ever seen a ten-year-old who's lost his hands because he was sent to work in a factory when he was too young to understand machinery? Or the bodies piled up by death squads, because people dared to speak out? Your CIA is a tool of capitalist interests, an imperialistic mercenary."

"Unlike the KGB, which is doing God's work, right? I suppose people come to you and ask to be sent to Siberia and be given mind-altering drugs in mental hospitals. The Berlin wall was built to keep your happy Communists in. You don't see Americans braving barbed wire and machine guns to get behind the Iron Curtain."

"Hearing yourself talk like that, can you wonder that I didn't just drop you a note and say, 'By the way, your real father works for the Evil Empire'? Let me tell you about Raymond,'' Petrov said abruptly. "Did you know he was a rabbi? And a guerilla fighter?"

"He never went to synagogue in his life."

"Only in his later years."

"I don't believe it."

"He was a rabbi in Warsaw. He tried prayer against the Nazis and saw his congregation swallowed by the camps. One night he saw two Nazi soldiers beating a young boy. He killed them, armed soldiers, with his bare hands.

"The Nazis demanded to know who had done it. They executed five entire blocks of Jews in the ghetto. Men, women, and children. He became a guerilla, leader of a small resistance cell. His group eliminated dozens of Nazis, disrupted supply lines, and provided vital information that was relayed to the Allies. He was instrumental in the Warsaw Ghetto uprising. He used the code name 'Moses.' Do you understand why?"

Eric shook his head.

"You should read the Bible. It is a fascinating document,'' Petrov said. "Moses couldn't get into the Holy Land because he had killed a man while defending a woman. Raymond saw himself as doomed. He was a man of peace, forced into war.

"Eventually he was herded to a concentration camp. The Nazis didn't know of his activities, only that he was a Jew. Hundreds were able to make it through because of him, his strength of will, his cunning at begging and stealing food from the guards.

"He was chosen for what the Nazis called experiments," Petrov said. "I don't know if even your mother knew."

"So how do you know?" Eric asked, his whisper so subdued that Petrov could barely hear it.

"When I thought your parents might be counterintelligence agents, I had them checked out. There was no file on your mother, but a thick one on Raymond, with full statements by survivors of the ghetto and the camps. He was worshiped. He had been approached by the Irgun and the Haganah, offered a leading position in the establishment of Israel.

"He predicted that Palestine would be a site of violence for generations to come. 'I have seen enough blood, enough horror, to last me until I die,' he told Ben-Gurion. He changed his name—he was born with the name Garfinkel—put that part of his life completely behind him, met your mother, and . . ." His voice trailed off.

The most basic assumptions of Eric's existence had been destroyed by the individual who sat facing him. The man who had raised him was not his father, and not the mild-mannered restaurateur he had appeared to be. His actual father was a GRU colonel, who had been used as a stud horse and fallen in love with the mare. His sweet mother had been the femme fatale at the center of an international tryst.

"Why are you defecting now?" Eric asked, trying to move the conversation to more manageable grounds.

"We can sort that out later," Petrov said. "I will answer any questions that I can tomorrow. I'm tired, and I am sure you must be."

Petrov didn't look tired to Eric, but he was already carrying his suitcase upstairs.

EIGHTEEN

SUPERFICIALLY THERE IS LITTLE TO DISTINGUISH CAMP PEARY from an ordinary military base. It has barracks, Quonset huts, weapons ranges, parachute-jump towers, obstacle courses, barbed-wire fences, and squads of military security men. But the lessons taught in "The Farm's" fifteen classrooms and on the training fields, which include such setups as a simulated closed border, are strictly for America's spooks.

The pilot of the Hughes HH5O helicopter transmitted the coded message that would authorize landing at Camp Peary. A false signal and he would be warned off. If he still attempted to land, he would be blasted out of the sky.

CIA director Wellington knew how important it was that the pilot get it exactly right. He didn't like helicopters to begin with, and knowing that surface-to-air missiles linked to radar were tracking them made him even more uncomfortable. Tuttle sat next to him, seemingly enjoying the flight—and Wellington's discomfort. The Director's aversion to helicopter flying had nearly overcome his concern over the unpleasant decision he knew he'd soon be making.

The twin General Electric turbine engines changed their

tone, and the craft slowed from its 175-mile-an-hour speed and began descending. The color returned to Wellington's face as the copter touched down; he gave the pilot a congratulatory tap on the shoulder and hurried into the detention facility.

The jail at The Farm is as secure as the highest-rated federal prison, though it has a capacity for only a few prisoners. It was here that Yuri Nosenko, a Soviet defector suspected of being a double agent, had been kept in a white room for three years while Agency brass tried to decide if his defection was legitimate.

"Doctor Attenborough is expecting us," Clandestine Ops Chief Tuttle said as they moved past the third layer of locked metal doors.

Attenborough was one of their finest psychiatrists. His predictions of the behavior of world leaders, even from thousands of miles away, were uncannily accurate. He specialized in deviant psychology, and had written outstanding profiles of Idi Amin and Muammar Khaddafi. If the papers had been formally published, they would have earned him international attention. But they had been classified top secret, and only a dozen people in the country had read them.

Attenborough had a deceptively disinterested expression on his face. He was wearing a white lab coat with a stethoscope hanging out of a pocket. He did not waste time on greetings.

"Do you wish to see the subject?" Attenborough asked. He never referred to patients by name, or even as patients. They were always subjects.

Wellington nodded. Attenborough waved, and a strapping orderly unlocked the door with a key chained to his wrist.

"We had to put him in a restraining jacket," Attenborough said. "He broke an orderly's arm and made it past the first two levels of security."

The door opened. Slater was sitting in an upholstered chair watching a TV, which was behind a heavy Plexiglas barrier. The room was part prison cell and part ordinary living room. There were no sharp objects and the windows were barred, but the walls were painted a cheery blue and the furnishings were of the sort found in a middle-priced motel.

Slater looked not very different from the way he had when Tuttle had last seen him, except for the white heavy-canvas straitjacket.

"Hello, Bert," Wellington said. "I trust you're being properly taken care of?"

A game show on the television held Slater's attention.

Wellington pointed to the TV, Attenborough waved his hand, and the television was cut off.

Slater faced them. His eyes—glowing like the inside of a blast furnace—locked on Wellington's face.

"You fuckers came by to see if they had broken me," Slater spewed. "Well, they haven't. You won't either."

He stared back at the quiet TV.

"How long has he been like this?" Wellington whispered to Attenborough.

"He disassembled last night."

"Bolshies! Filthy stinking Bolshies!" Slater suddenly screamed. "I won't talk, you stinking Commie bastards! Fuck you and the Kremlin, too."

Wellington walked into the corridor. The TV set clicked on, and Slater calmly resumed watching.

"Go for the refrigerator," he said to the screen, as the orderly gently shut the door behind himself.

The orderly left, and Attenborough and his two guests stood outside Slater's room.

"Sad," Tuttle said.

"I read your report," Wellington said to Attenborough. "Not very optimistic, are you?"

"My conclusions are based on solid clinical evidence.

We gave him MMPI and Thematic Apperception Tests, as well as a battery of our own projective and personality inventory exams. In addition, I called in several consultants and showed them the subject's records, taking the usual precautions to ensure secrecy.'' The doctor fiddled with his stethoscope. "Espionage by its very nature tends to attract unstable people.''

Tuttle snorted.

"It provides an opportunity for respectable citizens to act like criminals, to rationalize they are doing it in their nation's interest.''

"Are you saying it's not?'' Tuttle challenged.

"It can be,'' Attenborough said. "Sometimes it isn't. Individuals overreact, they do things they are ashamed of, and the only way they can accept it is to make the enemy less than human. When an agent is tortured, it sets up even more complex 'why am I being punished?' neuroses and psychoses. Issues are reduced to black and white, and the subject becomes capable of anything. But all the while, the dichotomous thinking is eating away at the subconscious values instilled in most of us as children.''

"Should we dissolve the Company and sign up for therapy?'' Tuttle asked sarcastically.

Attenborough faced the Director. "I've put forth the problem to you in memoranda in the past. Taking young men and women, relatively innocent, from the universities and putting them into a twisted, treacherous world is unfair to all parties concerned. I think our screening methods need to be improved.''

"What about Mr. Slater?'' Wellington asked. "Is it too late?''

"With a few months of intensive treatment, we can make him functional again,'' Attenborough responded. "Any stress and he would relapse. I believe he would be capable of murder if, for example, a shopkeeper closed up before he could get in.''

"He'll have to be terminated," Tuttle said. "With extreme prejudice."

"There's got to be another solution," Wellington said.

"Even after treatment, he could resurface as a dangerous embarrassment," Tuttle said. "We don't need another crazy mercenary claiming he's still with the Company while he trains bandits to slit throats. We can't afford another Wilson-Terpil fiasco."

"Maybe permanent institutionalization?"

"Impractical. With his training, he'll be a permanent escape risk. Besides, is it really more humane locking someone up in a nuthouse for life?"

Attenborough gave Tuttle a sharp glance. Wellington looked troubled.

"We can't risk Slater making a worse mess of Borzoi," Tuttle said. "Believe me, it hurts me. I've known him for years."

"How would it be done?" Wellington asked.

"Quite painlessly," Attenborough said. "His food will be drugged. Then we'll inject an overdose of a sedative. It's like putting a rabid dog to sleep."

On the helicopter flight back, Wellington asked, "What about Borzoi?"

"Damage control is operational. Everything's in place for plausible denial if Garfield is captured. We might as well let it run its course."

Wellington nibbled his lip as they passed over the lush green fields of Virginia.

The next morning Petrov and Eric sat on the front porch and watched the sun burn the dew off the grass.

"Let's discuss how we reach Leningrad," Eric said. "The sooner we get back to America, the better."

"You don't want to see a bit of the Soviet Union? The *rodina* is a great country, one sixth of the world's land area. We have a culture going back to when America wasn't even known in the civilized world."

"I'm more interested in knowing how we get past the border guards. It's going to be tough slipping out of one of the most repressive countries on earth."

"The Soviet Union is not one of the most repressive countries on earth."

"Tell that to the refuseniks in the mental hospitals getting pumped full of drugs."

"You have more people in your prisons than we have in ours," Petrov said. "As for drugs, we do not have children buying drugs in our schoolyards."

"No, you have them drinking vodka. You know there are more alcoholics in the Soviet Union than anywhere else?"

"We are changing that. We do not have a permanent class of poor, which your capitalist economy depends on."

"But you do have a permanent elite. The six percent who are members of the Communist Party."

"In America you have four point four percent controlling seventy percent of the wealth through interlocking directorates. They control half of the real estate and two-thirds of the natural resources."

They argued, throwing countries and incidents back and forth: the Vietnam War; the Stalinist purges; the genocide of the American Indian; the slave labor camps; the Bay of Pigs; Afghanistan; the Shah of Iran; the U-2 incident; the attempted assassination of the Pope.

"You can browbeat me all you want, but you can't change the truth," Eric said. "It's *you* who want to defect. Why is that, anyway, if we're so terrible?"

"That was to get you here under the right circumstances."

"What!" Eric jumped up. "You mean you're not going to?"

"I want you to understand Russia, not fear it the way most Americans do."

"So you trick me into coming over here. That's just great. That really is just great."

"I didn't trick you. I told the CIA. They were the ones who tricked you."

"Let's not split hairs, okay? Whoever did what, you instigated something and I wind up risking my life. For what? Do you realize how much danger you put me in?"

"I can handle it. You're protected."

"What happens if one of the border guards in this great and wonderful country of yours has an itchy trigger finger? A little slip on a Kalashnikov, and I'm your late son. Would that make you happy? For me to die on Soviet soil?"

Petrov leaned forward, his face only a few inches from his son's. "It is not without risk for both of us. I have broken enough rules for me to spend the rest of my life in prison. The country I love would disown me. But I thought it was worth it. Maybe I was wrong."

He jabbed his hand into his pocket. "I will arrange to get you out of the country soon. Before you go, I will tell you something for your CIA masters that will make the trip worthwhile." The colonel was an awesome presence, his rage barely under control.

"I don't want any Russian secrets. I just want to live my own life, be able to make my own choices."

Petrov dug out what he had been rooting for—an antique gold pocketwatch. He handed it to Eric. "This was from my father. I want you to have it." Before Eric could respond, Petrov said, "I am going next door."

Eric opened the lid over the crystal. On one side was a watch face with Roman numerals. On the other was a picture of Petrov and Eric's mother. Their heads were pressed together. It had been taken in a photos-while-you-wait booth, and been trimmed to fit into the watch. Eric stared at the picture and tried to make sense of what he had been through.

As soon as Petrov stepped away, he grinned. He hoped Eric had been impressed by his display of temper.

He walked across the lawn, found the break in the thick hedges, and strode to the front of Vasilev's house. The door was answered by Mrs. Vasilev after two quick knocks. They exchanged greetings. The General's wife was a stout, pleasant woman who lived completely in her husband's shadow.

Petrov found the General in the basement, already wielding a saber. "I've been practicing for you, Petrov. I will show no quarter."

"I would expect no less from you, Grigori Grigorevich."

"My wife said your nephew arrived late last night."

"He did. It's been difficult. He's young," Petrov said, as if it was a disease.

"That's a curse I wish I suffered from." Vasilev set his sword down and stretched. Joints popped and cracked as he moved his bulky frame.

Petrov also stretched, his leaner body less complaining. "I need a distraction. My nephew— Ah, let's begin."

"If you want to exchange stories, I can go on for days. At least you'll be rid of him soon. My Katya, I'd marry her to a Chukchi at this point," Vasilev said. "Probably only a Chukchi would take her. She's twenty-four and more trouble than the Chinese."

Petrov slashed the air with his sword. "When we were young, things were different."

"Stalin. Sometimes I wonder if we'd be better off with someone like him again, a good leader, not like these senile incompetents we have now," Vasilev said.

"You're a brave man to talk that way in front of an intelligence officer," Petrov said.

For a moment Vasilev tensed, but he saw Petrov had a mocking smile on his face.

"Since we are not under Stalin you don't have to worry about *etap*. Though I hear they have made big improvements in Siberia."

"You tease me, Petrov," Vasilev said, lifting his saber

and tapping the colonel's shoulder with the covered point. "I don't like that."

Petrov stepped onto the runway and pulled his mask on. He lifted his saber into the salute position as Vasilev faced him and put his own mask on.

"*En garde*, Petrov," Vasilev said with a growl.

Eric wondered if he could simply go back to the National Hotel, pretend none of this had happened. But he had slipped the surveillance team. There would be questions. His false identity might not be able to hold up. He might not be able to hold up. He'd better stick with the Leningrad escape route the Agency had provided. Don't improvise unless you have to. Had that been Number Six of Bert's rules? Headquarters has the big picture, obstacles the agent in the field can't see. He had to have confidence in himself, in the lessons Bert had taught him.

Eric went to the room he had slept in and dug the forged Eric Garber and Canadian papers out of the hidden pocket in his coat. He found a metal ruler and used it to unscrew a wall switch. He tucked the forged documents into the space. If the house was searched, the only papers lying around showed his face with the name Konstantin Petrov.

He was surprised at his own feelings—he wanted to make up with Petrov. How could he hate a man who had risked his life and career for their reunion?

The woman who opened the door at the neighbors' house gave him a welcoming smile. "You must be Konstantin."

"Yes. Pleased to meet you," Eric said in Russian. "Is Colonel Petrov here?"

"Your uncle's downstairs," she said.

From the basement Eric heard the sound of steel on steel.

NINETEEN

KATYA VASILEV DIDN'T HEAR HER MOTHER COME INTO THE room. Linda Ronstadt was singing too loud through the earphones clamped to her head. Katya's back was to the door, and she didn't realize that Mrs. Vasilev was watching as she swayed to "Love Is a Rose." Katya felt the heavy tap on her shoulder and eased off the headphones.

She had short-cut dark-blond hair, laughing blue eyes, and an upturned nose. Although she was attractive, she remained self-conscious about the buck teeth that protruded slightly and nestled on her full lips.

"Yes?" she asked her mother.

Mrs. Vasilev looked around the room disapprovingly. The walls were covered with posters of rock groups from the West.

"I want you to bring lemonade to your father and his guests," the general's wife said.

Why would her mother come up a flight of stairs to get her to go down two flights of stairs on a simple errand? Katya wondered. It had to be the guests. Probably an eligible male. Some up-and-coming soldier whom they would try to pair her off with. He would be more interested in making a good impression on her father than in getting to know her. Her parents were very concerned about her being an old maid.

"Put on some decent clothing," her mother said, making a disgusted face as she looked at Katya's outfit: a T-shirt with "The Grateful Dead" silk-screened on it and Jordache jeans. She was barefoot, and her toenails were painted red. She had drawn a hammer and sickle on each of her big-toe nails.

Her parents didn't know where she got the clothing, but they suspected her hooligan friends in Moscow. That was why they dragged her out to the dacha as often as possible.

"Wear a bra," her mother ordered before marching out.

Katya peeled off her top. She had a firm, slender body, only a couple of pounds heavier than the one she had swung across uneven parallel bars in tenth grade. She had done well at the Olympic tryouts, but not quite well enough for the team.

That was one place the general couldn't use his *blat* to get what he wanted for his darling Katusha. Her life had been shaped by the general's clout. If she did poorly in school, he showed up at the Administrator's office in full uniform, with medals, and somehow her grades improved, even though she didn't study harder.

She had gotten cynical young and, being the only girl with three older brothers, spoiled. Her brothers had gone on to join the Party and secure responsible jobs. She had dropped out of medical school and never held a job longer than a year.

She was very bright and a hard worker, when she chose to be. She spoke fluent English, because for her, America was a fantasy world. She had a collection of several dozen postcards showing sites like the Statue of Liberty and the Hollywood sign. Touting America's virtues was a great way to infuriate her parents.

She decided not to wear a bra, and put on her favorite T-shirt, the one her parents hated most.

Without her mother noticing, the barefoot Katya picked up the tray for the men. It held a pitcher of lemonade, glasses, and a bowl of *volba,* the Russian snack food of dried, salted fish. She padded downstairs. Her father and Colonel Petrov were too absorbed in their fencing to see her. The guy on the couch, however, quickly shifted his attention to her. He wasn't wearing a uniform. His clothes didn't have a shoddy domestic look. Not quite Western, though. Probably East European. He didn't have that tightass, serious expression most military men had.

He was cute. That was a plus. Her mind tried to find the American word. A hulk. No. A hunk. Yes. With his warm hazel eyes on her, she made a slow entrance. She wished she was wearing more makeup. She smiled mischievously, making sure her teeth didn't show.

In mid-bout, Vasilev spotted her. He retreated and banged his foot twice on the floor, signaling a break. Both men removed their masks.

"Konstantin," Vasilev said to Eric, "this is my daughter, Katya."

She lowered the tray. Vasilev turned as dark as borscht. Petrov pressed his lips together. Eric burst out laughing. Her T-shirt bore a silk-screened composite face that was half Vladimir Lenin and half John Lennon, ringed by the words "Working-class Hero—John Lenin."

She poured glasses of lemonade. The general and Petrov gave her terse thanks. She handed a glass to Eric and sat down on the couch next to him.

Eric had been listening to an impassioned lesson on fencing. Vasilev had insisted—"Here you are, the nephew of one of the Soviet Union's greatest masters"—on showing the fundamentals to Eric. He had watched as the swordsmen executed lunges, parries, ripostes, and cutovers. The men were beginning to demonstrate tactics when Katya walked in, and Eric lost interest in how to feint and redouble.

The colonel and the general stood a few feet away, their backs to the young people, drinking lemonade and discussing each other's fencing style in hushed voices. Eric sipped his drink while Katya boldly eyed him.

"You like my shirt?" she asked, thrusting her chest out a barely perceptible amount.

"Very much," he said in Russian. She had nice breasts, Eric saw, and her nipples made tiny bumps in the cotton.

"My father doesn't. He says it makes fun of Lenin. Do you like the Beatles?"

"Yes. And you?"

"Not as much as the Rolling Stones. Do you know who they are?"

Eric hummed "Satisfaction," and she sang the words in English. She had a fair singing voice, and her pronunciation was good.

Eric joined in the chorus.

"Do you know much English?" she asked.

"I studied it for many years," Eric answered, glad to be able to talk in his native tongue.

"You sound terrific. We can practice it together. Have you seen lake?"

He shook his head. She took his hand and gave a tug. "Let's go."

He got up and looked over to where Petrov and Vasilev had resumed dueling. "Excuse me, we're going to the lake," he said in Russian.

This time it was Petrov who retreated, and stamped twice. Vasilev lowered his sword.

"Be careful, Konstantin," Petrov warned.

"Don't worry, I know how to swim," Eric said, and followed Katya up the stairs.

"Well, they seem to have hit it off," Vasilev said to the colonel.

"Yes. It'll be good for him to get out. He's a very serious young man."

"I hope some of it rubs off on Katya," Vasilev said.

The reflection of the pines surrounding the lake shimmered on the cold, blue waters. A light breeze blew, making a whistling noise and bringing fresh, outdoorsy smells to their nostrils. He felt he could be at any small lake in the Catskills.

After seeing deer, rabbits, and countless birds as they strolled the perimeter, they took the general's rowboat out onto the lake. The spring sun was warm, and Eric removed his jacket, and then his shirt. The rowing motion was similar to his movements on the exercise machine back in the safe house. His powerful strokes moved them smoothly along.

"Did you know John Lennon was killed by worker upset by his bourgeoisie decadence?" she asked, nearly as happy to be speaking English as he was.

"He was killed, but by a crazy. Nothing to do with the workers' struggle. Where did you hear that?"

"From friend. Who heard it from friend. How do *you* know so much about the West?"

"I've studied it quite a bit," Eric said.

"At MIMO?"

"No." MIMO was the acronym for the Institute of Foreign Relations, a common training ground for KGB agents. Eric didn't want to name a school and get sucked into the tricky game of "Do you know so and so?"

"Where did you go to school?"

"Many places."

Katya seemed to lose interest in talking about school. She rolled up her T-shirt to expose her midriff, and rubbed suntan lotion on her flat belly. Without asking, she slowly rubbed lotion across his shoulders.

"I know why you know about the West," she said coyly.

"How?"

"Maybe I won't tell you. Maybe I will be mysterious, like you." She patted his arm on the word "you." She had a tendency to pat or touch him at every excuse.

"C'mon. Tell me, or I'll . . ."

"You will do what?"

"I'll tickle you."

"You will not."

They wrestled in the boat, rocking back and forth and nearly toppling into the water. She kicked and laughed as his hands brushed over her body.

"Is that what they teach in spy school?"

"What do you mean?" he asked, sitting upright.

"I know your secret."

He tried to sound casual. "What do you mean?" His eyes shifted to the shoreline. Had she told anyone? How had she found out?

"It is obvious," she said teasingly, and her hand brushed his face. This time, her touch chilled him. "Don't try to play fool with me. You know about the West. You speak perfect English. You are KGB."

Eric sighed with relief.

"I am sure you are very good at impersonating American," she continued. "I bet you are good spy. Have you seduced many beautiful women?"

"Hundreds. And you're next."

"I'm not beautiful."

"Yes you are."

"Look at these teeth. If I was in America, I could get them fixed. My parents say I'm lucky I don't have steel ones. Can you picture me with steel teeth?"

"You would still have a mouth meant for kissing," he

said. He leaned over and pressed his lips to hers. She opened her mouth to him. They slid down low in the rowboat.

After a few minutes they both were breathing hard. She pulled away and lay back, sunbathing like a contented cat.

"Have you ever tortured anyone?" she asked.

"What?"

"If I thought you had, I would never talk to you again, Konstantin." She shuddered, and then laughed. "Who thought ever I would find Soviet spy cute. Katya Vasilev, the girl who told her Komsomol leader that people were freer in America, and I would move there in a minute."

"Would you?"

"Perhaps. Will you report me?"

"I'm not GRU or KGB. Honest."

"Of course, you have to say that."

"How can I convince you I'm not a spy?"

"You can't. Lie back and enjoy sun. I like you anyway."

He moved so they could lie side by side in the rowboat, her head resting on his shoulder. He relaxed as the boat bobbed gently on the water.

He didn't notice the glint of sunlight on glass in a clump of shrubbery on the shoreline.

"Look at those boobs," Vesky said, as he focused the telephoto lens on Katya's breasts. He clicked the shutter twice. "Oh yeah, I forgot, that's not your taste."

"I keep my mind on my work," Blok said. In truth, Blok had been eyeing Eric.

"I know the marshal will want these for his collection. Did he ever let you see his collection?"

Blok shook his head.

"I haven't seen it either," Vesky said. "But I've heard about it. One day I'll get him to show it to me."

Blok nodded, but thought, "That'll be a hot day in Siberia.'' He was disgusted by Vesky. The big man lifted the binoculars to his eyes and studied Eric.

A breeze brought the sound of a few words across the lake.

"That didn't sound like Russian to me," Vesky said.

"It was English," Blok said. "American English. I understand the words 'record album.' "

They strained their ears trying to hear more, but the wind shifted.

"I wish we had a parabolic mike," Vesky complained.

"Next shift we will. For now, call in to Centre. Check with the second chief directorate for any American fitting his description coming into the country recently."

TWENTY

"I HAVE BUSINESS TO ATTEND TO IN MOSCOW," THE COLONEL told Eric the next morning over breakfast. "I'll be back by mid-afternoon."

"I'll be here," Eric said. "Or maybe next door."

The colonel repressed his smile. He could tell the boy and Katya were growing fond of each other. She was just Western enough to appeal to Eric.

The colonel drove to the city. The incident at *Detsky Mir* bothered him. The KGB agent named Blok had recognized him too quickly.

He made a few inquiries and found out that Blok worked for Krovili, and that the foul-mouthed KGBer was Viktor Vesky, another Krovili aide.

Petrov went to the Dynamo Gymnasium to mull over what that meant. He remembered Krovili, though he hadn't dwelled on the marshal the way Krovili dwelled on him. Could it be a coincidence that Krovili's aides had happened to bump into him like that?

The gym was gigantic, as large as two soccer fields. It had the best gymnastic, weight-lifting, and fencing facilities in the Soviet Union. Olympic teams trained there. On any given day a half dozen former Olympic medal winners would pass through the doors.

Petrov had a low-numbered locker, nearly as much an honor as the Hero of the Soviet Union medal. He changed into his gear and went out to the fencing room.

He spotted Defense Minister Gorchev. Gorchev liked to slip in and put on his mask. He said that otherwise his opponents would know who he was and be intimidated. In reality, word spread quickly when he arrived. Ambitious members of the military lined up to lose graciously to him.

But not Petrov. He strode out onto the floor. Gorchev saw him and signaled to end the bout with the major he was beating.

Petrov and Gorchev soon faced each other and the match began. Petrov fought to the best of his ability. Gorchev was skilled with an epee, but Petrov won.

"My congratulations, *tovarich*," Gorchev said.

"I was lucky, Comrade Minister," Petrov said.

Gorchev peeled off his mask. "You see through me."

"I recognize your style. Like Marshal Zhukov driving toward Berlin. Relentless."

Gorchev chuckled. "Come with me. I want to talk."

They showered and then went to the steam room. An orderly brought them Stolichnaya on a silver tray. Gorchev dismissed him. Petrov and the defense minister were alone. They sat on the marble, shrouded in clouds of steam.

"This is one of the few places I don't worry about our neighbors bugging us," Gorchev said.

"One day they will have microphones that can resist the heat and humidity," Petrov said, his voice not betraying the tension he felt. Could Gorchev know about Eric?

"I want to talk with you about Alvin Winters," Gorchev said, and Petrov relaxed. "As I recall, you recruited him."

"Yes, Comrade Minister."

"Come, come, Anatoli Vasilivech. Call me Nikolai."

"I am honored, Comrade."

"Tell me about Winters. What do you think of the man?"

"He was a worthwhile asset," Petrov said. "I regretted it when our neighbors took him."

"What about as a man?"

"Unstable. He suffers from migraines brought on by emotional pressures. I believe it's dangerous for us to encourage his rise in any way. He murdered his partner while under the influence of one of his debilitating headaches. What will happen if there is an international incident and he gets a headache?"

"I too am concerned. I voiced my opinion to the Politburo. Levski did not take it very well."

"What did General Secretary Zaroslavski say, if I may ask?"

"He coughed."

"How is his health?"

"Worrisome. And I don't think our foreign minister's is much better. We need more young men in power."

"What will Levski do?"

"I don't know. Would you like to be promoted to Chief of the GRU?"

The suggestion took Petrov by surprise. "I—I am honored, Comrade Minister. But why?"

"Our current chief has certain problems in his background. If Levski begins a campaign of slanderous smears, it could be an embarrassment. You know how riddled even our service is with KGB *stukachi*. They've always had a hand in how the GRU was run. It is time for someone of independence and integrity. I know your background. No one is more distinguished. No one is more dedicated."

"But I am only a colonel."

"An oversight that I can correct with a wave of a pen. Think it over."

"I will. And thank you."

179

"Don't thank me. It's in the interest of the Motherland. By the way, do you know the KGB is investigating you?"

"Uh—I had heard rumors."

"I presume they are anticipating me. Is there any other reason why the KGB would have a renewed interest? You can trust me, Anatoli."

"No."

"Good then. You will let me know tomorrow."

Gorchev was concerned as he dressed at his locker. Petrov should have jumped at the chance to head the GRU. Something was wrong. Could Petrov have made a bargain with the KGB? There were many cases of such cross-pollination in the past. But Petrov was a soldier, a military man. He would not fit in with the hooligans of the KGB. Still, Gorchev wondered. Was Petrov hiding something?

He went to the private phone and made a call. "Can you see me today?" he asked.

"Come right over," the voice at the other end responded.

Gorchev had several outfits in his large locker (which had a single-digit number): a dress uniform, complete with a fruit salad of medals; two custom-tailored Western suits; and a plain Soviet suit. He put on the Russian one, the coarse fabric uncomfortable against his body.

He snuck out a side entrance of the gym and rode public transportation to a house in the Lenin Hills. There were two KGB guards in front, sitting in a parked car. He walked past the house, around the block, and by climbing over a fence slipped into the backyard. The sliding glass door at the rear had been left open.

First Secretary Zaroslavski was in his den. A humidifier purred. Zaroslavski had a list of the members of the Politburo in front of him with zeros, plusses, or minus signs next to the names.

"Have you finished your evaluations?" Gorchev asked.

"Yes. We can count on the foreign minister, the minis-

ter of heavy industry, and the news media minister.''
Zaroslavski's breaths came easily. He looked five years
younger than he had at the previous Politburo meeting.
Gorchev decided he thrived on intrigue.

"The others?"

"Will blow with the wind."

"Levski may try something more direct," Gorchev said.
After Zaroslavski nodded, the defense minister said, "I can
assign a few men to keep watch. Do you have someone
tasting your food?"

"My wife prepares it."

"She can be trusted?"

Zaroslavski nodded.

"Still, someone can get to it before it is cooked."

"I will accept your advice regarding my security. I
don't have many months left, but I plan to enjoy them."

On the drive back to his dacha, Petrov concluded he could
not accept the position. The affair with his son made him
too vulnerable to blackmail by the CIA. He would have to
come up with a plausible excuse to give Gorchev.

But for now, it meant that he was in the defense minister's good graces. He had time to concentrate on his son.
If Eric would agree to stay in the Soviet Union, he might
even be able to take the job. The CIA could not hold
Garfield's future over his head. His having gotten them to
deliver his son to him, even by using a pretense that
implied treachery to the Motherland, might be explainable.
But he would have to go slowly with Eric. If he pushed
too hard, he knew he would lose him forever.

When Eric returned to the dacha from his stroll with
Katya, he found all the living room furniture pushed to the
side. His first reaction was that someone had searched the
house. But then he saw how orderly the dacha was. Petrov
came downstairs carrying two foils.

"It is time for you to take up the sword," Petrov said. "A gentleman should know how to defend himself."

"A wise gentleman is able to avoid trouble," Eric said.

"Sometimes you have no choice. Like now."

Petrov tossed Eric a foil and began demonstrating. Raymond Garfield had regarded sports as a waste of time. Eric, who had envied other youths playing Little League, was quickly caught up in the lesson, and Petrov clearly was thrilled to be teaching his son.

"When you go like this," Petrov explained, slapping Eric's blade aside with a swipe, "you overcommit yourself. The idea is to make as small a movement as possible, to be ready to riposte."

Eric kept thinking about Katya. His time with her was like an island on a turbulent sea. Could he really judge what she was like after only a day together?

"I wonder what it would be like to live in the Soviet Union," he said.

Petrov lowered his sword. "It could be arranged."

"How?"

"There are always malcontents who want to leave," Petrov said. "Through Yuri, we could find a suitable candidate who would like to go out as Eric Garber. You could take over his identity, or we could make up one for you."

Eric lunged suddenly, tapping his father's chest with his sword tip. "You didn't stamp your foot twice. Gotcha."

Petrov frowned, and then laughed. "Already you know how to play dirty." He laughed again, and Eric smiled.

"You seem to have hit it off with the General's daughter," Petrov said.

"She speaks great English," Eric said.

"I'm sure that's the only reason you two hit it off," Petrov joked.

"She's nice. She's smart, and cute, and funny."

"If she's so smart, how come she forgets to wear a bra?"

They laughed together. "Sexy, too," Eric said. "I'm going out with her tonight. She's nuts about music."

"It is too easy to let your guard down, Eric. Women can do that to a man. That's why every intelligence service in the world uses prostitutes. There's a temptation to talk openly or show off when you have a pretty girl on your arm. Your Russian is far from flawless, and your vocabulary is limited. If you speak English at the *tants ploshchadka*, you could call attention to yourself. There's lots of drinking, lots of fights."

"Are you telling me not to go?"

"That is your decision. If you do go, you must be very, very careful."

"Well, that sure will put a damper on my enjoyment. Let's make plans for my getting out of your wonderful country. I should head to Leningrad."

"Who did they give you as a contact there?"

"I think it's best if I don't tell you."

Petrov rattled off a half dozen names. Eric blinked his eyes rapidly on the third.

"So—it's Smironov they're using. He's a drunk and a fool," Petrov said contemptuously. "He has been a known CIA stooge for a decade, him and his smuggling."

"Why do you let him operate then?" Eric asked numbly.

"Better to have a known incompetent than an unknown who might actually be good at his work."

"If he's allowed to operate, I can still go with him," Garfield said.

"No. He's okay for smuggling out an unimportant troublemaker and bringing in a few Bibles. If you tried to get out using him, they would scoop you up before you knew it."

General Krovili looked at the pictures. He held up the visa

183

photos supplied by the second chief directorate. There was no question about it. The man in the boat was the American, Eric Garber.

"Look at those tits," Vesky said, leering over Katya's image. "You can see the nipples sticking up."

"Who is she?" Krovili asked tersely. The toadie Vesky had no right to talk that way to him. "What is her relationship with Garber? What is Garber's relationship to Petrov?"

"He is Petrov's house guest," Blok said, while the rebuked Vesky nervously toyed with the eight by tens.

"Do you think they are queer?" Krovili asked.

"It's hard to tell, but if I had to guess, I'd say no," Blok said. "The girl is Katrina Vasilev. She's the daughter of Petrov's neighbor, General Grigori Vasilev. We have a dossier on her. All petty incidents, but her ideology is suspect. Her father has had to use his *blat* to keep her from discipline a number of times."

"General Vasilev. Better and better. Another military man for the list."

"His wife is the sister of the Foreign Minister," Vesky piped up.

"Very informative," Krovili said sarcastically. "Why don't you tell me vodka makes you drunk. Let's keep two men out there at all times. Who do we have there now?"

"Skuratov and Zenin."

"Shit!" Krovili muttered. "Those swaggering idiots." The duo had risen to the elite squad solely through their family connections. Zenin, who was the nephew of KGB Chairman Levski's wife, was one of the worst. Both were lazy when they should be alert, and aggressive when they should hang back. "Okay, you get some sleep. I want you at Petrov's dacha in six hours."

The two subordinates headed for the door.

"Vesky!"

The man turned.

"Leave those photos on the desk."

Vesky took the dozen eight by tens and set them down on Krovili's desk. He gave Krovili an ingratiating smile and hurried from the room.

Krovili leaned back and gazed at the pictures. Had he stumbled onto a conspiracy? What was Petrov doing alone with the American at his dacha?

"I was afraid you wouldn't come," Katya said. Eric hugged her and they kissed deeply. His hands began to squeeze her tight bottom.

"Later," she said with a giggle. She led him through the woods to her car. As she drove, she asked, "You look so tense. What is it?"

He had a passing temptation to tell her, to see her reaction: My father, whom you think is my uncle, has to help smuggle me, an amateur American spy, back to the United States. The CIA's man in Leningrad is known by the KGB. Do you have any suggestions, Katya dear? Instead, he slid over on the seat and put his arm around her.

"Tell me what they teach you in spy school about America," Katya said.

"I didn't go to spy school."

"Okay, have it that way. What do you know about America? Do they have Negro persons starving in streets? Can you always get jeans in stores? Do newspapers really print anything they want? Are government officials controlled by Mafia?"

Eric laughed. "No. Yes. Within limits. Only some."

"Tell me what they tell you. What is America like? Am I as pretty as American girls?"

Eric pretended he was really considering the question. She slapped him playfully. "That you should know answer to right away."

The phone at Petrov's dacha shrilled.

185

"Hello, Colonel, bad news. I may be out of work tomorrow. I feel sick."

"How sick?" Petrov asked.

"Very sick."

"Too bad. I hope you feel better."

"I hope I do, too. Very soon."

Petrov hung up. The words he and his aide had exchanged were their prearranged plain-language code. Something had gone wrong—Yuri was on his way over.

They parked and hurried toward the square, which was ringed by row houses that looked as if they dated back to before the Revolution. There was a statue in the square, a noble worker triumphantly holding up a pitchfork. It was draped, as were several of the buildings, with strings of light bulbs. Only a few strands of light were glowing. On a makeshift wooden stage four Hawaiian-shirted musicians belted out "Blue Suede Shoes." There were two guitarists, a drummer, and a singer. They were as good as a second-rate Vegas lounge act. Their name, Caviar, was written on the front of the bass drum in English. The drumskin was patched.

The crowd of about a hundred men and women, ranging in age from late teens to early thirties, shouted requests and danced. There was a rowdy cheerfulness about them, fueled by beer and vodka. About a third of the men were in uniform—either the khaki of the Army or the gray-blue of the militia.

Periodically a squat man in an expensive gray suit would hop onto the stage and whisper in the singer's ear. The singer would then offer a patriotic song, about the strides the Party was making, how hard work helped the masses, what a great man Lenin was. His voice had the hint of a sarcastic lilt when he sang the forced songs.

Eric and Katya danced in the midst of the crowd. Katya prattled on and on about rock music, comparing Soviet groups like Time Machine and Arsenal with their American and British counterparts. She boasted of her large collection of *magnitizdat,* bootlegged cassette tapes.

Eric felt he was blending in. With Katya pressing against him, he could almost let go of his problems. The idea of living in the Soviet Union didn't seem quite as farfetched. Not probable, but maybe possible. Wouldn't that be weird, to change identities in mid-life?

"What are you thinking?" she asked.

"How I'd like to carry you away and make wild passionate love to you for hours on end," he answered.

She laughed. "You really have studied how to be an American."

"What do you mean?"

"Russian man would just drag me off by my hair."

The band switched to a bluesy number. Eric felt calm, horny, happy. As the song ended, they kissed, until people around them made clucking noises, and they separated.

"*Amoralka,*" one woman said.

A few more echoed the criticism.

The band played a patriotic song, and then the crowd's favorite, the Beatles' "Back in the U.S.S.R." A rowdy group of soldiers began clapping their hands and shoving their way through the dancers.

"Hey, Comrade, share the wealth," said a boozy soldier, throwing an arm over Eric's shoulder. The soldier had curly hair poking out from his cap, which sat crookedly on his head. His breath was as strong as the arm that squeezed Eric's in a gesture more of intimidation than friendship.

A second soldier, smaller and less drunk, came up to them. "How about doing something for the gallant Red Army that protects the Motherland?" His hand moved behind Katya. She jumped, and the soldier laughed crudely.

"Get away," Katya said. She tried to slap the soldier

who had goosed her, but he caught her hand, tugged her to him, and planted a beery, wet kiss on her lips.

"Come with me, sweet *kotik,* and I'll make you the czarina of our barracks."

"All right, Comrades, enough," Eric said placatingly in Russian. The soldiers snickered, and the smaller one tried to fondle Katya. Eric broke free of the big soldier and shoved the small one aside.

The big one swung a clumsy roundhouse right at Eric's head. Eric ducked and slammed a raised-knuckle punch into his midriff. The smaller one rushed Eric. Eric pushed the big one into him, and the smaller soldier fell to the floor.

The big drunk reached for his holstered gun. Eric slashed his throat with the edge of his hand, then tossed him on top of the smaller one with a *taoitoshi.*

Whistles blew and militiamen surrounded Eric. The two soldiers were lying on the floor, groaning. The police yanked them to their feet and led Eric and Katya to a quiet side street.

"Where were you when they attacked us?" Katya demanded of the leader, a lieutenant with a black goatee and thinning hair who obviously was trying to look like Lenin.

"You're in no position to make accusations," the lieutentant said. "You're in trouble."

"It's you who are in trouble if you don't let us go immediately. Do you know who he is?" she said, pointing at Eric. "Tell him, Konstantin."

The lieutenant turned to Eric. "Yes, tell me. I want to see your papers."

Eric cleared his throat. He looked for a way to flee and saw none.

"Don't be shy, show him," Katya said. "Then I will tell him who I am. We will see if he wants to be counting birches in Siberia for the rest of his career."

Katya stood, arms folded, a smug expression on her

face. It was clear she was one of the *zolotaya molodyozh*, the "golden youth" who had powerful parents, access to rubles and foreign currency, and privileges most Soviet citizens could only dream about.

"Don't be shy, Konstantin," Katya said.

The lieutenant was faltering. "Who are you?" he asked her politely.

"The daughter of General Vasilev. And Konstantin is the nephew of Colonel Petrov of the GRU. A Hero of the Soviet Union. And Konstantin himself is—"

"No more," Eric barked. "Take us to headquarters."

The lieutenant raised his hands. "It isn't necessary. We can straighten it out here. Obviously there's been some mistake. I should've known by the way you handled yourself, *tovarich*. These uniformed hooligans will be disciplined."

One soldier was trying to stop a bleeding nose. The other's arm was held at a strange angle. Katya looked at them sympathetically. "They're just a couple of drunks. There's no need for them to be reported."

"I agree," Eric said.

"Yes, sir," the lieutenant said, though he was ten years older than Eric. He signaled his men to follow him back to the square. The stunned soldiers were dragged along.

"I don't think I can sleep," she said, as she parked the car in the driveway to her parents' dacha. They were the first words she had spoken since they had left the dance.

"Neither can I. Want to go for a walk?"

Hand in hand, they entered the forest area adjoining their parents' dachas.

"Is something the matter?" he asked her, sensing her remoteness.

"I could very easy fall madly in love with you. But I could never love someone who works for the government security organs."

"I don't, I told you."

"At the dance, you took charge so easily. You handled those soldiers like they were children, and then bulldozed the lieutenant."

She began walking. Eric had to move quickly to catch up. He took her in his arms and spun her to face him. They were wrapped in the dark woods. A cool night breeze blew the scent of pine around them.

She pulled away and said, "I feel undercurrents. I like your uncle, and you know how I feel about you. But too many people have disappeared in the night because of KGB. Not only foreigners—Russian people. People who were speaking as truthful as me."

"Katya, please, believe me, I'm not KGB."

"I wish I could. But if anyone knows how to lie good, it is KGB. Even if you are GRU, I could never let myself love you."

"I'm not GRU. Honest."

"So what are you?"

"Can't you just accept me as Colonel Petrov's nephew?"

"I sense secrets in you I don't like. We can never get together."

They were by the water. He heard the small waves lapping. Katya was silhouetted against the moonlit lake.

They reached for each other. Her hands explored his body while his wandered over hers. Then he was pulling at her clothing, and their bodies met.

"I need you, Katya," he blurted.

"Just hold me close," she said.

"Katya, I have to tell you something. I am—"

She put her hand on his lips. "Don't say anything more, please. Maybe I am being punished for all times I flirted and teased. Maybe you have done something wrong. Whatever it is, we will never see each other again." She dressed quickly. "Let's remember this. Good-bye." She disappeared.

He sat on a rock, staring out over the lake and wondering what was going on beneath its calm surface. He started walking to Petrov's house. He was two-thirds of the way back when he heard a walkie-talkie crackle.

He dropped to the pine-needle-covered floor, and scanned the forest but couldn't see anyone. Had he imagined it? Had Katya set him up to be killed? Eric lay on the ground and silently shivered.

TWENTY-ONE

"WE MUST GET YOUR SON OUT TONIGHT," YURI TOLD PETROV as they sat in front of the empty fireplace.

"Has someone found out?"

"I don't know. A friend who is a secretary at the Politburo says Chairman Levski and Defense Minister Gorchev are warring. Marshal Krovili has been putting snow in Levski's pants."

"That shouldn't affect us."

"It does. I have it from a good source that Levski and Krovili will attack the military. You know the way it works—first the stories appear in *Pravda* about problems in the army, then the scandal is exposed by our brave KGB neighbors, then the procurator steps in, the show trials, the transfers, et cetera. If they turn up Eric, it will mean more than just smearing your name. Krovili will make sure you sound like a spy for the Americans, a traitor who had a CIA guest at your dacha. You'll be blamed for everything from the cold winter to Zaroslavski's emphysema."

"We still have time."

"I'm afraid not. There is worse news. Someone at the

second chief directorate informed me Eric Garber's pictures were ordered up. By Krovili.''

Petrov wished he had allowed his men to kill Krovili during the Great Patriotic War. "Did you contact Turkin?''

Yuri looked down.

"What is it?''

"Turkin is also under suspicion. They shifted him from transport.''

Petrov inhaled deeply and released the air in a long, melancholy sigh. The hope for enjoying years with Eric, for promotion, for happiness, faded. All he could do now was save his son. "Is there any other way to get Eric on a military plane?''

"I have been trying," Yuri said. "My whole family has been working on it.''

"I have several thousand in gold coins. Will that help?''

"It's not that, Colonel. Your son had the misfortune to come when a shit storm was beginning. I think you might get caught in it. The farther he is from you, the better for everyone. He should get to a border town. I'll drive him myself, tonight.''

"I can't ask you to do that.''

"No, but I can volunteer. Tell him to pack.''

Petrov gave Yuri a hug and kissed him on both cheeks—a gesture common among Russian men, but this was the first time Petrov had ever acted so warmly with anyone.

"My son is due back soon.''

Yuri lit a Bulgarian cigarette. He smoked only when he was very nervous. Petrov went upstairs and packed Eric's suitcase. It was almost midnight.

Eric came in a few minutes later. Petrov was pacing about. Yuri sat in an overstuffed armchair, a half-full ashtray at his side.

"Were you or Yuri in the woods tonight?'' Eric asked.

"No.''

"I thought I heard a walkie-talkie. I searched and didn't see anyone. I guess I was wrong."

Yuri took out a Czech revolver. "This gun is untraceable. I'll welcome our KGB neighbors."

"What's going on?" Eric asked.

"Trouble," Petrov said, and turned to Yuri. "I will take care of the rats in the woods. What of the future? I have made arrangements for myself. But what about you, Yuri?"

"I'm a survivor, Colonel. I will tell a story how you fooled me or forced me to commit vile deeds. I'll win such sympathy, probably get a promotion."

"What's going on?" Eric repeated.

Petrov ignored him and put his arm on Yuri. He squeezed his *tolkach* affectionately. "See if you can see anything through the window."

Petrov made a sketch of the house, surrounding grounds, and lake. "Where were you when you heard the noise?"

Eric studied the paper. With a few quick lines, Petrov had neatly captured the area.

"Right about here," Eric said, indicating a spot.

Petrov made a mark. "There are hills over here and thick shrubbery here and here," he mused. "To view the house best, there are only two possible positions someone could take. Since he had a walkie-talkie, we have to assume he was communicating with at least one other man. Probably farther back in the woods, near the road."

"Who are they?" Eric asked. "What's going on?"

Petrov hurried upstairs.

"What will he do?" Eric asked.

"Whatever it is, you can be sure it's the right thing," Yuri said. He stood next to the window, off to one side so he wouldn't be silhouetted.

The colonel returned, dressed in black, with shoe polish covering his face and hands. He carried a foil with its protective tip removed. It was a three-foot-long icepick.

"Yuri, take my son and leave. Make as much noise as possible. Keep their attention on you. Pretend you are going for a trip into Moscow. Wait for me a quarter mile up the road."

Yuri went to hand him the gun.

"I won't need that," Petrov said.

"Why can't we all just leave?" Eric asked.

"If it is routine, your father will shoo them away," Yuri explained, his tone brisk with annoyance at Eric. "If he runs away, it will be recorded as a sign of a guilty conscience. If they are scouts, they can relay word that we've fled. The opposition will be able to block us in."

"Did he see you?" Petrov asked Eric.

"I don't know."

Petrov nodded and turned to Yuri. "Make some noise, Yuri. Count to fifty and go."

Yuri grabbed Eric's arm and headed for the door.

"*Odin, dva, tri. . .*" Yuri began.

Petrov went to a rear window. He could feel his heart pounding under his ribs. He was sixty-three years old, in good shape, but hardly the age when springing after enemies in dark forests was recommended.

He heard the front door open, and Yuri's loud voice bellowing to Eric, "Come on. We have to get back to Moscow. They're waiting for us at the party. Hurry up, Konstantin. Get the lead out of your bottom."

At the exact moment Yuri started the car, Petrov dropped to the ground outside, rolled into a ball, and crawled a few yards.

Yuri raced the engine as Petrov scurried across the lawn to the edge of the woods. He moved cautiously, crouched low. He heard the crackling of a walkie-talkie from the ridge where he had guessed the man would be. He kept circling, the blackened foil held against his chest.

The man had dug a hole and buried himself. Only a few

inches of his head and neck protruded, and he had a black cap pulled low.

Petrov slipped behind him and laid the needle-sharp tip at the base of his skull. The man froze.

"How many are there?"

"Only me."

Petrov pricked the back of his head. "Again, how many?"

"One other."

"Where?"

"By the road. We're onto you, Petrov. You might as well put that stupid pig sticker down and give up. You'll get off with a few years in a labor camp."

"It is you who are in trouble. We'll find out who is behind this intrusion. Get up and come with me."

"Arrogant dolt. Do you know who I am? Do you know who you are talking to? By tomorrow at this time, you'll be wiping grease from tank treads in Irkutsk." As he spoke, the man moved his fingers, millimeter by millimeter, to his handgun. Grasping the butt, he opened his mouth to yell. Petrov clamped a hand over his mouth. The man jerked Petrov off balance. The colonel fell and the foil blade snapped. The two men scuffled.

The watcher bit down on Petrov's hand. When the colonel pulled it back, the man opened his mouth to shout for help. Petrov rammed a wad of dirt in. The man gagged. He squeezed the trigger on his Makarov. The pistol had a two-centimeter silencer on a nine-centimeter barrel. It made a sound like someone clapping his hands. The bullet thumped into a tree trunk.

Petrov grabbed his foil and shoved it into the man's ear. He kicked convulsively, like a frog that had been pithed.

Petrov rifled the man's pockets and found papers identifying him as Corporal Zenin in the KGB's elite counterintelligence unit. He felt his stomach flip as he realized he had killed the nephew of the head of the KGB. The walkie-talkie crackled. "This is *nozh*. Come in, *lozhka*.

Did you make a noise? Come in?'' Petrov could hear the panic in the man's voice. ''They're making a break for it. I'm going to let loose a few shots to keep them from getting away.''

Petrov grabbed Zenin's Makarov and walkie-talkie and raced through the woods. He was where he guessed the second man would be, a high point allowing a view of the road and the house. But there was no one in sight. Could the watcher have moved once he got no answer from Zenin?

Petrov depressed the Speak switch on the walkie-talkie. He made a garbled noise that could've been anyone's voice. He heard the crackle only a few yards away.

Then he saw him, ten feet off the ground, perched in the crotch of one of the oaks that dotted the landscape. He had a Stechkin 9mm automatic pistol APS, with wooden shoulder stock, pointed at the car. The gun could fire half its twenty-shot magazine in less than a second.

Petrov lifted Zenin's pistol as the sniper fired. The colonel's bullets caught the sniper in the chest, and the man dropped from the tree. Petrov raced to him and made sure he was dead. His eyes had already rolled up. There were three moist holes in his dark outfit.

The colonel ran to the car, presuming there were only two watchers or the others would have attacked. He had to move quickly. An old soldier like Vasilev would recognize the sound of gunshots. They had had trouble with poachers before, but if Vasilev decided to investigate . . .

He heard someone gasping. At the center of spiderweb cracks in the windshield were kopeck-sized holes. Yuri sat in the driver's seat, a bullet hole making his face even uglier. Eric was next to him, wide-eyed with terror and gasping for air.

Petrov tore open the door on the passenger side and hauled Eric out. Reaching into the glove compartment and removing a powerful flashlight, he took the keys from the ignition, opened the trunk, and grabbed the suitcase.

Petrov ran back to where he had killed the man in the tree. There has to be a car, he thought, his eyes scanning the woods. Every few yards he snapped on the flashlight and played it over the soft shoulders of the road.

He saw tire marks and followed them into the woods. A black Volga was concealed in a dense growth. The key was in the ignition. He started the engine. It was one of the KGB special cars, with a supercharged Chaika engine under the hood. Eric stood numbly outside the car.

"Get in," Petrov ordered, and Eric obeyed.

The colonel stepped on the gas. They passed the car where Yuri lay. Petrov thought of setting it afire, to make it harder to identify the body, but there wasn't time. He depressed the accelerator and headed north. Tears streamed down his cheeks.

TWENTY-TWO

GARFIELD AND PETROV HAD BEEN RIDING THROUGH THE DARK Russian countryside for a half hour before Eric spoke.

"Why did they kill Yuri?"

"Why? Because they are KGB idiots in love with their guns, punks not fit to clean Yuri's shoes," Petrov growled. He sighed. "Poor, dear Yuri. The world is like that. One minute you are living a full life. The next minute a trust is betrayed, a car skids, a bullet strikes, and life is over."

Eric didn't know how to respond to the colonel's pain. "Where are we going?"

"Probably Odessa."

"But it seems to me like we're heading north."

"We are. To throw the dogs off the scent."

Petrov spotted a farmhouse with a light on and rode to the front.

"Crouch out of view and stay here," Petrov ordered. "I won't be long." He walked up to the farm door and rapped forcefully.

The person who eventually opened the door had a grizzled face that was as Russian as the Urals. Strong, proud lines cut into deep features. He squinted at Petrov, whose shoe-polish camouflage was streaked.

"What is it?" the farmer demanded.

"KGB," Petrov said, flashing Zenin's identification quickly. "State security business. I need to wash up."

The farmer opened the screen door and waved Petrov in. His manner changed from belligerence to subservience.

"I know what it is," the farmer said. Despite the cold night air, he was sweating. "That lying Vanya makes up stories about me. My loyalty is to the Party. Forever."

Petrov marched straight to the kitchen sink. He turned the tap on, and a weak stream of reddish water flowed out. He scrubbed his face.

"We know about you, and Vanya too. You don't have to worry," Petrov said. "All I need is to wash and get food for the road."

"What can I do for you? It is a privilege to be able to help in the glorious workers' struggle. If I have it, it's yours. If not, I can run up the road and—"

"Bread, salami, cheese if you have it. Wine?"

"Bread and cheese, yes. All I have to drink is milk and kvass. Would you like cabbage rolls? My wife would be honored to make it for you."

As if waiting for a cue—and no doubt listening the whole time from the other side of the door—a red-nosed woman came in and curtsied to Petrov.

"Our daughter is a leader in the Young Pioneers," she said, taking a picture down from where it was tacked to the wall. She showed it to Petrov, further proof that they were good Communists.

"Very nice," he said. He tried to sound sincere, but it came across as cold and ruthless. He made the farm couple jittery.

The couple scurried about, getting food.

"One other thing. The road to Leningrad, how is it?"

"The glorious volunteer labor corps has been working

on it daily," the farmer said. "There is fresh asphalt for miles."

"There was a show on television the other night," his wife piped up. "Soon we will have four-lane highways stretching from Vladivostok to Kiev. Everyone will have a private car. We are lucky indeed, comrade."

"Do you have gasoline?" Petrov asked. It was a sensitive subject. Shortages meant tractors often sat idle in the fields without their petroleum lifeblood.

The man and his wife exchanged pregnant glances. "I need only a few liters," Petrov said.

The woman nodded. She handed over a napkin filled with food and a big bottle of kvass. The farmer went behind his house and came back with a dented jerry can full of gas.

Petrov thanked the man and returned to the stolen car. The farmer stood on the front steps of his house, watching as Petrov tossed the food in the backseat and drove away. The man's father probably had had the same relieved look as Cossacks galloped off: He was happy to share the little he had, as long as they didn't burn his house, rape his wife, or slit his throat.

KGB Chairman Fyodor Levski leaned against the dishwasher in the kitchen of his seven-room apartment on Kutuzovsky Prospekt. The kitchen included every appliance known to man, from microwave oven to popcorn popper. If it hadn't been such a large room, it would've been packed tight with cooking hardware.

Marshal Vladimir Krovili had personally delivered the bad news about the incident at the Toyma dacha of Colonel Petrov. The men were in the kitchen because Levski's wife was in the living room, moaning and sobbing over the death of her beloved nephew Zenin.

"Zenin was always a shit-for-brains kid," Levski said, almost loud enough for his wife to hear. "But he was the old cow's favorite. She'll go into mourning for a month. I remember the fuss she made until I transferred him into a top unit. Your unit.''

Krovili continued sipping his *chifir*, the thick, rebrewed tea burning his throat. His boss's face reddened as he worked himself into a rage.

"That son-of-a-bitch bastard prick Petrov," Levski said, smacking the dishwasher. "It's not the right time yet for the shake-up. I need to lay the groundwork with the no-balls mastodons on the Politburo. I can't knock out Gorchev just yet.

"I want you to fabricate a suitable reason why there were two KGB men in the woods outside Petrov's dacha. I want Petrov. We must find out what he has told the Americans. The borders must be closed off tighter than a virgin's pussy.'' The veins in Levski's neck and temples bulged.

"We can't circulate a photo of Petrov," Krovili said. "Too many people know who he is. But we have good photographs of this Eric Garber.''

"What else?"

"He seems to have spent quite a lot of time with the daughter of Petrov's neighbor, General Grigori Vasilev. The girl has a history of being a troublemaker.''

"Bring her in.''

"But the general is—"

"Bring her in.''

"Yes, Chairman.''

"You must use only your own special squad. No one must know. You've fucked up, Krovili. Don't do it again.''

"Yes, Chairman.''

Levski went to console his wife. Krovili left the apartment, teeth grimly set. He had been awake for nearly twenty-four hours. But the indignity of having to put up with that cretin's abuse—the man wouldn't know Tchaikovsky from Shostakovich—had riled him.

There was only one way to let out the fury. Krovili dug out his address book. One of his *kotiki* would get a surprise early-morning raid by the Little Czar.

Two hours before the scheduled emergency session of the Politburo, five of the leaders were cloistered in a secret meeting. The small room was reserved for private conferences. President Zaroslavski's personal security staff went over it daily. It was starkly furnished—a wooden table and four straight-back wooden chairs—to provide fewer places for an assassin or spy to hide bombs or bugs.

The unlit Uppman Cuban cigar Minister of Defense Gorchev was chomping made him look even more like a tank. Also at the table were the minister of news media, the minister of heavy industry, the foreign minister, and Zaroslavski. The elderly boss of the Politburo finished his speech and sat coughing at the far end of the table.

"What you've just told us—you have it from a good source?" the minister of heavy industry asked.

"Do you think I like getting up this early and sneaking in like a factory worker out to swipe parts?" Zaroslavski asked.

"I'm sorry," the cowed minister said. "But I'm stunned. I knew Levski was ambitious, but to plan such a thing, to dare to attack a fellow member of the Politburo."

"You're naive," the foreign minister said. "Our good comrade chairman can't wait to step into the general secretary's seat. He's got the makings of another Stalin."

"What do you recommend?" Zaroslavski asked.

The foreign minister spoke hesitantly. "Aside from those present, no one in the Politburo has the courage to take on Levski. They will go along with him."

"That is hardly encouraging," Gorchev said.

"Of the illustrious heads of the government security organs who have served the Union of Soviet Socialist Republics in the past," the foreign minister said, dragging out each word for suspense, "Yagoda, Yezhov, Beria, Merkulov, and Abakumov were executed. Menzhinsky was poisoned by his successor. There is even some question over the death of Dzerzhinsky, whether his heart attack was induced or not."

Zaroslavski coughed.

"Chairman Levski is known to be a volatile man," said the minister of culture as the idea dawned on him. "There is the possibility that he could suffer a heart attack. An alternative is he is murdered by CIA-sponsored terrorists, say Afghani *Moujahadeen*. It could help morale for the troops."

"Assassinate the head of the KGB," Zaroslavski said. From his level tone, it was impossible to tell whether he was endorsing the idea, just mulling it over, or offended by the proposal. He looked at Gorchev.

"He has two bodyguards with him when he travels," the defense minister said. "But I'm sure there are times when he is vulnerable. Who will handle the task?"

"You have the *spetsnaz,*" the foreign minister said, referring to the GRU's special-assignment troops of strong-arms recruited from the ranks of the military. "We can, as the Americans say, kill two birds with one rock. Can you find a suitable man or men who could perform a *mokrie dela* and be linked to the *Moujahadeen?*"

"I have another question. What about the sleeper operation Levski told us about?" Gorchev asked.

"We should let it continue," Zaroslavski said. "The upcoming confusion at the KGB should not affect things. We can always cancel it at a later date."

"What if Petrov has already told the Americans about Alvin Winters?" Gorchev said. "Though I still don't believe he would betray the *rodina.* I knew him back at Frunze Military Academy. I find it much easier to believe Levski's tricks than Petrov's betrayal."

"My source has seen the pictures of Petrov together

with the American, at his dacha in Toyma," Zaroslavski said.

"How did the KGB manage to take over the Winters operation from the GRU anyway?" the minister of culture asked.

"Petrov was working as an illegal under the name of Glenn Kelly," Gorchev said. "He developed this Alvin Winters as an asset. Somewhere along the way there was a leak from the GRU to the KGB—it happens all the time—and they moved in and stole Winters. They tried to steal Petrov too, but he turned them down. They provided the backing for Winters to go into politics. He doesn't know that Russians are behind him. He thinks it is Sicilian gangsters."

"Intriguing," the foreign minister said. He glanced at his watch. "We shouldn't be seen together before the meeting today. *Tovarich* Gorchev, you still have not said yes or no to the proposal."

"Who will lead the KGB after Levski's unfortunate death?" Gorchev responded.

TWENTY-THREE

PETROV AND ERIC HAD BEEN ON THE ROAD FOR SIX HOURS. They had passed fallow collective farms, small run-down plots of land, and enormous, dirty-looking factories. There were none of the distractions or attractions of American roadsides. No billboards, cozy motels, or Golden Arches. No streetlights, and few road signs. The main relief from the tedium was avoiding the large potholes. Often the road was not much more than a single lane winding through birch or oak forests.

Petrov had avoided small towns where Russian inquisitiveness could be a problem. For them, cities were safer. They got lost only once. Outside of Bryansk, Petrov had to pull to the side of the road to get his bearings. Eric rummaged in the glove compartment, hoping for a map. Petrov chuckled dryly.

"I forgot. You people are so uptight, you don't even print road maps," Eric said. "The ones you print have deliberate disinformation. Why are Russians so secretive?" Eric asked.

"Americans don't know what it's like to see invaders in the street," Petrov said. "We've had Tartars, Poles, Czechs,

Swedes, French, and Germans invade us. If an enemy army were to show up on your doorstep, you have maps guiding them to every military base, armory, and naval facility—available at any gas station.''

"Don't you think an enemy army would have that information? Isn't a lot of time wasted by people getting lost?''

"For most Russian people, they have what they need within a few miles of home,'' Petrov said.

"Can you tell me what's going to happen? Are you coming with me to America?''

"I will get you on a ship at Odessa. I have friends there who can help.''

"And you?''

"I'm like Antaeus, the giant who was strong only when he touched the earth,'' Petrov said. "The only earth worth touching is here.''

"But they will kill you.''

Petrov shrugged. "They won't,'' he said in a way that made it clear the conversation had ended. If only it hadn't been the nephew of the KGB boss he'd been forced to kill. He knew there was a good chance he would be executed. But he also knew that getting Eric alone out of the country was tough enough—for the two of them to escape would be impossible.

Kiev was Petrov's first choice, despite Eric's concern over the Chernobyl disaster.

"Trace radioactivity is the least of our problems,'' Petrov said.

But because of the accident, tourism in the city had dropped to near zero, and they would be particularly conspicuous on the once crowded streets, Petrov decided.

Heading toward Kharkov, a regional capital with a million and a half population, would make it harder for the hounds to figure out where the fox was headed. Kharkov had air, rail, and road connections with as many cities as Kiev.

"Change your appearance as much as you can," he told Eric as they neared the city.

Eric opened the suitcase and found makeup, wigs, and foam-rubber pads. He put a wig on, lightened his eyebrows with a blond pencil, and put a piece of foam in his mouth to puff up his cheeks.

"You're going to drop me in town, then return here and wait. If I'm not back in a half hour, leave for Odessa. It is due southeast, about four hundred miles. Get to Major Ustinov at the border station. Do you understand?"

"Major Ustinov, at the border. Who is he?"

"We have been friends since we graduated from the Academy. He's a fine man and a first-rate fencer."

"What happens then?"

"He will arrange passage on a foreign liner. There are many places to hide on a big ship. His family were smugglers, going way back."

"Aren't you afraid he might turn us in?"

"Would you turn me in?"

"Of course not."

"You are my son. He is like a brother."

Petrov found a side road and pulled off. Traffic had increased on the north-south route they had been following. More than half of the vehicles were trucks, usually several years old, belching foul clouds from their scabrous exhaust pipes. The cars were either official and new or private and old.

"What are you going to do in town?" Eric asked, after he took over driving.

"Steal a car. By now the word will have been spread to look for this one." Petrov blackened his gray hair and coarsened his eyebrows with mascara. He fished out a bushy black mustache that looked like something a bartender from the Gay Nineties would have worn.

Eric grinned.

"They'll remember the mustache, not the face," Petrov

211

said seriously as he glued the hairy prop into place. He quickly slipped into a workman's outfit—baggy twill pants, loosefitting plaid shirt, bulky woolen overcoat. Into one pocket he put a lock-picking set, into the other the identification he had taken off the dead KGB man.

"I'll come with you and help," Eric volunteered. "I can be your lookout."

"I don't need help," Petrov said.

Eric drove to the plaza at the center of town. Branching off the 750-yard-long square, which was part square and part circle, was Lenin Prospekt. They had gone a few blocks up the avenue when Petrov signaled Eric to stop. Petrov got out and watched as Eric drove off. The colonel knew just the kind of car he wanted—a late-model Volga Gaz 24 belonging to a Party official. It would be better maintained than a citizen's car, and helpful in bluffing his way past roadblocks.

Petrov ambled casually down the street, heading for the official buildings at the center of town. The gun felt heavy in his pocket. He hoped he wouldn't have to shoot a *militsia* man who was only doing his job. But he would if he had to. Saving his son was all that mattered.

TWENTY-FOUR

PETROV PULLED THE VOLGA GAZ 24 ONTO THE DIRT ROAD about a hundred miles out of Kharkov. "The next stretch is open," he said. "We'll be too easy to see by helicopter. We'll find a place to stay until dark."

They came to an abandoned building, a ramshackle structure that might have once been a warehouse. Petrov tried unsuccessfully to pick the rusted lock. He used the pry bar from the jack in the trunk to pop it off and drove the car in. Eric smoothed out the tracks the tires had left on the dirt road.

They sat in the car, in the warehouse, trying to sleep. Holes in the wall and roof let little patches of sun into the darkness. Eric dozed for a few minutes. Petrov's eyes were closed, but his ears strained for any sound. He heard the helicopter long before Eric. When his son finally did, he jerked upright.

"We should be safe," Petrov said reassuringly. "Just relax."

The big blades of the chopper seemed to be inside Eric's head as it *thump-thump*ed right above the building. Clouds of dust rose. Petrov sat quietly.

"Where's the gun?" Eric asked.

"That's a Mil Mi-8 helicopter," Petrov said. "It's fully armored and can hold twenty-six soldiers, combat loaded. It carries fifty-seven-millimeter unguided rockets and anti-tank guided missiles. Up to seven hundred fifty kilograms of conventional or chemical bombs. I have six shots left in this pistol. I don't think *they* have to be concerned."

The chopper, which had been droning overhead like a menacing wasp, flew off. Eric sagged into his seat, too tense to sleep. He stared at the patterns of light and dark.

"So many abandoned buildings, unfulfilled promises," Petrov said softly. "Broken dreams."

Impulsively, Eric reached out and squeezed the Colonel's arm. "Come to America."

"America." He repeated the word a few times. "You don't know how they treat a defector. First they suck out everything they can, checking to make sure he's not a double agent. When they're done, they toss away what's left like a dried-up orange."

"It can't be that bad," Eric said.

Petrov sighed. "I would never betray my countrymen. There is nothing worse than a traitor. I know, I've dealt with many over the years."

Petrov gave a sad smile. He patted his son's arm. They were silent for a while.

"Broken dreams. For my country, then with your mother, then with you coming to live here. I remember the night I decided to come back." He paused, and focused the image in his mind. "Toward the end of our relationship, I had gotten in the habit of riding the subways at night. I couldn't understand why. I'd take the train all the way up to the Bronx, down to Brooklyn, out to Queens.

"One night I was out in Coney Island. Looking at the water. There's nothing to make you feel smaller and more alone than staring at the ocean. The waves crashing, whitecaps occasionally visible, cold, damp. Buoys flashing in the dark.

"I heard the sound behind me. There were two hooligans with knives. Suddenly I knew why I had been riding. New York was not as bad back then, but there were places you did not go. I had been going to them. Hoping, deep down, to find what I found that night on the pier.

"I hurt them both. More than I had to. I knew the love inside me for your mother was turning to hate. Of myself, of her, of the man who raised you. Even of you. I knew if I didn't get away, something evil would happen.

"But the hate inside me made me good at my job. Before then I had been an untempered blade. After that night I knew what was in me.

"In all my later assignments, I could think of those moments and know I could do what had to be done. I earned many honors."

Petrov wiped his eyes. Eric couldn't tell whether they were tearing from the dust the copter had kicked up or stirred memories.

"I insisted on fieldwork. No desk job for me. In Istanbul, Hong Kong, Paris, Tokyo. I used my hurt. There has to be coldness in your heart to recruit an asset. You must seduce, blackmail, threaten.

"I recruited a businessman who killed his partner. I covered it up for him, but took evidence that would hang him if ever he rebelled. I nurtured him with secret loans, inside information. He became very successful. He unwittingly provided stacks of defense information. Then the KGB got jealous. They took him over, made him political, an agent of influence. He was an even bigger success. His name is Alvin Winters."

"*The* Alvin Winters?"

Petrov nodded.

"But that's impossible. He's more right wing than the John Birch Society."

"It's called a false-flag recruitment. It's common. The asset doesn't know who he's really working for. He thought I was with the Cosa Nostra."

"But why encourage someone who is a rabid conservative?"

"From what I've heard, it's part of a five-year plan. The hard-liners believe Winters will bankrupt the country, waste money on foolish defense projects, cut back the domestic programs that give Americans the soft life. Education, welfare, farm subsidies, pensions. He'll instigate a national identity-card program, supposedly to restrict illegal aliens. Provocateurs will begin to heat up the American people."

"What about Congress, the Supreme Court, checks and balances and all that?"

"That plan is what the hard-liners believe. They see your power structure through a rigid Soviet perspective. The more clever members merely want to put a few sleepers in key positions. We have assets at the lower levels of government, in academia, in the corporate world. They could be brought into the administration and provide us with an invaluable pipeline. The Defense, Treasury, and State Departments are the prime targets."

"Do you think the plan can work?"

"Who can say? Capitalism carried to the extreme, ruining itself. The danger is that Winters is a hate-filled man who has been blackmailed for many years. He has proven that he can lash out violently, irrationally. Also, if the American public ever finds out about our meddling, we will be closer to war. This risky plan is a sign of our own leaders' lack of confidence in the eventual victory of socialism.

"I spoke out against using Winters like that once. Only my past record kept me from being sent to an institution for correction. Maybe that's why I wanted to see you so much. Maybe there won't be a world a few years from now."

Awkwardly, in the confined space of the car, Eric reached over and hugged his father.

The chief of the CIA's intelligence division rushed into the office of Director Robert Wellington. "All hell's breaking loose in Moscow."

Wellington set down the weekly report on the activities of allied intelligence agencies and lifted an eyebrow expectantly. His intelligence chief was not a man given to dramatics.

"KGB Chairman Levski was assassinated by Islamic warriors," the intelligence chief said. "The Soviets are making the usual noises about us being behind it, but our sources say the attack was not entirely unexpected. There's talk of a link with the disappearance of a GRU colonel, but details are sketchy. They say we're also behind that."

The chief looked at Wellington questioningly.

"Don't be silly," Wellington said. "These problems are entirely of their own making."

"There've been demotions and transfers," the chief continued. "A few Levski loyalists have been locked up or shunted aside. Marshal Vladimir Pavlovich Krovili is acting KGB chairman. I brought his file up for you."

"Thank you. I'm sure I'll be briefing the President."

"It's too soon to tell, but it looks like Levski exceeded his authority. There was a skirmish with Nikolai Gorchev, the defense minister. Sort of like when Joe McCarthy took on the Army."

"An interesting comparison," Wellington said.

"Gorchev appears to have formed an alliance with the foreign minister. Zaroslavski seems to have given at least tacit approval. It could be a new troika, or we may be seeing the preparation for them passing on the crown."

"Very good," Wellington said. "Will you have something for me by this afternoon? You know what I need: minibios of the players, who's neo-Stalinist, who's progressive. Estimates, timetables, the usual stuff. Will they commit more troops to Afghanistan?''

''There's also the flare-up with the Chinese along their border,'' the chief said. ''This could affect the president's reelection, the way Carter was ultimately beaten by politics outside the country. The Ayatollah held—''

Wellington cut the other man off with a wave. He knew the chief could go on talking for hours, detailing the history and future of the world with equal enthusiasm. ''Thanks for getting the word to me so quickly. I'd better get back to these reports.''

As soon as he was out of the office, Wellington hit the intercom and had his secretary summon Tuttle, ''Forthwith.''

Eric and Petrov had been on the road for twenty hours.

''It's going well so far,'' Eric said cheerily.

''There's probably chaos at Centre. It'll act in our favor. By the time the bureaucrats are done covering their asses, you may be home.''

They hit a stretch of road with potholes as deep as bomb craters. ''These roads were built by German POWs during the Great Patriotic War,'' Petrov said. ''They did a good job. It's unfortunate that our leaders have not had them repaired since then.''

Eric felt Petrov getting gloomier with each bumpy mile they passed. ''Tell me about your parents,'' Eric said. ''My grandparents.''

Petrov's face relaxed, as if he were going through a box of pleasant memories looking for the best one to pick out and show.

''My father, your grandfather, was a great man,'' Petrov began. ''Nikolai Petrov was so great, he did not need to stand out. He stayed with ordinary people and helped them. He was the son of a serf, the first in the family to read and write. One of the few in the village who could. By the time he was fourteen, he was treated like a town elder.

"He was drafted into the czar's army and became a sergeant. He was a hero in the Russo-Japanese War. Several nobles wanted him to come to their estates and train their men, but he refused. He went back to Kaluga. The army had given him a chance to see Russia, to meet comrades from across the nation. Like many others, he could sense that it was time for a change.

"He was active in the Revolution of 1905, and badly wounded when Czar Nicholas's soldiers opened fire on the crowd on Bloody Sunday. He was given up for dead, but a young nurse named Svetlana took a special interest in him and brought him through. Afterward, he took a special interest in her. They were married the next year.

"He had a bad limp, but still he was at every demonstration. He would never take the podium, but he would write leaflets, get the crowd together, stand in front and cheer. Lenin called him one of his best men.

"After the Revolution Lenin gave him a choice of jobs. He became a commissar for the area just north of Moscow. He settled down, and he and Svetlana had six children. I was the youngest of five brothers. Two of my brothers died of childhood diseases, the others fighting the Germans in the Great Patriotic War. I had hoped you would meet my sister, your aunt, but it didn't work out."

"I would've liked that," Eric said. "What happened to Nikolai?"

"Stalin took power and it all soured. Lenin had warned us against him, but Stalin was too strong. Your grandfather disappeared during the purges of 1938. We tried to find out what happened to him, and they threatened to take my mother too."

"Sounds like he was a helluva guy," Eric said.

"A helluva guy," Petrov repeated.

The countryside began to get more and more beautiful. There were fewer abandoned structures, more signs of a healthy economy. They passed huge hydroelectric projects along the Dnieper River, thriving farms with rich black earth, newer vehicles on the road.

Petrov told Eric about his family. There was the black sheep, a notorious train robber; the great-aunt who married into nobility after passing herself as the daughter of a count; peasants who tilled the soil and worked themselves to death. And brave soldiers, loving wives, adorable children.

Eric had never had a sense of family. It was simply not discussed when he was growing up, he assumed because his father's relatives had been killed in concentration camps.

By the time Petrov was done shaking the family tree, the sun was rising and they were on the outskirts of Odessa. They drove into "the pearl of the Black Sea," a major attraction for those Soviets lucky enough to be allowed to travel. There are postcard-perfect views of the Black Sea, a temperate climate, lush green parks, and mud and mineral waters that purportedly have curative powers. It is also a "Hero City," along with Moscow, Leningrad, and Kiev, because of a seige by 300,000 Axis soldiers during World War II.

The town was crowded with visitors, but it was too early in the morning for most of them to be out of bed. Although not as crazy as Fort Lauderdale during Easter recess, Odessa had a wild night life for a Soviet city.

"Stay with me, but walk about twenty meters back," Petrov said. "If I scratch the back of my head, it means something is wrong. Take off and meet me by the car. If I don't show up within fifteen minutes, find Major Ustinov yourself. Tell him your story. Tell him you know about the time he pissed in the commandant's beer. I'm the only one who could've told you that."

"He really did that?"

"He did. And I took the blame for it." The smile disappeared from Petrov's face. "If I drop my cap, come up to me. Act as if you're constantly being watched, because you probably are." He handed Eric a pack of Stolichnaya cigarettes. "Come to me and ask for a light."

He drove to the Krasnaya Hotel on Pushkin Street and parked the car in the lot filled with foreigners' vehicles. If anyone noticed the car, he hoped they would assume it belonged to a Party official having a fling at the hotel.

Petrov put on dark sunglasses and gave a pair to Eric. "Let's go."

The Colonel sauntered down the acacia-lined street. Eric waited until he was a respectable distance ahead and then followed. They walked down Pushkin Street and over to Primorsky Boulevard. Petrov walked slowly, seemingly without a care in the world. Knowing the danger they were in made Eric admire his father's cool facade.

The street was lined with impressive buildings—ornate columns, statuary, and friezes—private residences from the nineteenth century now used as museums and office buildings.

The slate-blue waters of Odessa Bay came into view. They descended a flight of long stone steps. The scent of freedom was as strong in Eric's nose as the smell of salt water. He experienced a strong sense of *déjà vu*. Was it a warning on a subconscious level?

He saw tourists at the bottom, taking pictures, and realized why the stairs were so familiar. The Potemkin Stairs, made famous in Eisenstein's classic film *Potemkin*, in which czarist soldiers massacre revolutionaries trying to link up with mutinying sailors. Eric recalled the famous scene with the baby carriage bouncing down the steps.

One of the tourists turned to take a picture of the harbor. Two *militsia* men confiscated the camera gruffly, growling the words "military security."

Eric followed Petrov toward the water. About half of the occupied berths were filled with ships from the Soviet whaling fleet. Sailors were scrubbing and cleaning the vessels. There were a half dozen yachts, three ocean liners, and a few naval vessels tied up, including a couple of the trawlers notorious for their sophisticated spying gear. One ship had more than fifteen antennae poking from its sloppy decks. There was an armed guard standing by the prow.

Petrov dropped his hat near the statue honoring the mutineers from the battleship *Potemkin*. As Eric neared Petrov, he took out a cigarette, then patted his pockets. Petrov lifted a finger.

"I have matches, comrade, if you have a spare cigarette," Petrov said.

Eric gave a cigarette to the Colonel. As they leaned in to each other, with Petrov cupping his hand around a match, he said, "Go buy a copy of *Pravda* and sit on the bench near the ferry. Glance at your watch often, like you're waiting impatiently for your girlfriend."

"Good luck," Eric said.

Petrov nodded and was off.

Eric accidentally took in a lungful of smoke and coughed. Had anyone been watching?

He got a copy of *Pravda*. The man inside the shipping-crate-sized wooden newsstand had weathered skin and a crossed eye. "Comrade, you like foreign cigarettes?"

"What—what do you mean?" Eric answered nervously in Russian.

"Not our domestic crap," the man said, wrinkling his nose. "Marlboros and Winstons."

"No thanks." He fought the urge to run. "I must go." Eric hurried off.

He looked beyond the chain link fence that encircled the wharf, to the wooden customs house. Was Petrov in a back room, being interrogated? Was the guard on the trawler staring at Eric? Was the newsstand operator a *stukach*, eager to betray Eric?

He was at the bench. Petrov was still inside. Eric faced the customs house and feigned reading *Pravda*. He gazed at the ships bobbing on the water. He fantasized swimming out to an ocean liner, climbing the anchor chain, and sailing to freedom.

Where was Petrov? What could be taking so long? Eric glanced at his watch impatiently.

TWENTY-FIVE

PETROV EMERGED FROM THE CUSTOMS HOUSE WITH HIS "TUN-dra Face" in place. Eric followed him at the prearranged distance. They rode the funicular adjacent to the Potemkin Stairs and walked down Primorsky Boulevard. They doubled back once. Assured they were not being followed, Petrov led him to Deribasovskaya, the busiest street in Odessa. At an open-air cafe he dropped his cap and retrieved it.

Eric joined him at a table. Petrov's hands roved under the table to make sure it wasn't miked. He scanned the faces of the tourists, shoppers, and workers passing on the broad boulevard.

"My friend was recalled to Centre," Petrov said, after the waiter had brought them water, rolls, and a menu. "It's not a good sign."

He picked up the copy of *Pravda* Eric had set on the table and turned to the last page. Important news was deemed "sensationalism" and, if reported, was buried at the rear of the paper. He let out a slow hiss as he read.

"What is it?" Eric asked.

"No wonder. The chairman of the KGB died," Petrov said. "There is no quote from Zaroslavski about what a fine job he was doing. Which means he was in disfavor. Krovili has taken his place."

"What do we do?"

"I had hoped to get you on a ship today," Petrov said. The waiter came and took their order.

"When I was here during the Great Patriotic War, I led a group of resistance fighters in the *katakombi*."

"Catacombs?"

"Caves that have been developed into tunnels. They run for about fifty kilometers, from basements in the city out into the countryside. In some spots they're as much as a hundred feet deep. They've always been used by smugglers." Petrov had a faraway look in his eyes.

"Still, how long can we stay down there?"

"During the war we had several thousand men and women down there for months. There were a bakery, a hospital, arms dumps, machine-gun nests, artesian wells. Even a sausage works, though you wouldn't want to know what went into the sausages. The Nazis tried gassing us out. Hundreds died, but we kept on fighting. More than two hundred thousand Odessites died during the 1941 siege. The catacombs allowed us to hit and run, to smuggle food, to have a place to hide."

"What if they've sealed them up since then?"

"You don't understand the Russian people. We would no sooner alter a war monument than you would renovate the Statue of Liberty."

"But we did."

Petrov smiled, as if Eric had just confirmed his worst impression of Americans. "In your country, you can get all the frills you want. Even your poor have cars and television. But there is no soul. There is a gaping hole in the middle of your sugar-sweet doughnut."

"Then why do your people defect to us? You don't hear of many Americans dying to live in the Soviet Union," Eric said.

"The masses are like children. They'll do anything for toys. They'll eat dung if it is coated with sugar. With socialism, man takes care of his fellow man. We don't have the survival-of-the-fittest mentality that has produced your decadent society, millionaires snorting drugs and driving fancy cars while mothers feed their children dog food."

"Things don't look so peachy to me over here."

The waiter brought their food and both men dug in. It was several minutes before Eric asked, "We can't live underground forever. Do you have a plan?"

"Several comrades in arms from the war still live here. Safe passage can be arranged. Odessa has quite a reputation. Benya Krik, our version of Robin Hood, was based here. The smart players know with connections and rubles, anything can be done in Odessa."

Petrov and Garfield retrieved the car from the Krasnaya parking lot and moved it to the Intourist Hotel. The procedure took over an hour—they had to be absolutely sure the car was not staked out.

Petrov removed a fistful of gold coins from the suitcase and gave Eric half of them. "If you must bribe, pay as little as you can," Petrov cautioned. "If you offer too much, they'll only think you're worth more."

It was late afternoon when they found one of Petrov's old buddies. Aleksei Desnovich lived on the outskirts of town, in a comfortable row house with a small garden in front. The flowers were blooming. Petrov rapped on the rough wooden door.

"Yes?" a gravelly voice bellowed.

"The bear doesn't have trouble finding a cave," Petrov said.

The door swung open.

227

"Anatoli?" the bear of a man inside asked. He looked at Petrov, broke into a huge grin, and swept the colonel into his arms, planting kisses on both of Petrov's cheeks.

The giant called for his wife, Irina, to come out. She was a sullen, pretty woman. "Who is this young man?" Irina asked after they were guided into the living room.

"My son," Petrov said.

Desnovich hugged Eric and kissed him on both cheeks. "I should have known. He's strong-looking. Irina, bring us something to fill our bellies."

Irina nodded and disappeared into the kitchen.

"I saw a couple of articles in *Izvestia* about you," Desnovich said to Petrov. "I'm surprised you can get around, with all the medals they hung on you." They were seated around the table. Aleksei set out bottles of Pertsovka vodka and filled their glasses. Desnovich's massive forearms, covered with tattoos, rested on the table.

"I may have put you in danger by coming here, Alyosha," Petrov said, using the affectionate form of Aleksei.

Desnovich waved a huge hand in a gesture of dismissal. "You want me to cut off my arm, right now, to show you how I feel about you? While the rest of the Ukraine was bending over and welcoming a German dick, you fought back. We'd all be speaking German and goose-stepping if it wasn't for what you did. To Anatoli Petrov. A friend returned," he said, belting back a vodka.

"*Nazdorovye,*" Petrov and Eric echoed, downing glasses of vodka.

"Your father is the bravest man I have ever known," Desnovich said. "Has he told you about the time he single-handedly kept a German patrol at bay for a whole day?"

"*Nyet,*" Eric said. The pepper-flavored vodka had burned a path to his stomach.

"He was always too modest," Desnovich said. "If he was typical, he would've been in charge of the Politburo by now."

"Alyosha, I must confide a secret. I want my son smuggled out of Russia. Can you do it?"

Desnovich nodded. "Sometimes I take off more than I am supposed to. Sometimes I put on more than I am supposed to. But it might cost. Not for me, for the inspectors."

Petrov dropped a couple of gold coins on the table.

Desnovich lifted a coin and tested it with his teeth. "Force of habit," he said apologetically. "It will be arranged." He turned to Eric. "Let me guess—did you knock up the daughter of a big man in the *apparatchiki?*" He grinned conspiratorially.

Irina came in with a plate full of cabbage rolls. She looked at the money, and at Petrov, and left the room again.

"When do you need it done?" Desnovich asked.

"Right away," Petrov said.

"There's a ship leaving for France late today. We'll go to the docks in a few hours when my contact is due on board. It's best to wait for nightfall. Don't worry."

Desnovich launched into accounts of their brave days together. When he left the room to drain off some of the vodka, Eric confronted Petrov.

"Please come with me. You'll only get in trouble if you stay."

"There will be more trouble if I leave."

"But you killed those men."

"I will say I thought they were American spies. They had no business hiding in the woods."

"I can't leave without you."

"You will. Even if I have to knock you on the head and throw your body in a sack. Enough talk."

From the other room, they could hear Desnovich and his

wife bickering. They couldn't make out the words. The couple stopped arguing and Desnovich returned. He proposed more toasts, though something was clearly troubling him.

Petrov and Desnovich talked about former comrades in arms. Desnovich filled and refilled the glasses. They danced the *kazachok* together.

"If you drink, you die," said a drunken Desnovich. "If you don't drink, you die. So you might as well drink."

He insisted Eric take another shot of vodka.

"Food, we need food," Desnovich bellowed. "Irina will make *shchi*. No one makes cabbage soup like my wife."

He stumbled from the room. They heard cursing from the kitchen. Desnovich ran back. "You must get out right away."

"What's the matter?" Petrov asked.

"That whore of a wife of mine. She listened in on our talk. She thought you were trying to trap me. She threatened to tell the KGB if I didn't report you. She's gone out to turn you in."

The gym at the KGB headquarters in Odessa was outfitted with a half dozen frayed mats for hand-to-hand combat practice and a few sets of barbells and dumbbells. Stefan Blok jerked a bar with a hundred kilograms over his head. Sweat trickled on his brow, veins bulged, his breath came in heaves. He had been dispatched to Odessa by acting KGB chairman Vladimir Krovili.

"You are my most trusted man," Krovili had said. He had taken over Levski's office, even before his predecessor was buried. The only changes in decor were the piano Krovili had put in and the removal of Levski's portrait from its place of honor next to Lenin.

Krovili had toyed with the piano keys while he spoke to

Blok. "I want you to go to Odessa. I'm convinced he'll go south."

"Why Odessa?"

"He had wartime success there. Many of his cronies still live or work there." Krovili hit a sour note and replayed a few bars. "Besides, from Odessa you can get to any of the southern ports quickly. There will be a helicopter at your disposal twenty-four hours a day. I will send our number-one *gryaznaya rabota* squad with you."

Armed with AK47s, sniper rifles, electronic-imaging and night-vision scopes, battering rams, rappelling gear, and stun grenades, the squad was the closest thing to a SWAT team that the KGB had. Its members were hand-picked, trained in armed and unarmed combat.

"What do you want done?" Blok asked.

"I'm restricted on this. There are orders from Zaroslavski himself. No one outside the squad is to know Petrov is involved. You'll go to the field office and circulate the photo of Garber. Tell them only that he is wanted for questioning. If you find Garber, you'll find Petrov. If you kill the American, it's no tragedy. But Petrov must be returned alive. We have to know how much he has told the Americans."

"About what?"

"I can't tell you. That's even more restricted."

Blok and the five-man squad had been helicoptered to Odessa, and had promptly thrown fear into the local field men. He put pressure on them, they put pressure on their *stukachi*. There was nothing Blok could do but wait, and so he'd begun exercising.

A fellow KGB officer, stripped to the waist, stood in the doorway, watching as Blok pumped iron. Blok worked even harder. The officer was fair-haired, muscular. Blok felt the blue eyes appraising him.

"Would you like to work out?" the man asked in a soft voice.

Blok set the weights down with a clank. There was a private shower room, with a door that could be locked. He would wrestle with the stranger, let him feel the power in his arms. And then . . .

The squad leader suddenly shoved past the stranger. "We just got a phone call. A man fitting our description showed up at the house of Aleksei Desnovich. He's using the name Konstantin Petrov. He's with one of our military *sosedi*. GRU Colonel Anatoli Petrov. They fled a few minutes ago."

Blok raced to the hook where his clothes hung. "I want every KGB man in the city looking for Garber. If they're assigned to a hotel, have them stand outside. If they're off duty, bring them in. Drop every surveillance on every tourist and dissident.

"The militia is to be notified that Garber is wanted for questioning, along with anyone he may be with. Get the squad and have them meet me in the garage in five minutes. I want two cars and a van available."

"That's going to be—"

"We're here on the direct orders of Acting KGB Chairman Krovili. Make them understand."

"It'll be done," the squad leader said.

Blok turned to the blue-eyed stranger who had been eyeing him. "What's your name?"

"Sasha."

"Come along with me. We'll talk later when this is done."

The stolen vehicle had been discovered. Uniformed militiamen swarmed in the parking lot of the Intourist Hotel. Everyone on the street was being questioned.

Petrov and Garfield retreated to a side street. They walked briskly to the Central Recreation Park. A few lovers were enjoying the blossoming flowers. Near the remains of the fortress built in 1793 there was a metal gate set into the side of a low hill. A heavy chain was looped through the gate's links.

The pick set, along with the flashlight, was in the trunk of the car. Petrov tried the lock. It was solid. He peeled off his jacket like a man about to attempt a feat of strength. He wrapped the fabric around the lock and fired one shot. The sound was muffled, not much louder than a clap. The coat was smoldering from powder burns. Petrov shook off the glowing embers. There was a thumb-size hole with char marks in the middle of the chest.

The lock clung sickly to the chain. Petrov knocked it off and pulled the gate open. After Eric stepped through, he entered, rewound the chain, and put the broken lock back through the links.

A yellowish twenty-watt bulb shone in the distance. They stumbled several times on rocks as big as soccer balls as they made their way toward the light. Cold, musty air whistled down the passageway.

"There's a great deal I must tell you," Petrov said. "First, if you imagine this stretch of tunnels from the air, it looks like a four-tined fork. We are about two thirds of the way down the handle. You want the second tine from the right. It branches again. Choose the right. It goes to the edge of town. The other tunnels either dead-end or open on places where you'll be noticed."

They kept walking, passing the dim bulb. As they proceeded a few hundred meters more, they were in total darkness. Petrov led the way, groping along the wall.

"Listen carefully. At the end of the second fork from the left is the National Museum, a memorial to the resistance movement," Petrov continued. "We must be careful. In places the sewer system runs next to the tunnel. There are pockets of methane gas. There are civil-defense shelters recessed in alcoves, where we can get supplies.

We must have contingency plans. Do you know how to steal a car?''

"No."

"Try to find a Zhiguli. Look for a black wire and a white one under the dashboard. Strip them and touch them together. You should get a spark, and the engine will kick over. Try to get to your contact in Leningrad.''

"I thought he's no good."

"No good is better than nothing at all."

TWENTY-SIX

BLOK WAS INSIDE THE MAIN MEETING ROOM OF KGB ODESSA headquarters. On the grim gray walls were thumbtacked maps of the streets and the catacombs.

Besides the seven KGB agents, there were three anxious civilians. They had been taken from their homes by local agents. The civilians now realized they were not going to be jailed, but they still were shaky. They had provided the maps and answered Blok's detailed questions. One was the civil engineer in charge of the sewage system. Another was the curator of the National Museum located in the catacombs. The third was the local Party chairman.

Blok was on the phone with Krovili, briefing him on what had happened. "A militiaman discovered a lock that had been shot open. We don't know yet if it was Petrov."

On the other end of the phone line, Krovili was sitting in what had been Petrov's dacha. He was like a bloodhound, sniffing the hunted man's belongings to better track him. He sat at Petrov's desk, with the man's file open before him.

"I'm sure it was," Krovili said. "Have you questioned Desnovich as to just where in the tunnels Petrov and he operated during the Great Patriotic War?"

"Uh, not yet."

"Get someone on it."

Blok moved his mouth from the phone and barked a command. Two KGB agents hurried to the detention room where Desnovich was being held.

"The entrances and exits are being guarded," Blok told his boss. "If he's down there, we have him. It's just that there are nearly fifty kilometers to cover."

"I want you to get tracking dogs and tear gas. Have there been any locations in the tunnel where there were major changes made since the war?"

"One moment." Blok hurried over to the maps and gestured the local Party chairman to his side. "Where have there been major changes since the war?"

The local leader pointed to two sites, his finger trembling a bit. He was portly, with a curly mustache, usually known for his bright smile. He was not smiling now.

"Here and here," the chairman said. "Cave-ins. We had to wall off two tunnels. And here. We had to dig deep to build the ten-story building that is a monument to the hardworking leadership of our illustrious First General Secretary."

Blok went back to the phone and repeated what the chairman had told him, without the backpatting.

"Drive Petrov to those dead ends he won't know about. Meanwhile, have someone fly me copies of the maps. I want to be kept posted every half hour. If you find positive proof he is in the tunnel, I will fly down immediately. Don't let those Odessa bunglers know what's going on. I'll send headquarters men.

"Remember, Petrov must be captured, not killed," Krovili repeated before hanging up.

Blok went to the uniform room and found a black jumpsuit that fit his oversize frame. He strapped a knife, modeled on the Fairbairn commando dagger, to his thigh. The foot-long piece of hard steel added to his confidence.

Sasha watched him dress. They rode out to the main tunnel entrance, legs pressing against each other.

There was no prohibition against killing Eric.

Petrov and Garfield crouched in the cramped room. Dim light was provided by the twenty-five-watt bulb out in the main corridor. Crates were piled up, nearly reaching the ceiling. There were cans of food, menacingly bloated or cracked and foul smelling; a crate of flashlights, but no batteries; and a few dented cans of kerosene.

Concealed behind the crates of useless goods were a half dozen newer cartons. Petrov pried them open. Light reflected off the liter-size bottles filled with a clear liquid labeled Narzan. The bottles were cushioned with styrofoam.

"This is not the usual packing for bottled water," Petrov said, unscrewing the lid and sniffing. "*Samogon*. In American you call it moonshine," he said, handing the bottle to Eric.

"Whew. It smells like pure alcohol."

"It's Polish vodka. A hundred and ninety proof. Do what I am doing." He poured out a third of the vodka, refilled the bottle with kerosene, and dropped in a few styrofoam chips. "The lasting monument to our former premier."

"Molotov cocktails," Eric said, as he began to unscrew a bottle. While he poured, Petrov tore up his coat and stuffed the strips of fabric into the mouth of the bottle.

"Do you think we'll need these?" Eric asked.

"I hope not."

They each carried two Molotov cocktails as they continued their flight north along the handle of the fork. At times their path was as steep as an underground mountain. They would be a hundred feet below the surface, and a few minutes later so close to the sidewalk they could hear people's footsteps above them. The floor was sometimes slick with moss, and they had to move forward slowly. They passed numerous holes leading to side passages.

"Where do they go?" Eric asked.

"I never explored them. Many return onto the main tunnel. Some lead to the basements of houses. Others—who knows," Petrov said.

They had traveled about five kilometers when they heard men's boots echoing down the tunnels. Petrov paused to confirm the sound.

"The second passage on the left is our best bet. There are the most exits," Petrov said.

They passed through a crack that was barely as wide as their shoulders—some parts of the tunnels were large enough to drive a car through—and came to where the passage divided three ways. The walls were cracked.

"I don't remember this division," Petrov said, studying the three tunnels. He sniffed the air. "Gas!"

They raced down a corridor and came to a dead end. Running back to the division in the passageway, Eric slipped and fell on a mossy patch. He wasn't hurt, but he had made noise. The sounds of their pursuers grew louder.

Stefan Blok was in a bad mood. The Odessa KGB did not have trained dogs, and he couldn't use the militia's dogs without their handlers. He didn't want anyone besides his squad in the tunnels, and he couldn't wait for the men to be called in from home. To add to his annoyance, the local stock of tear-gas grenades was in sorry shape, way past their expiration dates. The KGB did not have to contend with large demonstrations or hostage rescues on a regular basis.

Behind the fuming Blok was Sasha, armed with an infrared scoped Kalashnikov assault rifle. The five other men, spread out every few meters, trailed. The group trotted down the corridor single file, advancing cautiously.

They heard the sound of someone falling and lifted their weapons. It was Sasha who first smelled the methane and signaled Blok. As they were putting the masks on, Petrov stepped from the crevice he'd been hiding in, lit the Molotov cocktail, and tossed it in one smooth motion. Eric tossed a second.

There were thirty meters between the pursuers and the pursued. The gas bombs landed on damp spots on the tunnel floor a few meters shy of the KGB squad. The Molotov cocktails flared and died.

Blok's squad had begun firing, their bullets ricocheting down the corridor. They were aiming low, to cripple, not kill.

Petrov stepped into view and tossed his last Molotov cocktail. It exploded on a pile of rotted timbers. The well-trained squad kept firing through the flames. The fire gobbled oxygen, and soon a strong wind was whipping down the corridor. It intensified the pocket of gas.

The KGB men kept shooting. Eric was pressed into a crevice in the wall. Petrov pressed flat to the floor, bullets whining over him and ricocheting off the rocks. His leg was twisted under him, and he couldn't have gotten up even if he had wanted to. An AK47 bullet had carved a path across his thigh.

The fire prevented the KGB men from advancing. But the waist-high flames were flickering and beginning to wane.

Petrov was bleeding from his thigh. The bullets stitched closer to him. Eric ignored the hail of fire, bent over, grabbed his father, and pulled him to safety.

The fire began to die.

"Get ready!" Blok shouted to his squad. The men put fresh clips into their guns. The ominous clicks echoed down the tunnel.

The fire was knee high and fading fast.

Petrov got out his pistol with the six shots. "Your only chance is to make it to the farthest passage. When I shoot, run for it," he told Eric.

"No way. We're getting out together."

Petrov looked down at his thigh as an answer.

The fire was nothing but glowing embers. The KGB squad advanced a few meters. Petrov fired two shots, and they ducked.

One of the KGB men assembled a plastic folding bullet-proof shield the size of a garbage-can cover. He set it in front of him and began wiggling down the corridor on his belly. The rest of the squad crawled behind him, like a long deadly snake. Petrov fired one shot, just to keep them from moving too quickly. They had a dozen meters to crawl on the rough, rock-strewn floor.

"Thank you for picking me up," Petrov said to Eric. "In war you would have earned at least a medal."

Petrov shrugged. "It is ironic, isn't it, for me to be killed where I made my first glory? To be killed by Russians." Petrov fired another shot. "All because of a man named Krovili, a KGB pig with an overactive penis. I am sorry I brought you into this mess."

"*Byvayet*, it happens," Eric said. There was no point in recriminations. It was too late for that.

Petrov took the Molotov cocktail from his son, lit it, and tossed it.

The bottle shattered on the cave roof above the man with the bulletproof shield. The burning man stood up screaming, dropped the shield, and ran. He got ten meters before he hit a pocket of methane.

There was a sound like a giant's belch, and then the KGB men were suddenly engulfed in a fireball that raced down the corridor toward Petrov and Eric. The hellish juggernaut filled the chamber with a light as bright as the sun, singeing their hair and eyebrows. A few meters from them it stopped like a wave run out of energy and receded. The KGB men hadn't even had a chance to scream.

Petrov and Eric reached the place where the catacombs divided. "We'll take this one," Petrov said. "A few kilometers more there should be a factory. We can steal a car from the lot and be on our way.''

Petrov yelped involuntarily when he moved too quickly. His wounded thigh nearly gave out. When the corridor was wide enough, they moved side by side, with Petrov leaning on Eric. When it was too narrow, the colonel limped along as fast as he could.

They had gone about a kilometer when they hit the first rubble. A few hundred meters more, and they came to the dead end.

"We'll have to try a side passage," Petrov said.

Eric followed his father into what looked like the largest side passage. Unlike the main corridor, it had no lights. They groped their way along the wall in the darkness. The wall was moist, slimy. At times they had to get on their hands and knees and crawl through spaces no wider than their shoulders. They moved quietly through the gloom, never knowing if they were about to bump into pursuers, hit a dead end, or step off the edge over a precipice. Once Eric banged his head on a jutting rock. He cried out.

They saw a faint glow. Then they were back in the main tunnel.

"We did it!" Eric said in a joyful whisper.

They trotted back to the main division.

From out of a side tunnel stepped Blok and Sasha.

"*Stoi!* Put your hands in the air," Blok ordered. His jumpsuit was burned in several spots, exposing patches of charred flesh. The Makarov in his steady hand was aimed at Petrov's middle. Sasha, who appeared untouched by the fire, trained his AK47 at Eric's chest.

TWENTY-SEVEN

"I'LL TAKE CARE OF YOURS, YOU KNOCK ASIDE THE GUN ON mine," Petrov said in English to Eric.

"What did you say?" Blok demanded in Russian.

"My friend doesn't understand Russian," Petrov said. "I told him to stay still and listen to instructions."

Blok waved his gun. "This speaks all languages."

Eric kept his hands raised, but remembered one of the tricks Bert had taught him—keep the arms as low as possible. The elbows should be level with the shoulders for the best chance at a successful attack.

"Let's go," Blok ordered. "No more talk."

Their feet made splashing noises as they walked through a streamlet flowing along the tunnel floor.

"When I stumble . . ." Petrov began in English.

Blok gave him a crack across the neck with his Makarov. Petrov staggered. Eric went to help him and got a sharp jab from Sasha's Kalashnikov.

"Another word and I break your arm," Blok threatened. "I've had enough of your cleverness, Petrov. If Sasha and I hadn't tried to find an alternate pathway, we'd have been fried in your trap like the others."

They walked down the hall. Petrov exaggerated his limp, then appeared to stumble.

Eric lunged for the huge KGB man, smashing the Makarov aside. At the same moment Petrov kicked Sasha in the groin with his good leg. Sasha tried to use the Kalashnikov, but Petrov got a grip on the long weapon and jammed it into Sasha's stomach.

Petrov's blows were sharp and efficient. The heel of his hand slammed on the bridge of Sasha's nose, dropped an inch, and shoved the bone fragments up into his brain. He was dead within seconds.

Eric rammed his elbow into the weight lifter's abdomen. Blok grunted. Eric threw what would've been a fatal blow to Blok's throat, but the big man blocked it. Blok swung the butt of his pistol and caught Eric's shoulder, numbing the right arm.

Petrov gripped Blok's gun hand and deflected it as the big man pulled the trigger. The bullet that had been aimed at Eric's chest ricocheted down the corridor.

Blok smashed Eric against the wall. He sagged into a dazed heap on the floor. He couldn't get his eyes to focus or his legs to stand.

Petrov knocked the Makarov pistol away from Blok. But when he tried to draw his own gun, Blok disarmed him as easily.

Blok could see Sasha's lifeless form lying on the floor. He forgot about his instructions to bring Petrov back alive. He drew the Fairbairn dagger and lunged, blade held low, almost out of sight, pointed up to do maximum damage to internal organs. But he was facing a man who had an international reputation as a fencer.

Petrov dodged the thrust and landed two punches on Blok's muscular frame. Blok lunged again, the slash narrowly missing the colonel. Petrov was hobbled by his wounded leg, unable to make the movements he was used to.

Eric stepped into the fray, but a swipe from Blok's paw sent him crashing back against the wall.

Petrov kicked Blok in the shin and knocked the KGB man's legs out from under him. Blok jerked Petrov down with him. Blok's powerful arms pushed the blade toward Petrov's throat. Blok bared his teeth in a feral grin.

Eric pulled himself to his feet and grabbed a rock. He brought it down as hard as he could on the KGB man's head. Blok swayed and momentarily let up on the pressure.

Petrov got a grip on Blok's knife hand and twisted. The blade fell. Blok reached and came up with his fallen gun.

"No!" Eric yelled.

Petrov had the knife and a millisecond to act. He buried the dagger in Blok's neck at the same time that Blok pulled the trigger.

The bullet tore into Petrov's chest.

Blok and Petrov glared at each other, both stunned, neither having the strength to use his weapon again.

The colonel had the satisfaction of seeing Blok's eyes roll and the big man fall dead.

Then Petrov toppled over.

"Dad! Dad!"

"Hurry, get out of here," Petrov ordered.

"I'll carry you out. We'll go to a doctor."

"Don't be foolish," Petrov said.

Eric put his hand under his father to lift him up.

"Go! You owe me nothing but to survive. You have my blood in your veins. More of the KGB men may be coming." Petrov shut his eyes.

"Don't die. Don't die. I love you—please don't die."

Petrov's eyelids fluttered. Eric felt for a pulse and found none. He took his father's body in his arms and rocked back and forth.

Eric, wearing Sasha's KGB jumpsuit, crawled along the floor, through a narrow hole in the catacomb wall. The sniper-scoped, night-vision-sighted Kalashnikov was slung over his shoulder.

He moved with the maximum combination of speed and silence. When would the KGB get reinforcements? Or flood the tunnels? Where would he go, even if he could blast his way out? Leningrad? How would he get there? It was a thousand miles away, over unfamiliar roads. A wrong turn and he could wind up in Siberia. Would he be able to steal a car after a one-minute lesson from his father?

He thought of Brooklyn, of the days when his problems were worrying about potholes and community planning board meetings. His mind jumped from thought to thought, from scene to scene, like an unedited movie in a high-speed projector.

A frame froze in place. Benjamin Franklin Sokolov! The man with the meat-pie bribe. His brother was a dissident, a truckdriver in Odessa. He struggled to recall what Sokolov had told him. From his brother's business you could see the Potemkin Stairs. There couldn't be that many trucking companies.

Eric lost track of time. The fire had knocked out the power in many spots. He used Sasha's flashlight to cut through the gloom. Several times he thought he heard footsteps. Once he nearly got wedged in a narrow passageway. He was beginning to think he would spend the rest of his life as an underground wanderer when he felt warm, fresh air blowing across his face. A breeze was coming in from a side passage. He advanced slowly in a half crouch.

He came to an exit. Two militamen were guarding it. Eric kept the gas mask over his face as he approached them. They had their guns drawn.

"What's going on in there?" one of the militiamen asked.

"Fire!" he said, his voice muffled by the gas mask. "Open the gate."

The militiamen had been told they were looking for an American. The figure before them spoke Russian, was dressed in the uniform of the elite KGB unit, and hadn't tried to use his AK47 on them.

One of the militiamen opened the gate. The other saluted Eric. Eric stepped out into daylight.

"KGB headquarters is the other way," one guard said, his gun still in his hand.

"But my car is not," Eric said as arrogantly as he could.

The militiaman shook his head, shamefaced.

Eric sighed like his father as he walked away.

There were three trucking businesses by the harbor within view of the Potemkin Stairs.

"Where's Boris Sokolov?" he demanded at the first he went to.

"He's three doors over," the woman behind the counter said. "Has he gotten into trouble again?"

Eric grunted authoritatively.

Sokolov looked like he was going to hit Eric when he strutted in and asked, "Are you Boris Sokolov?"

"Yeah."

A woman timidly working in the background edged closer.

"I must talk to you. Alone."

"There's only one of you. I expected more," Sokolov said, his fists balled up. "A goon squad was already here. They terrorized my wife. She's home in bed now. This time you're talking to a man."

Eric unslung the Kalashnikov. "I must talk to you alone. Please."

"Please" was not a word in the KGB vocabulary. Boris signaled with his hand, and the timid woman went into the back.

Eric whispered, "My name is Eric Garfield. I'm a friend of your brother's from America. I need help."

247

Sokolov, a stocky man with a stubbled face and a nose that had been broken at least once, studied Eric. "This could be a trick."

"The KGB doesn't need tricks to take you in," Eric said, struggling to complete the Russian sentences. "Benjamin told me about the *samizdat* you've smuggled. Please!"

Sokolov hesitated, then nodded. "My bookkeeper might be a *stukach*. Let's argue. Make like you want me and my truck to go to your station."

"All right," Eric said, suddenly raising his voice and unslinging the AK47. "Come with me."

"Where do you want me to go?"

Eric was careful not to point the gun directly at Sokolov. "Enough talk."

"Feh."

"Move out."

Eric gave Sokolov a shove with the gun barrel. "How long will I be gone?" the trucker asked.

"Shut up," Eric yelled.

With a nudge of the gun barrel he led Sokolov from the office.

"You weren't rotten enough," Sokolov said as soon as they were in the street. "You don't make a believable KGB man. My van's around back."

Sokolov led him to an Ikarus van, a red Hungarian truck with better than one hundred thousand miles on it. Eric got in and crouched low in the passenger seat.

"I'll take you home and we'll talk," Sokolov said.

Sokolov lived way out of town in a house that dated back more than a hundred years. The walls were mud and weathered wood. The garage built next to the house was strikingly modern. Sokolov pulled his van in and shut the garage door.

"I'll go in first and explain," Sokolov said. "If Ludmilla sees you without knowing why, she'll have a heart attack."

Sokolov came out after a few minutes. Ludmilla Sokolov

was a moon-faced woman who looked at Eric nervously. But when she saw how weak he was, maternal instincts overrode her fear. She took him away from her husband and helped him into the bathroom. She was very strong, but her voice was soft, and she crooned to Eric like he was a baby.

"Just you don't worry, I'll take care of everything."

He relaxed in her arms. He didn't resist as she undressed him and eased him into their claw-foot tub.

She wiped his wounds with alcohol, making soothing, motherly noises. It was only when he felt the antiseptic sting on his forehead that he realized he'd cut his head somewhere in the catacombs. The blood had caked into a crusty mass along his hairline.

"Borenka, make tea," she ordered her husband in the middle of her ministrations. Boris complained, but Eric heard him puttering around the kitchen.

She poured buckets of water over him—there was no shower—and washed his head. Eric enjoyed vague childhood memories of his mother bathing him.

"I'll see what I can do about clothing," she said when he was scrubbed.

She disappeared, and Eric lay back in the tub. The porcelain was cracked and stained. He dozed. He awoke to Boris gently shaking his shoulder. His host was holding a hot cup of tea. "Drink," Boris said.

The strong brew was nearly as thick as coffee, so hot it burned Eric's mouth. It felt great.

"My wife adjusted our son's clothing so it could fit you," Boris said, laying an outfit on the straw hamper next to the tub. "If you got caught by the KGB wearing one of their uniforms, they would not be nice. Get dressed and come out. Ludmilla's made you food."

Eric dried off and joined the Sokolovs at their small dinette table. There was a copy of the sayings of Lenin under one leg to make it even with the others. Still, the table wobbled. The noisy refrigerator could've been sold in the United States as an antique.

In broken Russian Eric told them about his father and the ploy that had brought him to Russia. Ludmilla cried as the story ended. Eric fished out the watch his father had given him and showed the Sokolovs the yellowed picture of Petrov and his mother. Eric began to cry. Boris joined in. Ludmilla's sobbing was punctuated by a honking noise as she blew her nose into a large kerchief.

Boris broke the sad mood by asking about his brother. Eric told him how well Benjamin was doing. They laughed together, and Boris recited tales of Ben's hijinks as a boy.

As they spoke, Eric had been wolfing down the kasha, eggs, and borscht Mrs. Sokolov had set out.

"You must travel all the way to Leningrad?" she asked.

"Yes. My contact to get out of the country is there."

"Borenka, can't you get him out?" she asked. "Maybe through Romania?"

"The KGB has my usual routes sewn up tight," Sokolov said. He looked over to see Ludmilla's concerned expression. "But I will get him to Leningrad. It's not going deeper into the *rodina* they worry about."

He took his wife's hand. Boris and his wife looked as happy as a couple in a cigarette ad.

"Could I do this without involving you?" Eric asked, speaking very slowly as he struggled for the right Russian words. "I could steal your truck; you'd report it missing and be in the clear."

"Wouldn't work," Boris said. "They probably have check-points on the road up north. You need me to show you the way."

"You'd better get going," Ludmilla said. "The longer you're here, the more of a risk. I'll go to the office, tell them you're staying home."

Eric kissed Mrs. Sokolov on the cheek. She hugged him so hard he yelped. He dug into his pocket and pulled out one of the gold pieces his father had given him.

"It's a small thanks for all you've done," he said.

She wouldn't take it.

Eric turned to Boris. "Listen, I forgot, your brother sent this for you."

"The only way he would get this kind of money is if he was robbing trucks," Boris said.

"How about for gas? Please, it's the only way I have to show my thanks."

"That's because you're a capitalist," Boris said with a grin. "If you were truly a Russian, it would be understood."

The two men went out to the van. They arranged Boris's smuggling cover—a large wooden crate under fifty-five-gallon drums filled with disgusting, pungent fluid.

"Fish oil," Sokolov said when Eric wrinkled his nose. "Even the most dedicated pissant doesn't want to get close to that. You'll go in the crate when we're passing checkpoints. It'll be cramped. There will be two drums on top, so you'll be stuck in there. I'll let you out after we get an hour or so away from town."

As Eric climbed into the crate, Mrs. Sokolov hurried out with a picnic basket and a few cartons of fruit.

"What's that for?" Eric asked.

"There's an old saying: 'Defend yourself against a robber with a club, against an official with a ruble,'" Boris said. He took the cartons from his wife. "We grow these here. They're worth more than rubles."

She kissed Eric affectionately, and her husband passionately.

"Come back soon, my hero," she said to Boris. He patted her ample bottom.

Eric climbed into the smelly darkness. Sokolov arranged the drums to cover the crate. "Okay?"

"Okay," Eric shouted back.

Then the van started and they were off.

TWENTY-EIGHT

THEY WERE STOPPED AT A ROADBLOCK ON THE OUTSKIRTS OF Odessa. Eric heard the guards grilling Sokolov, who had the proper mixture of indignation and resignation as they checked his internal passport and cargo. The guards "confiscated" a basket of fruit and let the truck through.

They drove northward. Eric was getting stir crazy in the crate. His bladder was swollen to near bursting, and the air was fetid. He kept imagining his father, still alive, suffering in the catacombs. At last Sokolov stopped and let him out.

"We should be okay for a while, at least till the north end of the Ukraine," Sokolov said.

Garfield raced to the bushes. Boris laughed at Eric's sigh of relief as he relieved himself.

Occasionally Eric recognized collectives and factories as they traveled on side roads he had ridden with his father. He wondered how many smugglers, secret policemen, and fugitives prowled the back roads. The Soviet Union is too large for even the most totalitarian regime to control completely.

At nightfall Eric took the wheel and Sokolov slept in the back. In the dark, many of the stretches didn't look very different from roads he had traveled in New England. Eric thought about his fathers.

Eric had to hide in the crate twice more when they passed through risky areas. By the time they were a hundred kilometers from Moscow, all the fruit was gone.

Fifty kilometers from the city, Sokolov told Eric to get back in the crate. "Around the cities they sometimes have surprise checkpoints. We won't go all the way into Moscow. Even ordinary Soviet citizens from other areas can't stay there more than three days without a police pass. But I have a *samizdat* friend on the outside of town. We can sleep there a few hours and get more gas and food."

Eric went into his box, Sokolov set the heavy drums on top, and they headed off. After about fifteen minutes, Eric heard a loud, "Oh no!"

The van slowed to a stop. Eric heard orders shouted and Sokolov getting out. He imagined Sokolov being hauled away, shots being fired and ripping into the carton.

The van's rear door was pulled open and the guards angrily berated Sokolov.

"Your name is familiar," one guard said. "When were you arrested?"

"Never."

"We'll see about that."

Eric heard them banging around the back of the van, opening oil drums. The men made disgusted noises as the pungent smell of the fluid was released into the air.

"Phew! What is that garbage you're hauling?" a guard demanded.

"Industrial waste. It can be refined into first-grade oil," Sokolov said. "Of course, in its present form it's very dangerous. Causes sterility and blindness if you're not careful."

The voices got more distant, as if everyone had taken a giant step backward. Eric heard a guard going through the glove compartment and passenger area of the van.

"Aha, what's this?" a voice said.

"Don't ask me. It's a company truck. Maybe someone left something," Sokolov said.

" 'The KGB is a cancer growing in the heart of Mother Russia,' " one of the guards read in a sarcastic voice. " 'It must be cut out to let the nation grow to the greatness that Lenin foresaw.' "

"*Samizdat*," another guard said, like a Salem priest pronouncing "Witch."

"I don't know how it got there. Just throw that garbage out," Sokolov said.

"Sokolov, get in the car over there," the leader ordered. "You're coming to headquarters."

"What about my van?"

"We're not going to touch that poison," a voice said. "We'll leave the load for the next shift to go through."

"My van will get stripped by hooligans," Sokolov said.

"You'll be back on your way soon enough—we'll just keep you overnight," another voice said, barely loud enough for Eric to hear. "Get in the car before you get in real trouble."

Sokolov sputtered and protested as he was led away.

Garfield, folded hands and knees to chest, couldn't shift to get leverage. He bucked against the top of the box, but the heavy drums on top made it impossible to lift. He strained like a trapped animal. Nothing happened. The cut on his head throbbed. His whole body was feverish.

Though it seemed like hours, he realized it was probably only minutes when he first heard someone prying something off the van. Then the back of the truck was opened.

"Did you get the wipers?" a hushed kid's voice asked.

"Yeah, yeah. Did you get the hubcaps?" another youth whispered.

"Only two. I've been looking out for the guard."

"Don't waste your time. It's their supper break. They always goof off for an hour or more."

Eric heard the scratch of metal on metal as the hooligans pried everything they could from the Ikarus.

"We must have a hundred rubles' worth," one said. "Let's get out of here."

"I want to see what's under the cans first."

"Whew! It smells like low tide at Sevastopol."

Someone climbed into the van. More metallic sounds. The drum was rolled off his crate.

"Whooooooooooooooo!" Eric howled.

A kid screamed, fell over, and then ran from the van.

"Hey, what's going on over there?" a guard in the distance shouted. There was the sound of people running.

Eric lifted the box lid off with his back. He looked out through the windows. The guards were chasing two rapidly disappearing figures. The car strippers had dropped jack, windshield wipers, hubcaps, spare tire, brake-light panels, and assorted bits of vehicular junk.

There were no other guards in sight. Eric sprinted into the woods. Heaving, leaning against a tree, his mind racing, his body stuck in first gear.

Where could he go? Had Sokolov said the name of his friend? Had Eric forgotten it? He'd take the subway to Leningrad. The D train, change at Times Square. Red Square.

He had to keep focused. Could he reach the American embassy and get asylum? He had no identification—how long could it take for the U.S. government to confirm his identity? But would they risk an international incident? Who really gave a damn about Eric Garfield?

They'd been traveling north on the road to Moscow. He was now to the southeast of it heading east. If he could sneak back to his father's dacha, get the Canadian passport he'd hidden, and then make it to Leningrad, he had a chance. As bad as his CIA contact might be, it was his only hope.

He stayed where the woods were thickest. The moon follows the sun, rising in the east and setting in the west, Bert had told him during their lessons on cross-country travel. Look for the north star. Man naturally tends to walk in a circle if he doesn't sight on landmarks. Relax and try to picture the scene when you last saw it. Things register that you don't consciously recall. He searched for anything familiar.

He figured if he was seen, wearing the clothes that Ludmilla had adjusted for him, which were short and tight, and with the scabby cut on his face and the desperate look in his eye, he would look like a down-and-out hobo. Did they have hobos in the Soviet Union? He walked by the side of the road. A couple of times vehicles passed and he hid in the drainage ditch.

He hummed songs to himself. Rock music from the sixties and seventies, Shostakovich, a disco beat, Russian folk songs. He saw people dancing on the road in front of him: Petrov and his mother; Desnovich and his wife; Sokolov and Ludmilla; Sussman and Shirley. He saw a grinning Katya beckoning him to dance with her. She was wearing the John Lenin T-shirt, and nothing else. He stepped toward her, and got thwacked in the face by a protruding branch.

Continuing eastward, he could see the faint light of dawn just over the trees. He had to find a place to curl up. He was exhausted, his body was wracked by periodic chills, and it would be too dangerous to travel by day.

He found a dense patch of beech trees and shrubs and dug what looked like a shallow grave. He lay down in it and piled leaves and branches over himself. All he could think of was sleep.

He awoke with a leaf in his mouth. It was late afternoon. He opened the watch Petrov had given him and gazed at the yellowed photo inside. He thought he was going to cry, but his eyes remained dry.

He dozed and jolted awake a couple of times. His body shook uncontrollably. Twilight was approaching. He was desperately thirsty, but he didn't dare move until it was darker—he heard too many cars on the road, and he wasn't that far from several houses.

Nightfall, and he began his trek. How far did he have to go? There was no way to guess. He came to a stream. His mouth was parched, his face was burning. The water was fast-moving and didn't appear to have any man-made contamination. He sniffed it, dipped his head in, and then took a gulp.

He drank until he could hold no more, then put his aching feet into the cold stream. Did it empty into the lake on his father's property? If only he could become a molecule of water. He imagined himself as a molecule, swept along by the current. Reluctantly, he put his shoes and socks back on and resumed his trek.

He saw in the distance the blinking lights on top of antennae. Where had he seen them before? On the way to the dacha that time with Yuri. He got his second wind.

Hours passed, but each time he saw a familiar sight, it gave him an energy boost. A fork in the road. A boulder in a clearing. A patch of trees that had been burned.

He hurried onward. The dacha came into view. There were lights on inside, a car in front. Someone was living in the house already.

He approached slowly, swaying. He would break in, get to the papers.

He saw Katya. The hallucination didn't fool him. She was leaning against a tree, a wood nymph in blue jeans. She was even more beautiful than he had remembered her. There was a light in her eyes that pulled him forward.

"Konstantin? What happened?"

Why was she calling him by the strange name? She touched his brow. Her hand was as cool as the stream water.

"You're burning up," she said.

He tried to push away the hallucination's hand. It was solid. He passed out.

TWENTY-NINE

THE CIA CHIEF OF CLANDESTINE OPERATIONS SPEARED A shrimp from his salad and slid it into his mouth.

"I thought you'd enjoy this place," Alvin Winters said. "It's off the beaten track, but the food can't be beat."

"Very nice," Tuttle murmured, lifting his glass of Vielles Pierres. "Congratulations. I understand you picked up a few more percentage points in the CBS poll."

"Thanks to the people you recommended. They've done an excellent job. The TV spots were brilliant."

"They had excellent material to work with," Tuttle said, indicating Winters with his wine glass.

"I feel almost like a lover slipping away for a tryst," Winters replied with a smile.

"You know how gossipy people are," Tuttle said. "Which reminds me, how do you get away from your Secret Service chaperones?"

"The same way JFK did," Winters said, giving a broad wink. "By the by, what about that defection you mentioned? How's it going? Of course, if you can't tell me . . ."

"The patient died, but the operation was a success," Tuttle said.

"Can you clarify?"

"We may have succeeded in destabilizing the KGB. We had a Soviet military intelligence colonel named Anatoli Petrov approach us. He requested a certain young man, who had no intelligence background, escort him out of the Soviet Union. We were quite puzzled by it.

"Turned out the boy was Petrov's long-lost son. Now he and the boy have disappeared, Chairman Levski is killed, and we suspect it was an inside job. Heads are rolling at the KGB. It looks like Defense Minister Gorchev and the military are making a power play. Our Kremlinologists are working overtime."

"Petrov and the boy are gone?"

"Disappeared. Dead, as far as we know. Unless they've got them on ice somewhere."

"How were you going to get them out?"

"Through Leningrad. But we pulled in our network. This boy had only a name and location, but it still could jeopardize our man in Leningrad. He's a worthy asset, done a lot of work for us."

"So they are on their own behind the Iron Curtain?"

"Frankly, I doubt if either of them is alive. But even if they crack the kid, it can't hurt us."

"I like your style, James. If I'm elected, I would hope to see more of these kinds of operations. The best defense is a stiff offense, and all that. Let's keep those Commies off balance."

"A wise policy," Tuttle agreed.

Winters was kneading his temples.

"Is everything okay?" Tuttle asked.

"Damn migraines. For a dozen years I haven't had more than one or two. In the past few months, I've fought them off several times. Cafergot and Sansert just don't help anymore. I hate the side effects anyway.

"I tell you, Jim, in the old days people used to choose leaders in trial by combat. Nowadays it's trial by ordeal. I don't think I've had more than five hours' sleep a night for the past three months. I probably haven't been in any city for longer than three days. The incumbent has it easier. His word is law—the press picks it up. I'm just a candidate. The press won't be the only ones who learn a few things when I get into the Oval Office."

"It must be a great deal of stress," Tuttle said soothingly.

"Stress? You want to talk about stress? I built my company from a fly-by-night operation with my own two hands. When the government started intruding in my affairs, I fought back. Well now, I—" Winters paused. "But of course you know about stress. It must be tough on you losing a field man like that. One of the proverbial unsung heroes."

"You wouldn't believe how difficult it is," Tuttle said. "Out there, all alone, with nothing but their wits about them. It's very hard."

"I'm sure," Winters said. "Would you care for dessert?"

There were vague visions of both of Eric's fathers and his mother on a picnic. They were laughing when the Russian Army, led by Bert and the troops in the catacombs, charged across the field. Eric was trying to run to his family, but he was stuck on marshy ground.

Garfield awoke on a soft bed in a strange room. He glanced around. He was in a girl's bedroom, ornate teak queen-size bed and matching dressers, night table, and vanity. Pink curtains, pink comforter, and teddy bears with pink bows. There was a large Oriental rug on the gleaming pine floor. On the night table was a note: *I'll be back soon. Love, Katya.*

It was quiet in the house. Eric dizzily stumbled to the bathroom and looked at himself in the mirror. He had lost a half dozen pounds and his skin was the color of a frog's belly. He had a cloth dressing on his head. He peeled it up. The ugly cut on his forehead seemed to be healing.

He took a few mouthfuls of cold water from the sink. He got too dizzy to stand up. He staggered back to bed and slid under the covers.

His first sight when he awoke was Katya.

"Hi," he said.

She planted a kiss on his lips. "You've been out two days," she said in English as she helped him to the bathroom. "I was thinking of taking you to hospital."

"I can't go anyplace like that."

"I figure as much. But I could not let you die."

She made him a meal and helped him shower and shave. She stroked his head and neck as he told her what had happened.

"I thought I really had control of my life," he concluded. "But then I was manipulated by the government, by Bert, by Petrov. In a way, you could say my parents manipulated me, my bosses, my friends."

"You are becoming too, too . . ." She searched for a word. "Cynical. Life is unbearable, but death is not so welcome either."

"I guess I never realized how easy it would be to be uprooted, programmed, and sent out. I never understood how ordinary guys could become vicious soldiers. It's manipulation and mind games."

"You are only indignant because of your American values," Katya said. "In Soviet Union, you would have learned government has all rights. Over here they say people must be pushed around for their own good. Of course people that say that are the ones doing pushing. You learn to say *byvayet*, it happens. Otherwise you go crazy. You know what happened to me?"

"What?"

"They took me in for questioning," she said. "They

had pictures of us. The KGB said our fathers were planning to overthrow the government together, like military coup.

"They didn't beat me, though they hinted they would. I was stripped and left in bare room for two days. I didn't know what would happen. I was terrified. There were bloodstains on wall. I heard screams at night.

"Then KGB boss came. He apologized for what had happened. He asked me about you." She looked embarrassed. "I told him what I knew, which wasn't much. He laughed when I said I thought you were KGB. He gave me back my clothes, and I was released.

"My father looks ten years older. It was his *blat* that got me out, but he's suffering deep inside that I was jailed and he was interrogated." Katya had begun toying with a strand of hair. "He and mother, they're afraid of things now."

"What about you? Are you afraid?"

She squeezed him as an answer. They hugged for a few minutes, trying to shut out the rest of the world.

"Who's living in Petrov's dacha?" Eric asked as Katya changed the dressing on his wound.

"That's funny thing. The man who was KGB boss moved in. The dachas are assigned by the state. As KGB chairman, he was entitled to much bigger one. But I guess he wanted that one. His name is Krovili. He told me to call him Vladimir Pavlovich. Though he was nice, he gives me creepers."

"You say he is the KGB chairman?"

"He was. He's been replaced. I'm not sure who is new chairman."

"How did I get here?" Eric asked.

Katya explained she had dragged his unconscious body to a car and then brought him to a friend's dacha. The friend wouldn't be back for another week.

"It's dangerous for anyone to know I'm here," Eric said.

"She doesn't know it's you. I told her it's lover my parents don't approve of."

"You've done so much for me, I don't know what to say. I owe you a helluva lot. I feel terrible that you and your family were involved. I hope you realize it wasn't intentional and if there was—"

She put her fingers on his lips. "Maybe it was best thing, my father getting taste of KGB hospitality. It opened his eyes. I always hated the bastards. I just have more to hate them for."

"I must get into my father's dacha to get my papers," Eric said, struggling as he did sit-ups. Katya held his ankles down.

"It will be hard. Since he lost his job, Krovili is in house all the time. He has food delivered. I looked in window. He plays chess with himself. Sometimes I hear piano playing. I think you did enough up-sits."

Eric sprawled. Katya lay next to him.

"You did a great job taking care of me," he said.

"I told you I dropped out of medical school."

"Why did you do that?"

"Being a doctor here is no thrill. That's why we have so many women doctors. Soviet medical system is bad except for *apparatchiki*. Pay is better working as mechanic in subway. Equipment is old, broken. Not enough doctors or nurses, or medicines. Corruption everywhere. My father pressured me to find something else. I haven't found it yet."

"What about becoming my personal physician?"

She gave him a peck on the lips. "How do you feel?"

As an answer, he took her in his arms. They made love tenderly, letting their passions build slowly.

Katya got up before him and wrapped a blanket around herself. "What are you thinking?"

"I was wondering how much longer we could go on like this, and what I'm going to do."

"So romantic."

Again he embraced her.

"I love you," she said.

He hugged her tight. "I love you, too. Can you come to America?"

"I can't leave my parents." She got up and got dressed. "They need me. We've become closer."

"I can't stay here. I must get out of the country," Eric said. "And soon. If your friend drops by for a surprise visit, or the KGB takes you in again, or—"

"I know, Eric, I know you must leave. I've been talking to the *fartsovshchik* who gets me my western clothes. He is very smart in black market. He can help you get out, make sure your papers have right stamps."

"How does he get this stuff? Are there any guarantees?"

"He has contacts in government, hookers on Gorky Street, forgers, connections at airport. There are no guarantees, but he has never let me down."

"Can he be trusted?"

"He doesn't know who I am asking for. He knows you can pay. Gold, American dollars, pounds, sterling. Anything but rubles."

"Can't he get you papers? Maybe you . . ."

She gave him a peck on the lips, smiled sadly, and walked out.

THIRTY

MARSHAL VLADIMIR KROVILI'S BLUNT FINGERS POUNDED THE keys as he tried to immerse himself in Rachmaninoff.

Those stupid mastodons on the Politburo.

"You failed at the mission we assigned you," he had been told. "Petrov is dead. We don't know where we stand. You don't have the modern touch needed."

Whom had they made chairman? That toad Vesky. Krovili understood now how it seemed that Zaroslavski knew his every move. That *stukach* Vesky had been keeping the First Secretary posted. In return, he got the reins to the Committee for State Security. A more subservient chairman than Krovili would have been. Oh, that Zaroslavski was a cunning old mastodon. Krovili had been returned to his old KGB position. But for how long?

The doorbell rang and the tart from next door appeared. She was a trifle old for his taste, but she had a young face and a body that was meant for the bedroom. He recalled the first time he had seen its contours, in the surveillance photos. Then he had savored the entire show, as she was questioned in the cell at Lubyanka.

Now they were sitting on the sofa in the living room.

She was chattering about how nice it was to have him next door, how kind he had been when she was in custody. He knew what she wanted. All these bitches wanted the Little Czar.

"Tell me about yourself," she said. "I heard you are a real hero of the Soviet people."

He told her. Some truth, a lot of lies. She was wide-eyed and cooing. After five minutes she put a record on the turntable and turned the volume up. It couldn't have been any better if he had done it himself. When she screamed, it would muffle the noise.

Eric crept to the side of the house and looked in. Katya and Krovili were sitting on the couch, a half meter apart. Shostakovich's Fifth Symphony was blasting from the stereo. Eric cautiously made his way to the other side of the house and eased open a window. He clambered in.

As he padded up the stairs, he was in full view of Krovili. But the Marshal was completely absorbed in his guest.

In his former bedroom he used a nail file to unscrew the wall plate, and then tried to use it to lift the papers. But they had slid down too low. He forced his hand in. He could touch the edge of the paper, but wasn't able to get a grip on it. He looked around the room for something to help him.

There was a pack of Italian chewing gum lying on the night table. He popped three pieces into his mouth and chewed until they were soft. He hurriedly went through drawers, but couldn't find string. He bent and pulled out a shoelace.

He pressed the gum to the shoelace and lowered the sticky mass into the hole in the wall. With his fingertips he was able to press the gum to the edge of the packet. How many times had he fished coins out of storm drains in New York using the same technique?

He slowly lifted it. For a fraction of a second it hung, stuck on something, then the precious papers were in his hand. He pocketed them, dropped the used gum into the hole in the wall, sealed the panel, and retied his shoelace.

Eric hadn't fully recovered from the infection, and the tension was as draining as a marathon run. He wanted to get revenge on Krovili, but returning to the U.S. and stopping Winters was more important. He swayed at the top of the stairs and looked into the living room.

Katya was bent over the couch, her nude buttocks in the air. She was tied, gagged, and wide-eyed with terror. Krovili, naked from the waist down, was swigging from a bottle of brandy and roughly pinching her thighs.

Eric bounded down the stairs.

The marshal avoided Eric's charge, and Garfield bashed into the couch. Krovili swung the bottle at Eric's head. Eric dodged, but the blow caught his right shoulder. Liquor sprayed into Eric's eyes as the bottle broke.

"Garber!" Krovili said.

Krovili surprised Eric with a punch in the stomach. Eric folded, and Krovili battered him. He got him in a headlock and slipped his wrists around Eric's throat. He was delirious with a manic strength. The man he had been searching for all over Russia had dropped into his hands, the criminal returning to the scene of the crime.

Eric was getting weaker. His eyes burned from the liquor. He struggled against the ever-tightening grip around his throat. The grotesque beast had a crushing power. Eric wanted to give up, lie down. He should've been recuperating, not battling for his life.

"You came here to get revenge for what I did to Petrov," Krovili said, breathing hard. "But we see who gets the last laugh. I will have rid the country of Petrov and his American spy."

The marshal's genitals were waggling centimeters from Eric's face. He grabbed Krovili's balls and yanked.

The marshal yowled, released Eric, and clutched at his crotch. Eric hit him once in the throat, then smashed him to the ground with an *ippon seoi-nage*.

The marshal tried to get up. Eric kicked him in the neck. Krovili stiffened as if he'd gotten an electric shock, then fell back.

Eric untied Katya, and she pulled her clothing on. He held her trembling body.

"Are you okay?" he asked.

She nodded, staring numbly at the marshal lying on the floor a meter away from her feet.

Was Krovili dead? Eric wondered. He'd have to check. And if he wasn't, what would he do? Even if Eric made it out of the country, Katya would spend the rest of her life in a labor camp if Krovili had his way.

Eric knelt. As he felt for Krovili's pulse, a hand snaked toward his ankle. Katya screamed as the marshal grabbed him. Eric fell and they grappled.

Krovili had the jagged brandy bottle in his hand. Eric pinned his hand to the floor. He got a grip on Krovili's throat and began to squeeze. The marshal's face changed from pink to red to purple. Eric held on until he was sure Krovili was dead.

More than Marshal Krovili had died at the Toyma dacha. When Katya came to Eric the next morning, she was as cold as if they had been strangers. She spoke in Russian, and wouldn't talk anything but business. She told him the price her *fartsovshchik* friend had quoted for the necessary paperwork.

"For a thousand rubles you get an exit visa to go with the passport from your father's house, and a suitcase of clothes so you don't look suspicious."

"Why'd you stop speaking English?"

"I'm tired, Eric. Do you have the money?"

He tried to embrace her, but she shoved him away.

"You killed that man in cold blood," she said.

"It was self-defense. After he tried to rape you."

"In cold blood. With your bare hands. There must have been something else you could've done."

"Like what?"

"Maybe I don't know you."

"Can't you understand?" He tried to hug her again, but she moved away.

"Let's make this easier on both of us," she said. "With any luck you'll be on your way back to your country in a day. You're leaving, Eric. Forever. Maybe we could get back what we had if there was more time. There isn't. It's that simple."

Eric wasn't as nervous as he had been coming into the country. Either he made it or he didn't, he thought fatalistically. He accepted the way things were. *Byvayet.* It happens.

The border guard questioned him in broken English. Eric answered in Brooklyn-accented American.

A prostitute had stolen the papers from an American businessman visiting Moscow. Katya's friend had swiftly doctored them and delivered them. By the time the businessman discovered his loss, reported it, and the Soviet bureaucracy geared up, Eric hoped to be safe in America.

He kept the proper attitude of annoyance with the Passport Control officer as the official pawed through the suitcase. It too had belonged to an incautious tourist. The guard found a couple of packs of Marlboros and confiscated them.

"Come back soon," the guard said.

Eric hefted the suitcase and walked down the long hallway. In the distance, a jet engine roared.

THIRTY-ONE

ERIC GARFIELD WAS CONFINED TO A STARK WHITE ROOM, A shielded light fixture and a mirror the only break in the monotony. He could see his stubbly, scruffy self in the mirror. He figured there were people on the other side of it, studying him.

"I want you to tell us again exactly what happened," an electronically distorted voice commanded. "From the time you were first contacted in Brooklyn until you showed up at the embassy in Helsinki."

"No. I'm sick of going through this," Eric said, folding his arms across his chest. "I'm an American citizen. You can't detain me like this." Eric glared at the mirror.

On the other side of the two-way mirror Dr. Attenborough made a note on Eric's chart. Beside him were Tuttle and Wellington.

"The stress evaluator and flutter box show he genuinely believes that Alvin Winters is a KGB pawn," the doctor said. "That doesn't tell us whether it's true or not. A classic story R. D. Laing once told me involved a mental patient put on a flutter box and asked if he was Napoleon. The man, wanting to get out, said no. The detector showed he was lying. It's not the truth, it's what the patient *believes* to be the truth.''

"Of course it's not the truth," Tuttle said. "I've met Winters. He's a fine American. Exactly the sort the KGB would want to torpedo with a disinformation campaign.''

Wellington peered in at Eric. "Maybe we should take a look into Winters' background.''

"The FBI's done that. He passed," Tuttle snapped. "Even the hint we were doing that could have negative ramifications. It exceeds the parameters of our charter. We are better off just neutralizing Garfield.''

Wellington threw him a sharp look. "Kill him?''

"There are other ways to neutralize. We could arrange through our Southeast Asia channels for a delivery of a large quantity of heroin," Tuttle said. "When the Drug Enforcement people find it in his apartment, it'll put them in a favorable light. Garfield, of course, will be discredited if he tries to make any sort of a ruckus.''

"It's a risk subjecting him to additional stress," Attenborough said. "I wouldn't want to hazard a guess as to the effect it would have on his psyche. He has weathered a traumatic period relatively well. I would surmise he has passed through denial and bargaining of the expected responses to grief. He is in the anger phase, with hints of depression. When he'll reach acceptance and hope, or if he will ever reach them, I can't predict.''

"Can you determine whether he's been brainwashed?" Wellington asked. "Is he a danger to Winters? And us?''

"His responses show none of the deviation we associate with hypnosis, psychoactive drugs, or behavior modification," Attenborough said. "I don't think we have a Manchurian Candidate situation on our hands.''

"But you don't know?" Tuttle challenged.

"We never do. There's been a remarkable change in certain basic traits, compared with the psy profile I worked up when you first contacted me. Neurotic response is significantly reduced. There's been a flattening out of his emotional curve. But all in all, he's come through admirably. It would've been difficult to predict that a subject with his background could emerge so well balanced.''

"How can you believe that an utter amateur made it there and back without becoming a KGB asset?" Tuttle demanded. "How can you even consider his preposterous story?"

"I favor releasing him, but keeping him under tight surveillance," Wellington insisted.

Tuttle walked to the door. "Fine. It's your decision."

Through the mirror, Wellington watched Eric. The director picked up the microphone. "All right, Eric, we have your report on Winters. It will be acted on. We'll handle this matter. We don't want you jeopardizing our operation. We want you to go home and recuperate. You'll be getting the bulk of your pay in a few months. Paperwork and all that. For now, a few hundred dollars will be mailed to you. You did a good job and we thank you."

Eric nodded. Sitting patiently on the edge of the bed, he stared at the thin gap in the white that revealed where the door was.

Wellington clicked off the mike.

"Interesting study," the doctor said.

"Very," Wellington answered. His mind was elsewhere. He had heard rumors of meetings between Tuttle and Winters. From his subordinate's overreaction, he now presumed they were true.

Garfield's story sounded farfetched. But was it any more unbelievable than Kim Philby? Or breaching the security on America's atom bomb project? Or the wholesale infiltration of the West German intelligence apparatus? Every institution was vulnerable. Every intelligence agency strove for agents of influence, as well as intelligence gatherers.

As he walked to the helicopter where Tuttle waited,

Wellington wondered whom he could trust to look into presidential candidate Alvin Winters.

Eric was trapped in his rent-stabilized Brooklyn Heights apartment. The CIA had sent him only a hundred dollars cash. His bank account had been frozen, his credit cards canceled. There was a mysterious lien on his money. The bank vowed to straighten it out, but it would take time.

Eric knew what was going on. The CIA was immobilizing him, giving him just enough to get by. They didn't want him to have the freedom that money allowed.

The Agency's presence was as oppressive as the KGB's had been. His phone line clicked and hummed. His mail had a mushiness along the flaps, as if it had been steamed open and resealed. Neighbors shunned him. He had spotted his keepers—there were at least six men guarding him at all times.

He'd jogged the wrong way down one-way streets to lose car surveillants. He'd gone walking in isolated parks. He hurried in and out of crowded department stores. He hadn't been able to shake them. They knew every trick. Of course they did—they had been taught by the same people who had taught Bert, who had taught him.

He gazed out his west-facing window at the Statue of Liberty and the Manhattan skyline. It would be easy enough to do what they wanted. Vegetate. Go back to Sussman's office. Resume his life.

Traffic noise drifted up from the harbor and the Brooklyn-Queens Expressway. Sea planes took off frequently from their lower-Manhattan base across the East River. He wondered what his father would do in similar circumstances. He switched the television on.

"Our top story tonight: Presidential candidate Alvin Winters is the front-runner in the CBS poll," said the anchorwoman. There was footage of Winters addressing a packed auditorium.

"I know about crime firsthand," Winters was saying in a speech to the International Chiefs of Police. "My first business partner, a beautiful, gentle genius, was killed by a robber. I promise you that my administration will crack down on the predators the way they've never been cracked down on before."

He got a standing ovation.

A CBS analyst came on and predicted that with the advancing age of four of the Supreme Court justices, Winters had a chance of packing the court. With Republican control of the Senate, and nearly equal representation in the House, Winters could be the most influential president since Franklin Roosevelt.

Garfield picked up the *Daily News*. There was a front-page photo of a smiling Winters pressing the flesh with a New Jersey crowd.

Eric brushed his hair back off his face. He looked remarkably like his father in the tiny picture in the pocket watch. He had lived through the grief of losing his father. Twice. Why had it happened? Who was to blame? Petrov? Krovili? The CIA? Himself? Could he have been stronger at the outset, refused the Agency's pressure? And what was he going to do now?

His thoughts were interrupted by horns honking and sirens wailing from the street below. He looked out the window.

The door to his apartment opened.

"I'm glad you were able to slip away," Tuttle said, as he and Alvin Winters met near the ruins of Fort De Russy in Rock Creek Park. The fort in the northwest Washington park was one of a circle of fortifications built to protect the city during the Civil War.

"I don't have much time. The campaign schedule is a killer," Winters said with his professional smile.

"I don't know exactly how to say this."

"Come on, James. I regard you as a friend."

"There may be an attempt on your life."

Winters chuckled. "The Secret Service gets a couple hundred threats a day. Lefties, sixties radicals, Communist sympathizers, as well as the usual screwballs."

"This one is different. He's been trained by us."

There was a long silence.

"Sometimes people go bad," Tuttle said apologetically. "He isn't an Agency employee. Strictly a contract worker, with a few weeks under his belt."

"Where is he?"

"Don't worry. We're keeping a watch on him. Over my objections, the director set him loose."

"Why is he interested in me?"

"It's ridiculous. I told the director that, but Wellington actually considered investigating the allegations. This psychotic claims you're a Communist dupe. Something about a fellow named Glenn Kelly in your past. Covering up the murder of your partner. It's really quite an imaginative bit of disinformation."

"Rather than going through channels, I have photos of him I'd like to have you give to the Secret Service," Tuttle said. "You could have them keep a lookout for him."

Winters extended his hand, and Tuttle gave him a five by seven of Eric from the passport. Winters stared at the face. "What's his name?"

"Eric Garfield. It's probably nothing. But I thought I should warn you."

"Right," Winters said, pocketing the photo. "Well, I better be going. Good day, James."

That should assure that Wellington was booted out as soon as Winters took office, Tuttle thought as he watched the candidate walk away.

"Who are you?" Eric demanded, facing the intruder.

The man looked like a frazzled Woody Allen. He didn't answer. He pointed to the walls and tapped his ear. He handed Eric a sheet of paper:

"My name is Deeb. I'm a friend of Bert's. I'm here to take you to the director. We have to get away from the surveillance team outside. No talking. Move quietly. Your apartment is bugged."

Eric grabbed his sport jacket. He followed Deeb into the hall, and they rode the elevator to the basement. They hurried out a side entrance.

The street was crowded with four police cars and three fire engines. The CIA pavement artists were being held at gunpoint, spread-eagled on their vehicles. Deeb and Eric walked briskly down the street. Another CIA man stepped out of a doorway.

"Hold it, what's—"

Deeb hit the man in the stomach, then on top of the head as he folded. The apparent milquetoast packed a knockout punch. They dashed to his car, got in, and drove away. Deeb didn't break any speed limits, but he didn't waste any time.

"What's going on?" Eric demanded.

"A power play in the company. The director didn't want anyone to know he was meeting you. He has a few more questions to ask."

"Where are we going?" Eric asked.

"A safe house. On Staten Island. I've been told about the good work you did. It's a pleasure to meet you." They shook hands.

"Did you phone in false alarms to get us out of there?" Eric asked.

Deeb nodded.

"Clever. Will there be any problems over you hitting that other guard?"

"I didn't really hit him. That was playacting." Deeb changed the subject and kept up a constant small-talk chatter about the weather, sports, the attractiveness of a passing woman. Every time Eric tried to get more information, Deeb would say, "I'm just a messenger; I don't know what's going on."

The forced congeniality grated on Eric's nerves. By the time they drove off the Verrazano Bridge, the hairs on the back of his neck were standing on end. He tried to appear as relaxed as possible as they rode along Hylan Boulevard on the western side of New York's least-developed borough.

He wondered if he should jump out and run. If he was wrong, Deeb would think he was an idiot. It would ruin his chance of talking personally to the CIA director. But if he was right, he could be on his way to becoming part of the Staten Island landfill.

Running was not the answer. Deeb would catch him. Eric remembered Bert's words: "If you go against a pro, give it all you've got. You won't get a second chance."

Deeb kept up the chatter and turned down a smaller street. Eric casually looked out the window. No one on the street. They came to a red light. Eric pretended to adjust his seat belt and covertly unbuckled it.

"I was wondering," Eric began, and then swung a knife-edge hand at Deeb's throat.

The smaller man blocked it quickly. But Eric had been expecting that. He slammed his fist, with all his strength, into Deeb's floating ribs. Deeb's foot came off the brake and they rolled into the intersection.

There was a click, and suddenly Deeb held an eight-inch-long switchblade. Eric blocked the first thrust and pinned Deeb's hand against the seat. Deeb surged at him, but the seat belt restricted his movements.

Then Eric landed a solid back fist against Deeb's temple, stunning the Agency man. A classic uppercut to the chin, and Deeb fell back against his seat. The car, doing no more than ten miles an hour, banged into a telephone pole.

Eric tore open Deeb's jacket. He had a .32 ACP Heckler & Koch HK4 with a short silencer in a spring-release shoulder holster. The gun was Parkerized—a black, no-glare finish from muzzle to stock. There was no serial number. An assassin's gun. Eric shoved the weapon into his belt. He took the wallet. There were two hundred dollars in it.

Calmly, Eric got out of the car and walked up the street. He didn't know whom Deeb represented. The CIA? A dissident CIA faction? The KGB? Alvin Winters? But it didn't matter. He couldn't trust anyone. He had to neutralize Winters by himself.

THIRTY-TWO

"YOU'RE NOT SUPPOSED TO CALL," VINCE PERSICO SAID.

"This is urgent," Winters responded. "I took precautions. There's someone named Eric Garfield who knows about Glenn Kelly. He thinks he's a Commie, though. Isn't that absurd?" There was an hysterical edge to Winters' tone.

"Calm down. Who told you this?"

"The CIA operations chief."

"It could be you fell for a ploy to test your reaction," Persico said. "I'll check into it."

"It's not just that. What if they reopen the investigation of Phil Dector's death?"

"Calm down. Go about your business."

"I have the big rally coming up. I can't take this pressure. What if the press finds out about you and Kelly? If I'm linked to the Mafia, I'll be dead."

"Don't worry," Persico said. "Glenn is gone. I'm your only link with that unfortunate episode. My record is clean. I'm just another real-estate speculator. I've got no arrests, no skeletons in my closet. Just calm down."

"My head hurts so much. I don't need this kind of pressure. I've got enough on my mind. It's not *fair!*"

"I'll handle things. You go about your business. There's only a couple of more months. Relax. We've come this far."

After hanging up on Winters, Persico shut off his video setup. He had been watching a cassette of his favorite film, *Casablanca,* on his six-foot video screen. Sitting on a plush sofa, in his silk robe, sipping champagne, enjoying a good old movie—that was the way to live.

Winters had ruined his mood. He had to get back to work.

The man Winters knew as Persico had been born Krikor Mikhailov. He was a KGB agent who had worked for three years in Italy before being assigned to America in the mid 1970s. He was handsome in a nondescript way, a prosperous businessman you'd meet on the plane and forget by the time you had reached the airport cab stand.

He had been afraid of this all along. But Mikhailov was too good an agent to object. And his future was riding on Winters' fortunes. Mikhailov had a Jaguar, a condo, a ten-room house, and every luxury appliance. There was nothing better than being a KGB operative with unlimited access to funds in a land of consumer decadence.

He put a cassette into his variable high-speed tape recorder and spoke into the microphone.

"Product not doing well under rigorous tests. Shows signs of a breakdown. Some question over whether rivals know about past performance. This is a serious matter requiring priority attention."

He put the cassette into the burst radio transmitter and set the timer. It would be broadcast at ultrahigh speed at exactly 10:53 A.M. If anyone intercepted the signal on its long-wave frequency, it would sound like an electronic burp.

Mikhailov put the champagne in the refrigerator. He got himself a Perrier and a twist of lemon. The liquid didn't help the rotten taste in his mouth.

It really was a pity about Winters.

"Hello, give me Steve Sussman," Eric said into the mouth-piece of the pay telephone. The hairs from the fake bushy beard tickled his nose.

"He's not available right now. Can I help you?"

"Shirley, I need to talk to him. It's Eric."

"Eric, where have you *been?* I've been worried sick about you. You wouldn't believe what's going on. That *meshuggener* they had take your place, he didn't know a bagel from a—"

"Shirley, I don't really have any time. When can I get ahold of Steve?"

"Wait a second. I've been telling everyone he's un-available. He's snowed under. For you, he's available."

"Eric, Eric, I was just thinking about you," Sussman said when he came on the line a few moments later. "I got rid of that other guy. I want you back as soon as possible."

"That's nice. Did you dump him as quickly as you dumped me?"

"Dump you? Dump you? I thought it was understood you were coming back. At a twenty-dollar-a-week raise."

"You must really be in trouble."

Sussman lowered his voice. "I'm up the creek without a paddle. That replacement had a good sense of politics, but no feel for the community. All the regulars did was ask for you. Then they stopped coming in. The guy put together a slick brochure, didn't cost me a cent. But someone broke the windows at Merman's campaign headquarters. Also sabotaged their van. I'm taking the heat for it. I was pretty sure this guy did it, so I canned him. I've been trying to run this show myself. Help!"

"I'll make you a deal, Steve. I want a ticket to the Alvin Winters rally tonight at the Garden."

"What? Where have you been?"

"I don't have time to explain. I want a ticket."

"Done."

"Not a bleacher seat. I want the kind that gets me access to the candidate. You know, like I was a thousand-dollar-a-plate supporter."

"That's tonight we're talking about? How am I going to scare that up?"

"Talk to your Republican buddies from the assembly. Twist some arms. You'll figure out something."

"Okay. When will I see your smiling face?"

"Tomorrow." Assuming I'm still alive, Eric thought.

"Where can I get ahold of you?" Sussman asked.

"I'll call you back."

Garfield went up the broad stairs between the two stone lions into the main branch of the New York Public Library. He requested several magazine articles and books on Madison Square Garden. When they were brought out, he sat at a long table and read.

The Garden is a 20,173-capacity arena, on the fifth to ninth floors of an entertainment complex located above Penn Station in midtown Manhattan. Lower floors include the Felt Forum and the Exposition Rotunda. Penn Station is a terminal for Amtrak and Long Island Railroad trains. Subway lines going in over a dozen directions also stop there.

Forget about that. There was no realistic way he would be able to escape after killing Winters. He had to accept the fact that he would probably spend the rest of his life in prison. Could he really do it? How much was he Petrov's son, and how much was he Raymond Garfield's son? Even the pacifist Raymond had killed when he had had to. What would it mean if a KGB-manipulated man became the president? What about the Agency? Why hadn't they acted? Were they waiting for Winters to be elected, so they could blackmail him with what Eric had told them?

The thought of what he had to do made his heart pound.

He got up and went to the counter where the library was having a book sale. He bought a textbook on mining, the biography of an obscure British politician, a legal text on maritime law prior to 1950, and a directory of New York State corporations, circa 1961.

"You have eclectic tastes," the librarian said as she sold him the thick volumes.

Eric smiled and hurried to the bathroom. He waited in a stall until the room was empty, set two of the books on top of the sink, and walked back a few paces. He quickly drew the silenced H & K and fired at the books.

Nothing happened.

He remembered the safety and clicked it off. He put the gun back under his jacket and tried the move again.

Thpit! The noise was not too much louder than a man clearing his throat. The gun had kicked up, the bullet barely catching the top edges of the books. It bored through the first and halfway into the second. Eric tucked the gun back into his belt and repeated the maneuver.

Thpit! Dead center on the third and fourth books. Of course he was only ten feet from the target. But he hoped to get that close anyway. There were seven shots left in the gun. He had a feel for the weapon's weight—about two pounds with the silencer; the size—he didn't want the front sight catching on his pants; the kick—which wasn't bad at all; and the noise.

The door opened and a man came in. Eric took the four books and casually dropped them in the trash.

John Tustin, the forty-first President of the United States, sat behind his desk twiddling a gold pen. As vice president, he had been a major disappointment. Brought onto the ticket as a moderate influence, the previous administration had allowed him not even the usual ceremonial trappings of power. Stories about presidential abuse of VPs are common—Eisenhower with Nixon, Kennedy with Johnson, Johnson with Humphrey—but Tustin suffered even more than most. When he did get a chance in the spotlight, his bitterness showed, and he came across badly.

So when the previous president retired, forced out by health problems, press pundits predicted the Tustin administration would be lackluster at best. But Tustin returned to his moderate stance with a vengeance, resuscitating social service programs, vigorously pursuing anti-trust cases, and in general undoing much of what his conservative predecessor had done.

Although popular with the people, Tustin managed to antagonize much of the establishment. With the backing of Big Business, Winters had very much become a serious threat.

Robert Wellington finished playing the recordings of Winters' call to Persico and Eric's call to Sussman.

"I hope we're not breaking laws with this taping. Or if we are, that we won't get caught," the president said. "Perhaps we can get Rosemary Woods to transcribe it."

Wellington grinned.

"I suppose it doesn't matter," the president said. "This could never go to court anyway. But if it did come out, the idea of a president using the CIA to investigate his opposition would go over like reactivating CREEP. What about this Garfield?"

"You should be aware, he has a gun. Apparently Jim Tuttle attempted to have him executed. Garfield overcame the assassin and stole his weapon. We found the man in Staten Island, trying to convince the locals not to charge him with drunk driving. He matched up with the individual who knocked out one of our agents when Garfield slipped surveillance."

"What do you think Garfield will do?"

"He's resourceful, embittered, and armed. I spoke to our psychiatrists. They say he might do nothing, he might attempt to kill Winters, he might kill himself."

"Doesn't sound like they were much help." The president dropped the pen and picked it up. He got out a sheet of paper. "Let's look at our options," he said, and began writing. "We pick up Garfield when he gets the ticket from Sussman and force Winters to withdraw from the race."

"We don't have any solid proof against Winters," Wellington said.

"True. How about we let Garfield get to Winters. Let's say he kills him—that certainly would give me the edge in the election."

Wellington looked up suddenly, relieved when he caught the president's wry smile. "The gun is untraceable. If he's caught attempting the murder, however, the whole story of the operation could conceivably come out."

"I think I recall Tuttle from my days with the Company. What did you wind up doing with him?"

"I had him put under house arrest."

"A possible scapegoat?"

"We're getting into a dangerous graymail situation," Wellington said. "Tuttle could be a major embarrassment."

"I could appeal to his patriotic instincts to keep his mouth shut. We do have the secrecy oath to hold over him," the president said. "If we decided to act, how long before you could get agents in the field?"

"I have a team standing by. Depending on travel, minutes or hours," Wellington said, glad that he had come prepared. The nation's leader was known for being decisive, almost impulsive. He was rarely wrong.

The president sat back and stared up at the painting of Theodore Roosevelt on the wall. Tustin had always been interested in Roosevelt. Like Roosevelt, he was a moderate Republican who came from the East Coast establishment, and had ascended to the highest office in the land on the premature departure of a previous president. Like TR, he had stepped on a lot of toes when he entered the Oval

Office, and like the twenty-sixth president, he had found he enjoyed it. He believed TR was the greatest president in this century. His desk was the one TR had used—made from the timbers of a British ship—and he had brought as much Roosevelt memorabilia as the White House staff could muster into the Oval Office.

" 'The nation that achieves greatness, like the individual who achieves greatness, can do so only at the cost of anxiety and bewilderment and heart-wearing effort,' " the president said. "Do you know who said that?"

Wellington, following the president's eyes to the TR portrait, and knowing the president's background, said, "Roosevelt."

The president smiled. "An astute piece of intelligence analysis." He walked to the window facing out on the Rose Garden. Secret Servicemen were planted in the garden like protective bushes. The president pulled the gold floor-to-ceiling drapes closed. He returned to his desk and picked up the phone.

The "hot line" is actually two linked, coded Telex machines. The leaders use it because of the precision of the printed word. But there is a secure telephone line that can be used for less formal contacts.

Despite his years as the chairman of a multinational corporation and at the highest levels of government service, Wellington felt a chill. Although the motions were the same as for the most casual phone call, even the president seemed tense as he lifted the handset to his mouth.

The president was connected with Soviet First General Secretary Zaroslavski. They made innocuous small talk, comparing notes on their families and party politics. The chitchat took the edge off. It was obvious the president had not called to say that a nuclear warhead had accidentally been launched. There was a few seconds' delay each time the conversational ball shifted back and forth, so the highest security translators could accurately interpret the words.

"We have an interesting situation here," the president began, his voice turning serious. "Would you know of a fellow named Persico? Lives in Detroit. He's an old friend of my political rival, Alvin Winters."

"Detroit is a big city, is it not?" Zaroslavski responded. "Why do you ask?"

"Well, we got wind of a fantastic plot. Frankly, it doesn't have your touch to it, but we're certainly going to look into it. Seems that Persico is controlling Winters." The president gave a dry chuckle. "If the American people thought for one minute the Soviet Union had tried something like that, well, I don't think it would go over too well."

Zaroslavski coughed. "You're right. It is a fantastic tale."

"If Winters were to drop out, I don't see any need to take this matter further."

"Your American politics are so intriguing," Zaroslavski said.

"Well, we never had a Catherine the Great or a Rasputin. But we try."

"I appreciate your calling to tell me this story," Zaroslavski said. "I'm curious. You said this fantastic plot does not have my touch to it. What would have my touch?"

"Oh, some sort of incident stirred up between us and the People's Republic. We fight it out and you pick up the pieces."

Zaroslavski laughed and then lapsed into a coughing fit. "The peace-loving Soviet peoples want only to achieve international communism through mutual acceptance."

"Sure, and General Motors doesn't care about making a profit."

"Which reminds me, there are certain trade restrictions I wanted to discuss."

"I tell you honestly, this Winters thing weighs on my mind. Perhaps when it is cleared up, I'll be able to concentrate on other matters."

"I understand," Zaroslavski said.

"I am sure you do."

Persico decoded the emergency contact message from Moscow. "Withdraw the product and return to Centre immediately."

Much as he hated to, he had to use the telephone. He dialed the private line of Winters' New York City campaign headquarters. He used an illegal black box, which tapped into a toll-free line. Not only did the device cheat the capitalists, but it made sure there was no record of the call on his phone bill.

Persico used the emergency code name that brought Winters right to the phone.

"You must withdraw from the race," Persico ordered.

"You're kidding!"

"Something has come up."

"You can't do this to me. It's not right."

"Don't make me warn you."

Winters exploded. "I've worked too hard. You rotten guinea bastards aren't going to play games with me. America needs me. I'm in for the duration."

Winters slammed down the phone.

Persico knew there was no point in calling back. He removed his passport and several thousand dollars in cash from the hidden strongbox. It had to look like he was just stepping out, as Burgess and Maclean had when they fled to Russia after betraying Britain. He'd have to leave his custom-tailored wardrobe and state-of-the-art appliances behind.

He hurried into the bedroom and put his Rolex on one wrist, gold ID bracelet on the other. Gold rings went on four of his fingers. He chose his best silk shirt, custom suit, and five-hundred-dollar ostrich-skin boots. He filled an attaché case with more finery, and tossed the cash and the passport on top.

The KGB agent had chosen Detroit because the Canadian border was just a cab ride away. He hurried downstairs. He hailed a taxi and hopped in. "Windsor Airport please. I'm in a rush."

"Sure enough," the cabbie said, and stepped on the gas.

They got stuck in traffic. The doors on either side of the cab opened suddenly. The cabdriver spun around, a dart gun in his hand. The men on either side grabbed Persico's arms. The dart stung his neck.

"Is this really necessary?" he asked, and then passed out.

Eric stopped in a theatrical supply store near Times Square and bought plastic putty, clear spectacles, and makeup. At a hardware store he purchased a wallplate-sized magnet and an indelible black Magic Marker. He went to a uniform supply store and bought a deliveryman's outfit.

He disguised himself in the bathroom of a Thirty-seventh Street bar. He attached the magnet to his gun and wandered over to Madison Square Garden. The building looked like a giant drum with a tan, precast concrete skin.

He studied the model of the huge auditorium set up in front of the ticket booths. It didn't show the interior or service corridors, just the red, orange, yellow, green, and blue seating areas.

For an hour he lounged across the street, nursing coffee, apparently girl watching, a typical loafer. The sky was clear, a warming breeze blew, and the air seemed to have been imported from Vermont.

A service road on Thirty-third Street led to a twelve-foot-four-inch-high trailer-truck ramp. Shorter trucks were driven right inside, where an elevator lifted them to the arena.

There was a steady stream of trucks. Deliverymen were carrying in miles of bunting, boxes of balloons, and a quarter ton of confetti. Workers unloaded liquor cartons and kegs of beer. Caterers brought truckloads of food.

When they began wheeling in carts from Zanville's, a chic West Side deli, Eric made his move. This was not food that would be left out for the hordes. It would be put where the inner circle hung out.

Eric helped a worker hump a waist-high Zanville's metal cart over a bump. While they waited to be checked in at the door by an officious man holding a clipboard like a shield, Garfield talked to the appreciative worker about getting a job at the deli. As he spoke, he took out the Magic Marker and made a mark on the corner of the cart.

Eric bent to tie his shoelace, his movements blocked by the bulk of the cart. He slipped the gun under the bottom, and felt the magnet bond to the metal.

Garfield chatted for a few minutes on how hard it was to get a job. When they were the next to see the officious man, Eric began his good-byes.

"You come by the deli sometime, I get you a free sandwich," the worker said. "See if you can talk to the boss."

"That's great. Thanks," Eric said, and wandered away.

Alvin Winters had locked himself inside a storage closet at campaign headquarters. He refused to talk to his wife or top aides. He paced in a tight circle, surrounded by steel shelves stacked with paper goods. Outside, his aides pressed their ears to the door. They murmured among themselves, unsure what to do.

Winters slammed his fist into his hand. "Sonofabitches. The president must've gone to bed with the spaghetti benders." He felt a tremor of nausea and the flashing lights that warned of pain to come. "Who's going to believe them anyway if they come up with an old piece of paper? A forgery. Experts will say so. They can't control me.''

Aides knocked on the door.

"Go away!" he yelled, and kicked the door. He paced some more.

Suddenly he knew what he could do. In his speech he would attack the mob, vow to smash organized crime. If they brought up his past, he would dismiss it as a crude smear.

The migraine precursors disappeared. He adjusted his tie. He would be the best damn president the country had had, waging a simultaneous war against Commies and mobsters. He would find his own J. Edgar Hoover, maybe that CIA man Tuttle, and get America back on the right track.

He unlocked the door. A half dozen people were anxiously staring at him. He gave his wife an affectionate peck on the lips.

"What's everyone dawdling for? Let's get this show on the road. We have only a few hours until the rally.''

THIRTY-THREE

THE PRESIDENT'S "MOLE" IN THE WINTERS' CAMPAIGN HAD RE-
layed details of Winters' strange behavior minutes after the
challenger had emerged from the closet. The president had
immediately summoned the CIA director from Langley.

"Just what we need, Joan of Arc for president," Wellington said after hearing the details.

"This job can make a sane man nuts. God only knows
what it will do to a fruitcake. What's been happening on
the Eastern front?"

"We snatched Persico. One of his coat buttons contained enough cyanide to kill three people. He's a tough
nut to crack. We've given him the maximum tolerable
dose of the new Pentothal derivatives. His name is
Mikhailov, but we still haven't gotten him to admit to his
mission. There's nothing evidentiary in his apartment."

"And Garfield?"

"We have a phone intercept on Sussman. Eric gave him
elaborate instructions for a rendezvous at the Atlantic Avenue subway station. To reel him in, overtly, would be easy
enough, but we'd need a small army for a covert surveillance."

The president toyed with his pen. "I could blow this conspiracy up in Zaroslavski's face. But I don't want to sit on top of a country screaming for war. Politically, it could be as dangerous confronting Winters." The leather chair squeaked as the president leaned back and pondered the options. "Okay," he finally said. "We let Garfield go ahead with getting the ticket. We let him get to Winters."

"You're going to let him kill Winters?"

"I'm going to have the Secret Service set up metal detectors at the door. Redouble security. I want to see what Garfield plans. Let him rattle Winters' cage. For Garfield's sake, I hope he doesn't show up there with that gun."

Eric wore a navy-blue blazer, white shirt, khaki slacks, and a red tie. His hair was darkened and brushed back, the way his father had had it. He looked very much the young Republican and fit in with the crowds surging along the mall into Madison Square Garden.

Busloads of teens had been brought from up and down the East Coast. Elderly shut-ins were driven up in specially equipped vans. Clean-cut, suited men and well-coiffed women in evening gowns arrived in limos. Celebrities were flown in from California. The air was thick with exuberant confidence, a championship team going into the playoffs.

"Al-vin, Al-vin, Al-vin," the crowd chanted.

Miles of red-white-and-blue bunting rippled in the air-conditioned breeze. Helium balloons bobbled above the heads of the crowd. Bags of confetti were distributed and tossed. Forty forty-foot portraits of a smiling Alvin Winters hung from the sixty-eight-foot-high ceiling.

"Al-vin, Al-vin, Al-vin."

Thousands unable to get in pressed against the blue "Police Line" sawhorses outside. As TV cameras panned the capacity crowd, the noise grew louder. It was like a revival meeting and rock concert combined.

"Al-vin, Al-vin, Al-vin."

Eric passed through a metal detector without it whining. He showed his restricted-access ticket to a perky blonde who cooed over it and insisted on pinning the special pass on Eric's blazer. At the second security check a Secret Service man brushed a metal detector over him, then passed him through.

The select crowd was more dignified: pearls and gowns on the women, dark three-piece suits on the men. Eric was one of the youngest people. He nursed a scotch and made small talk with the heavy hitters, major contributors to the Winters campaign. He buttonholed a Winters aide and mentioned his desire to donate more money.

"Between me and my company, you can figure us for another thirty thou," Eric said. "There's financial disclosure laws we'll have to skirt, since I've already put in the legal limit."

"I'm sure our comptroller can work out something," the aide said cheerily.

"I'm sure he can too," Eric said, winking at the young woman. "I'd like to speak to Al personally beforehand."

"After his speech there'll be a reception."

"I need to speak to him now."

"That's not possible."

"Try. Tell him Glenn Kelly Junior is here and needs a minute of his time."

The aide hurried to the smaller hospitality room where Winters and his inner circle had established their camp.

"Are you sure you're up to going out, honey?" his wife asked. They were alone in one of the dressing rooms. A string of hundred-watt bulbs around the makeup mirror made it as bright as midday in the Mojave.

"I have never felt better," Winters said truthfully. He

gave his petite wife a peck on the lips and whispered in her ear. "The only thing I'd like to do more than go out and mingle is haul you into a closet and ravage you."

She giggled. She had a charming giggle, and it added to his excitement. She said, "How does it feel to be so perfect?"

"Can you imagine making love in the White House?"

"Constantly."

"I hope I have time for affairs of state."

"You won't have time for any affairs," she said.

They kissed, and he gave her a wink and opened the door. There were about a dozen people in the room, top campaign coordinators, administrators, and organizers. A pair of Secret Service men stood by the entrance.

Through the open door came the sound of the chatter of heavy contributors, and beyond them the roar of the workers, volunteers, and assorted supporters out in the main hall. "Al-vin, Al-vin, Al-vin."

"Gentlemen, gentlemen," Winters said to his inner circle. He winked at the two women who were high in his campaign. "And ladies. I want to thank you for the absolutely outstanding work you've done. You have my undying appreciation. Soon the nation will appreciate your long hours and hard work in the trenches."

The people in the room applauded. He worked the crowd, radiating warmth and charm. Between the pleasantries and the pep talk he got updates on media coverage, event timing, and honored dignitaries who were in the audience.

An aide handed him a note. His wife noticed the way he patted his left temple.

"Are you okay?" she whispered.

"There's someone I have to see."

The Secret Service men followed Winters' every move, like faithful dogs just before their mealtime.

"You boys go and have a drink. I'll be fine," Winters said. "There's someone I have to speak to privately."

"We have orders to stay right with you, sir," the senior man said.

Winters patted him on the shoulder. "I like a man who knows how to follow orders. I also like a man who shows a little imagination. I tell you what—I'll go off in the corner and speak with this person. You can keep an eye on us while I talk to him. That sound fair?"

The agents exchanged a look, and the senior man nodded.

Winters signaled for the aide to go and get "Kelly."

Eric hurriedly buttoned his jacket as he saw the aide approaching, beaming with self-importance. He knew the answer before she opened her mouth.

"Mr. Winters will see you," she said.

"Thanks a million. I knew you could do it," Eric said with an appropriate smile. He was led down a narrow, fluorescent-lit corridor. The huzzah of the crowd reverberated off the cinder-block walls.

"It's a great moment, isn't it?" the aide asked.

"Yes." Eric unconsciously adjusted his tie and collar. He was meeting an important man. He had to look right. His hand was still fiddling as he was admitted into the hospitality area.

It was a thirty-foot square, with a bank of phones on a table on one side and a buffet table on the other. There were empty coffee cups and full ashtrays everywhere. On the wall, charts and graphs.

Eric easily spotted the Secret Service men. Both wore dark suits, walkie-talkie earplugs, and emotionless expressions. They appraised him as he entered.

It seemed that everyone was watching him, as if they knew what he had in mind. But it was just the attentiveness of insiders, wondering who was getting or giving favors. What connection did he have with Winters?

Winters feigned indifference. The man who would be president was talking to his media consultant about a new television commercial. The ad featured a Russian bear mauling the American flag.

"I want to do something blasting the Mafia," Winters was saying. "They make good villains. Maybe dealing drugs to children in the school yard or forcing young women into white slavery."

"No offense, sir, but that's a trifle cartoony," said the consultant, a portly man with a neatly trimmed beard.

"I'm talking symbolically. You know what I mean. Keep 'em entertained," Winters said. "What am I telling you that for? That's like me telling Shakespeare how to write." He gave the consultant a friendly pat, then pretended to see Eric for the first time. He gestured for Eric to approach as the consultant moved off.

Eric kept his gestures slow, his movements easy. No point in getting the watchdogs' adrenaline up. He was three feet from the candidate. The Secret Service men were about seven feet off to Eric's right. On the other side a few aides were clustered about fifteen feet away, reviewing a computer printout.

"It's a pleasure to meet you, young man," Winters said, taking Eric's hand with a two-handed political grasp. "I'm very fond of your father. How is he?"

Eric's resemblance to his father was having its effect. The candidate's gaze kept sweeping over Eric's features. He had trouble meeting Eric's eyes.

"He was murdered a few days ago," Eric said coldly.

Winters put his arm across Eric's shoulder and guided him into the corner. The Secret Service men sidled closer.

"Occupational hazard, I suppose. I am sorry to hear that. I liked him much better than Persico."

"Who?"

"Don't play coy with me, kid," Winters whispered. "I know Persico must've given a report to his capo. They sent you, counting on old times' sake. Well, it doesn't work." Winters' voice was a low growl. But his friendly posture made it impossible for anyone watching to realize what was being said. "Your grease-ball buddies tried to get me to pull out already. Why'd they send a punk like you here? I told them I'm in."

Eric had seen that look before. The political animal. The scent of power as stimulating as fresh blood to a leopard, the roar of the crowd as deliciously maddening as chum to a great white shark.

"Forget about any message to drop out," Eric said, his voice growing husky. "There's been some confusion within the organization. That's why my father, the don, was murdered. He had a lot of respect for you, and what you could do for us." Eric hoped he wasn't sounding too much like Marlon Brando as Don Corleone. "I came here to make peace. You will have our continued help. And guidance."

"What do you mean, guidance?"

"We've been carrying you all these years, Al," Eric said, getting into the role. "The gun, the confession, they've been sitting in the vault, earning interest."

Winters' face was pale, Faust just learning whom he'd made his bargain with. "What do you want?"

"The family has ideas about who'll be a good Secretary of Labor, of the Treasury, and especially the Justice Department."

"You can't force me into anything."

"Al, everybody's vulnerable. There's *paisani* who wanted to whack you out. Remember JFK."

"You—you people really did that?"

"You think it's a coincidence Valachi started squealing, Bobby Kennedy's busting our balls, and a month later JFK gets blown away?" Garfield said.

Winters rubbed his left temple. "You can't scare me. You're lucky I didn't give the Secret Service the pictures Tuttle gave me, or you'd be in prison right now."

"I'm not trying to scare you, Al," Eric said, not understanding what Winters was talking about but not wanting to lose momentum. "We want you just where you are. As long as you know who put you there. You figure you're safe right now. Don't you?"

Winters nervously scanned the room, looking for a hostile face. He turned back to Eric. "What do you mean?"

The Secret Service men had been intently watching the strained conversation. They moved a few steps closer.

"Come with me," Eric said. "Just over to the buffet. But first, why not clear this place? The show should be starting soon."

Winters nodded. Eric could feel him falling under control. "Friends, friends," Winters said. He didn't need to shout. Everyone had been watching his conversation with the mysterious young man. "It's time to join the loyal masses," he quipped. "I'll be out in a few minutes."

"I'll stay with you," Winters' top aide volunteered.

"Get outside," Winters barked.

The aide looked at him questioningly, then left. The only ones besides Eric and Winters were the candidate's wife and the two Secret Service men.

Eric led Winters to the buffet. "You're saying someone could poison me? I can get a food taster."

They came to the marked cart. "The Secret Service, they go over an area pretty good," Eric responded. "Bomb-sniffing dogs, background checks, the whole shebang. But nobody's perfect. Do me a favor, reach down under the corner there and see what you feel."

"This is ridiculous."

"Do me a personal favor. For my old man's sake."

Winters knelt and felt under the cart. He pulled the gun out and held it in his hand, staring at the all-black, silencer-equipped assassin's gun.

The Secret Service men slammed Eric against the wall and frisked him.

"No weapon," one said, while the other snapped cuffs

on Eric's wrists. Winters' wife tugged at her horrified husband, guiding him away.

The Secret Service men each kept a hand on one arm as they led Eric down the hall. The senior agent recited the Miranda-warning litany.

Garfield was spirited down a service corridor and loaded into a van. He was transported to the federal detention center in lower Manhattan. He declined to make any phone calls. There was no one he wanted to speak to. His rights were read to him again. A Secret Service man began to question him, but he refused to talk.

A speaker in the wall played rock music. Eric stared at the chipped blue paint on the cell door.

The music was interrupted at 9:56 P.M.

"We take you now live to the Alvin Winters rally at Madison Square Garden, where Juan Palomo has the report," the announcer said.

A new voice came on. In the background a tumultuous crowd could be heard. "The mood is ugly here tonight after Alvin Winters' speech. From the moment he took the stage, it was clear something wasn't right. He kept anxiously scanning the crowd, as if he was looking for someone. When a balloon broke, he ducked behind the podium. Then came this shocking moment."

Winters' voice came through the jail speaker. "My administration will sweep organized crime out from under the rocks where they hide. They're trying to get me and ruin America. But they won't. We will persevere. The lights are too bright. Ahhh. Turn them down." There was the sound of a crash.

"The noise you heard was Winters knocking the microphone to the floor," Palomo said. "He began clutching his head, and was helped from the stage by two aides. I'll be going out into the crowd now to get the reaction to this startling development. Back to you, Dave."

"Thanks, Juan. We have in our studio political analyst Dr. Randall Rothenberg. Dr. Rothenberg, what does it all mean?"

"Well, it reminds me of then-presidential candidate Muskie breaking down in tears. There have been rumors that Winters' health is not all it should be, but his staff has succeeded up to now in convincing everyone he was fine. You might recall the complete check-up and bill of good health he got recently. The question everyone will be asking is, 'Is Alvin Winters in sound-enough shape to be in the White House?' I think you'll find . . ."

The radio was shut off for the night. The lights in the cell also went off automatically. A dim bulb burned in the hallway outside the cell.

A few hours later, a guard opened the door.

"You're free to go. No charges are being pressed," the guard said as Eric was led to the property room. He retrieved his belt, shoelaces, and valuables.

The streets of lower Manhattan were quiet. Eric walked over the Brooklyn Bridge. He paused in the middle of the span and gazed at the lights of the city reflecting off the dark waters of the East River.

EPILOGUE

THE DAY AFTER WINTERS' COLLAPSE AT THE RALLY HE DROPPED twenty-five percent in CBS and Gallup polls. *The New York Times* and Harris polls showed him losing only twenty percent. There were conflicting statements from the Winters campaign as to whether he would remain in the race. Unnamed sources in the Democratic party vowed they were behind him a thousand percent. Other unnamed sources said the senior Senator from Pennsylvania, who had previously withdrawn from the race, was being groomed as a last-minute replacement candidate.

There was a slew of polls, vicious infighting, and a hurried primary. The divisive atmosphere at the nominating convention did nothing to help the Democratic cause. The Pennsylvania senator emerged triumphant, but not unscarred.

Winters refused to drop out, and ran as an independent, splitting the vote with the senator. Winters and the senator combined got less than forty percent of the vote.

In Brooklyn, Assemblyman Steve Sussman became Congressman Steve Sussman with eighty-nine percent of the vote. His was traditonally a Democratic district—and he had been expected to win—but his victory was by the greatest margin in the district's history.

His administrative aide, Eric Garfield, had said that he would resign immediately after Sussman was elected. But the fledgling congressman convinced Eric to come with him to set up the Washington, D.C., office.

Sussman had a knack for getting bipartisan support for his ideas. He was awarded membership on the prestigious Ways and Means Committee and a large suite in the Longworth House Office Building. He and Eric were invited to all the right parties. *The Washington Post* did a major profile of the congressman. A key housing bill with Sussman's name on it was signed into law.

Eric didn't really know what he wanted to do. He brooded about Russia, and of the living and the dead he had left there. Katya occupied nearly as many of his memories as his father. There was so much he should have said to both of them, but hadn't.

Eric earned a reputation as an unsmiling workaholic. Sussman tried to cheer him up—arranging blind dates, taking him to important functions, sending him on junkets. But Garfield would flash back to visions of his father, lying dead in the catacombs. And Katya, what had nearly happened with Krovili, and what could happen if the KGB found out about her helping him. Despite his position of power and respect, the thoughts made him feel helpless.

Alvin Winters was indicted on twenty-seven counts of campaign-funding irregularities. It only added to Eric's depression when Winters pleaded guilty to one count, and got off with four months in jail.

Six months after Sussman became a congressman, he and his aide were summoned to the White House for a private meeting with the president.

They were ushered into the Oval Office separately.

Sussman went first, and came out glowing like a Medal of Honor winner. Then the White House usher led Eric in.

"I've heard a lot about you," the president said, rising from behind his desk to shake Eric's hand. "From Robert Wellington. Your contribution to the nation's security is recognized and respected."

"Thank you."

"I know you've had a difficult time. As Theodore Roosevelt said, however, 'The democratic ideal must be that of subordinating chaos to order, of subordinating the individual to the community, of subordinating individual selfishness to collective self-sacrifice for a lofty ideal, of training every man to realize that no one is entitled to citizenship in a great free commonwealth unless he does his full duty to his neighbor, his full duty to his family life, and his full duty to the nation.' "

"But what if they conflict?" Eric asked.

Tustin was silent for a moment, then burst out laughing. "As TR would say, bully. It's not often anyone questions me when I get long-winded. I used to memorize TR the way some swains do poetry. Not as effective for romancing the ladies, but they do make great conversation stoppers.

"I told Steve he has senatorial potential. I made it clear that's only if you remain his aide. If you do leave him, let me know. We can always use someone of your abilities around here. Perhaps as a general troubleshooter. Maybe you'd prefer to work for the Agency?"

"No sir."

The president took a copy of *The Words of Theodore Roosevelt* from his desk drawer and presented it to Eric. Inside, he had inscribed, "To the kind of man TR would have approved of," and signed his name.

"Read it," the president said. "It's uplifting without being hokey. 'It is hard to fail, but it is far worse never to have tried to succeed.' "

"Thank you." Eric's expression remained unchanged.

"I know what happened in Russia, and I'm sorry. But I do have good news that might brighten your day." He tapped his fingers against the desk, letting Eric wait.

"We recently had a major defection. It's been hushed up until this general was sufficiently debriefed. He provided reams of valuable details about the Soviet order of battle in the event of a conventional war.

"This general insisted on bringing his whole family with him. It was quite a tall order, but apparently well worth it. The DIA and the CIA pulled off a first-rate joint operation. A small plane picked them up and flew them under radar to Turkey. I shouldn't say more—it's still very classified. But I presume you'll get the details."

Eric didn't understand why the president was telling him this. "That's nice," he said politely.

"The general's name is Vasilev."

Eric ran and hugged Tustin, who responded awkwardly. Then Eric realized what he had done and jumped back. "Sorry, sir."

The president laughed. "You better save your affection. Your gal's been making quite a fuss, demanding to see you. She's at a safe house about fifteen minutes from here. There's an unmarked car at the entrance by the north portico. The driver is cleared. You better get there before she causes an international incident."

"Thank you, thank you very much."

The president watched Eric race out of his office. The nation's leader returned to his chair and leaned back. Signing bills that provided billions in aid was well and good, but it was seldom that he got to enjoy helping someone on such a personal, immediate basis.

Wellington had requested that Eric be offered a position with the Agency. Garfield would be a significant asset, Wellington had said.

But the president didn't feel like forcing the issue. He

wanted to let Garfield enjoy his time with his girlfriend. There'd be plenty of opportunities for recruitment later on.

He reached into Roosevelt's desk and took out his own well-worn copy of TR's sayings. He thumbed to a favorite page and savored the words: "All daring and courage, all iron endurance of misfortune, make for a nobler type of manhood."